Also by Josef Skvorecky

The Cowards

Josef Škvorecký

Miss Silver's Past

translated from the Czech by Peter Kussi
foreword by Graham Greene

Ecco Press
New York

Issued in 1985 by The Ecco Press
18 West 30th Street, New York, N.Y. 10001

Published simultaneously in Canada by
Stoddart, a subsidiary of
General Publishing Co., Ltd. Don Mills

Printed in the United States of America

Library of Congress Cataloging in Publication Data

Skvorecky, Josef.
Miss Silver's past.

Translation of Lvice.

I. Title.

PG5038.S527L913 1985 891.8'635 84-13691
ISBN 0-88001-074-6 (pbk.)

Dedicated to Vladimir Justl and to all my friends in the publishing world for their Blumenfeldian efforts.

Their struggle for the freedom of literature in my country seems lost now; but I believe Dasha Blumenfeld is right and they won't have to milk the cows for too long.

Preface
by Graham Greene

Exile is like some herb which gives its distinct bitter flavour to many different forms of writing: the comic, the ironic, the tragic. You can taste it in the irony of Conrad – it is completely absent from the home-based tragedies of Hardy – it is there in *The Cherry Orchard*. For to experience exile a man doesn't necessarily have to leave his country. The sense of banishment can be felt on one's own hearthstone. Exile is a deprivation – to be an exile is to be unable to communicate freely.

Josef Škvorecký was an exile long before he left his country for a university post in Toronto some months after the Russian invasion. One can argue that all his writing life, like Conrad's, has been spent in exile, like those of his fellow countrymen Kundera, Havel, and Hrabal, who are still in Czechoslovakia. The scene of his remarkable novel, *The Cowards*, was laid in a small Czech border town during the last days of the German occupation: the point of view was that of a high school student as much interested in saxophone-playing and Negro jazz as he was interested in the retreat of German troops, the arrival of Russian ones. It offended the Communist authorities by its lack of socialist realism and false heroics, by its praise of the 'decadent' jazz music of the West, perhaps above all by its '*poésie du départ*', for the good Marxist need never dream of personal movement, only the movement of revolution; he needn't search for the good life for he has already found it. The lyrical freedom with which the novel ends must surely have been the subject of prolonged debate in the publishing committees which are described with such a fine comic sense in *Miss Silver's Past*.

The Cowards was published in 1958, attacked by the conservative reviewers of the Party, and banned. Škvorecký lost his job as an editor of *World Literature*, and he had to publish several novels under the name of a friend. Only after 1963, in the pre-Dubček period, was he allowed to publish a few non-controversial books. His serious work had to wait for the brief spring of Dubček and for his exile in Canada.

Of all his works my favourite are the two *nouvelles* which have not yet found a publisher in English:* *The Legend of Emöke* and the strange poetic *The Bass Saxophone*, about a student who cannot resist the dangerous temptation when he is invited to play the instrument, of which he has always dreamed, in a German dance band during the war. The sadness in comedy, the comedy in sadness – of this Škvorecký is a master and this too is the mark of exile, of a writer who has not been granted the common gift of a home, who has to study, if he is to survive, a long indifference – '*Cette indifférence qui est notre mère, notre salut, notre perte ...*' (I quote from the French translation of *Emöke*.)

Miss Silver's Past (the Czech title was a better one: *The Lion Cub*) is the last of his books to have appeared in Prague, (*The Tank Corps*, which should have appeared the same year, 1969, was banned in advance), and reading it now one feels astonished at the degree of freedom that came to writers under Dubček. The background of the novel – part love story, part detective story – is a State publishing house, where morality must be defended as strictly as Marxism, and the endless committee meetings, the private cabals, and the heated discussions which surround the question whether or not to accept a certain first novel. To quote the report of the publisher's reader:

> The novel shows signs of an uncritical acceptance of fashionable Western literary phenomena, such as a decadent interest in degenerate aspects of life, the mixing of chronological planes, emphasis on sex, alcoholism and a variety of esoteric allusions ... I have no doubt that Cibulka's novel would be greeted by the snobbish circles with the greatest enthusiasm. It is therefore the duty of a socialist publisher to reject such a work and to exert an educational influence upon the author, urging her to think more deeply about the significance of her work so that her future creativity would be free of modish piquancy and so that she would try to portray the whole truth about our lives – lives which certainly have their difficult moments but in which hope and good cheer predominate.

* Published together in Picador as *The Bass Saxophone*, 1980

It would all be hilariously funny if it were fantasy, if it were not the truth, if the livelihood of a writer in Czechoslovakia did not depend on the politic decision of one publisher and the distant menace of that figure whom we never actually meet called 'Comrade Kaiser'.

Graham Greene

Author's preface

The statement that all persons and events described in this book are completely fictitious, and that any resemblance to real persons and events is purely coincidental will not be taken seriously by anyone – because it is the truth. This is neither a psychological novel nor a social novel, but a detective story. As such it does not portray real people, but only real attitudes in their rudimentary manifestations. It serves two main purposes: to discover the murderer, and to divert the reader. But if you are not satisfied merely to follow the adventures of our cynical editor and our beautiful girl from Bio-Ex, and are determined to amuse yourself in a more demanding way, do not try to identify your friends or enemies with my fictional characters. Instead, analyse your own conscience. There you are likely to find the germs of at least one or two attitudes and traits of my characters – even if you have never set foot inside a publishing house.

'. . . there are certain crimes which the law cannot touch, and therefore, to some extent, justify private revenge.'

Sherlock Holmes in
Charles Augustus Milverton

I *At the Moldau*

'Over there – that's her. The one in the blue bathing suit,' said Vasek.
'The bikini?' I asked.
'Right,' said Vasek, keeping his eyes fixed on her.
I, too, looked intently at the approaching girl. She was wearing a real bikini, one that barely covered her breasts and loins. She was walking towards us over the grass. In one hand she held a white towel, from the other swung a plastic bag stamped with the words 'Scandinavian Airways'. Her eyes were hidden by silver-coated sunglasses. She had glossy black hair, cut short in a boyish way. She was slim, very beautiful, and she walked proudly without glancing to the left or right.
Vasek's mock cough caught her attention. White teeth glistened in the golden-brown face, the sun flared in her mirroring glasses. The girl's whole body, even the cleft between her breasts, was an exquisite golden tan. Obviously she had been sunning herself in the nude.
'Good afternoon, Professor,' she said, and again teeth glinted in the dusky face.
'Good afternoon, Lenka,' answered Vasek, in an odd voice.
'This is my editor friend, Mr Leden. And this is Lenka. Lenka Silver.'
'Glad to meet you,' said the girl, extending a hand. I glimpsed a small scar near the elbow, pink against the tanned arm.
'My pleasure,' I said, and put on my most dazzling smile, even though Vasek was one of my best friends.

Vasek and I stretched out on the trampled grass, on either side of the girl's bath towel. She was lying on her back, her thoughts concealed behind glasses which dimly reflected the world. She welcomed the sun with her whole body, as if offering it up as a sacrifice. Prickly sensations raced through my nerves like ants. I had not known this tingling for a long, long time. I had the feeling of being in the presence of a new phenomenon; an enigmatic creature with long, slim legs and false eyes that knew too much – eyes I had only sensed, not seen. It felt good to be alive.

Multicoloured umbrellas flared outside the restaurant, and the surface of the river reflected the gay tumult of the swimmers. The water sparkled under the blue sky, the sun blazed like an atomic furnace. I breathed in the moist, somewhat bitter smell of the river, the odour of wet bodies and the new, mysterious, vital aroma of the girl's body.

'I'm dying to know who's going to win,' babbled Vasek from the other side. 'The Russians have better technique, but the Japanese are better at free form.' Nobody was interested; the girl surrendered herself to her celebration of the sun. 'What do you think, Lenka?' asked Vasek.

'I don't understand those things,' she answered curtly. That squelched him.

I recalled that I was there only to help Vasek make out with the girl. But deep down I already knew that I was more likely to help myself. I said: 'Why don't we all go? Do you want to come with us? Or aren't you interested in gymnastics?'

The boyish head turned slightly, but only a grassy slope dotted with half-nude bathers looked back at me. The mystery of the girl's eyes was still impenetrable.

'I might. How much would it cost?'

I smiled at that dark landscape of a face, white clouds afloat on the black sky of the glasses.

'We'll take care of the tickets. Just give us the pleasure of your company.'

The corners of the girl's mouth lifted. 'You might be sorry. If I go at all, I like to sit in the front row.'

'Surely you don't think we're cheap ...' I began, but Vasek interrupted me enthusiastically: 'Don't worry! I have a friend on the Sports Council. I get a discount. No problem at all.'

I winced. It was hard to see what went on behind the glasses.

Vasek, naturally, was oblivious of all the byplay. I stopped paying any attention to him and turned over on my stomach. The girl's golden arm lay stretched out beside me, and the scar was plainly visible. It was a small pink rectangle, as if someone had rubbed off a strip of skin and the wound had remained pink ever since. I put the tip of my finger on this interesting spot. It felt hot, combining inner and outer warmth. Vasek had exhausted his current topic, and the girl again turned her black mirrors towards me.

'What happened here?' I asked, and like an apostle of Christ I left my finger on the wound.

She lifted her arm and looked at the elbow. She didn't return the arm to its former place alongside her body, but rested it on her bare, beautifully hollowed stomach. My hand remained on the towel, the finger pointing indecently.

'Oh, that,' she said. 'You'll make fun of me. I had a tattoo once.'

'Really? You mean you travelled with a rough crowd?'

'You might say so – pretty rough.'

That encouraged me to place my hand on her arm. 'What was it? A heart and arrow? An anchor?'

'An inscription,' she said.

'I see. Somebody's name?'

The girl turned her cropped head, the anonymous eyes taking in the sky. 'Yes. Somebody's name.'

'Whose?'

'Aren't you being just a bit nosy?' she asked of the sky.

'Sorry.'

'In individual competition it will probably be Gubov,' Vasek's voice broke the silence. 'But there's also a chance . . .'

The girl suddenly stood up. Gracefully, athletically. The sun drenched her bare back and painted two tiny shadows around a pair of dimples quite low along the spine. She stretched and turned towards us. She loomed against the glowing sky and her reflecting glasses seemed to burn through me with black rays. She asked, 'Aren't you going for a swim?'

'Great idea!' Vasek shouted. I could tell that he didn't like the idea at all. He got up obediently.

For a brief moment I gazed into those artificial black eyes. They told me nothing. The girl stood there, motionless. At last I said, grinning: 'I'll join you in a minute.'

The girl tossed her head at Vasek and smiled at him. Then she took off her glasses and threw them down on the towel, but she had already turned her back on me, so the mystery of her eyes remained unsolved. She strode gracefully among the reclining bodies towards the wooden cabanas. Vasek skipped along by her side like a fool.

She disappeared in the waves, and then her tousled head popped up on the sparkling surface like a black olive. I got up, jogged down to the piers and dove into the water. Chilled by several days of rain, it was cold.

I swam slowly through a throng of whooping children and searched for the tousled black head. A white sightseeing boat jammed with a holiday crowd steamed by, the waves churned up by its huge wheels, making swimmers' heads bob like corks. The sun's glare blinded me, and I had to close my eyes. Plunging under the surface, I opened them. In the greenish shade ahead, I saw a woman's thighs flapping next to a man who was trying to ram his big belly between her legs. In the water, I thought, people shed a lot of their hypocritical habits. The thought gave me fresh courage for my next move.

I came up and scanned the surface for a black, boyish head and Vasek Zamberk's sandy mop. A paddleboat glided slowly towards me, trailing foam. I heard a resonant, familiar voice: 'Karel!'

My Chief. He was sitting on the paddleboat in his swimming trunks, his head protected from the sun by a hideous blue and green cap. Pedalling alongside him was his nondescript wife.

I returned his greeting and, in a friendlier voice, said 'Good afternoon, Ella' to his wife.

'How come you're all alone?' she asked from the perch. 'Where is your girlfriend?'

Her husband reproached her theatrically: 'Really, Ella! Can't Karel have one day of rest?'

He gave a Don Juanish laugh. I was annoyed. Apparently Annie had gossiped to him about my difficulties with Vera. Annie always pricked up her ears when Vera phoned. And though I tried to sound casual when I talked to Vera, Annie could tell the difference. Like most women, she had a sharp ear for nuances.

'I'm here with some friends, but they seem to have disappeared,' I said, looking around. A bit too quickly, I added: 'Oh, *there* they are. I'd better swim along.'

'Swim along then,' Ella said, with obvious irony.

For some time now I had had the impression that the focus of this woman's flighty interests had centred on me. No, thanks. My Chief's friendship is too holy to me. With strong strokes I left the two of them behind.

Vasek and the girl were obviously heading for the opposite shore, since they had already swum nearly halfway across. I frowned. I had always hated the strange desire that seemed to possess pretty, athletic young women to swim across the Moldau. I had already been forced to perform this feat on two occasions, and I was certainly far from an Olympic swimmer. Of course Vasek was a professor of physical culture, so it was quite possible that he was the one who had suggested it. He probably thought this would be a good way to impress the girl.

The cry for help rang out as I was lazily floating on my back near a boat in which a portly gentleman was relaxing. The call sounded weak and distant, but it was perfectly clear.

Quickly I turned my head to find where this voice that suddenly silenced the shore and the river was coming from. Far away, close to the opposite shore, a little black head surfaced and went under and popped up again. Whoever the head belonged to was obviously caught up in some kind of violent struggle. From all sides swimmers struck out for the spot. From the corner of my eye I noticed the lifeguard reaching for a life preserver.

I swam over to the boat as fast as I could and scrambled in. The fat man, roused from his nap, started to protest but I shouted: 'Excuse me, my friend's drowning!' When I grabbed the oars, the man stopped protesting and obediently plunged in, butt first, over the side. I pulled hard on the oars. The bow slammed into the waves. The boat skipped through the water.

I glanced over my shoulder. The little black head was still bobbing on the surface. Close by it, Vasek's blond mop popped out of the water. A few more hard strokes took me past several furiously kicking and splashing Australian-crawl champs. I looked around again. The sun glistened on a tanned wet arm holding Vasek under the chin. I was quite close now. I manoeuvred the boat over to the girl.

At that moment I saw her eyes for the first time. I had never seen such eyes in my life – big, black, and without any irises at all. Just two small black discs, as opaque as the silvered glasses she had worn earlier. Her eyes, too, mirrored the water, reflecting tiny sparks of sunlight. Whatever secret lay behind those strange eyes was not revealed in that brief instant our glances met.

The prow of the boat nudged in against Vasek, and the girl reached for it with one hand. She didn't say anything. Drops of water were running down her face and her mouth was twisted from exertion. But she still looked beautiful. She had that rare kind of face which no grimace can turn ugly. I leaned out and grasped Vasek under the arm. With the girl's help I managed to haul him into the boat. Then I reached for her, but she nimbly scrambled over the side by herself. The soaked bikini was glued to her body; her nipples stood out in bold relief.

She glanced at me. I quickly lifted my eyes from her halter. 'You'll row?' she asked.

'Of course.'

I sat down behind the oars. She sat on the seat opposite and placed Vasek's head on her lap. I strained at the oars, but my pleasant interlude as Charon was soon interrupted. The lifeguard had caught up with us and he expertly brought his boat alongside ours. 'Is he breathing?' he asked.

'Yes,' answered Lenka Silver.

The lifeguard told Lenka to get into his boat. 'That will be easier than moving him. We've got to get him ashore as fast as possible.'

Lenka fixed me with her black pupils, smiled as if to excuse herself, shrugged her shoulders, rose and lightly jumped into the lifeguard's boat. This moment was probably decisive. That motion of hopping from one boat into the other, that instant when her slender legs opened slightly, as if inviting me to enter a nook of delights, that mysterious smile in the mysterious eyes – I knew how it would end. It was fate; nothing could be done to avert it. Not that I had any intention of doing anything to avert it. Vasek or no Vasek.

I leaned back, pulling on the oars, and, accompanied by the lifeguard's boat, I rowed the semiconscious swimming champ to the pier.

The doctor diagnosed Vasek's condition with a technical expression, the point of which was that he would be fine in a few minutes. 'Don't go into the water any more today,' he told Vasek, adding that people shouldn't jump into the river when they are all heated up. What he meant was not the way it sounded.

As soon as the doctor and lifeguard left, Vasek said gloomily: 'Well, I sure pissed away my chances.'

'Nonsense,' I replied. 'It could have happened to anybody.'

'It didn't have to happen to me, though.'

'Oh, come off it! It's no great tragedy. She fished you out when you were going under, that's all. You've got to see the whole thing as a joke. Maybe this is the very thing needed to ... to ...' I was groping for a word, knowing that any word was bound to ring false, that even if I used the cunning of a Goebbels, Vasek had already formed an unshakable conviction of failure – and I was glad. '... to bring you closer.' I finished the sentence and gazed out of the window.

Vasek shook his head. 'Not a chance. I'm not lucky with women. Today was just one more example. Remember last year with Kveta? Same thing. I was teaching her mountain climbing, and like a bloody fool I slipped from a rock that a child could have climbed, and sprained my ankle.'

'And you've never called her since, have you? Naturally, she thought you didn't give a damn about her.'

'Like hell she did. She started running around with Joska Kral and he gave her advanced courses in alpinism at Boucek's place on Hruba Skala,' he said with unexpected bitterness, which I interpreted as an ominous sign.

I quickly answered with all the cynicism I could muster: 'You should have straightened her out in bed!'

His belligerent sarcasm evaporated: 'Yeah, sure, sure. For six months I put on this mountain-climbing act and then I fall flat on my face ...'

'Elementary, my dear boy. Never boast to a girl. The higher you puff yourself up, the harder you fall.'

'But what else can I do?' asked Vasek in desperation. 'I can't bull-shit about books the way you can.'

'Less talk and more action,' I instructed him. 'As soon as you feel a little better we'll go after this Silver girl again.'

But Vasek said firmly: 'Not me!'

Just then the curtain in front of the door parted and Lenka Silver's black head popped in.

'May I come in?'

'Please do!' I said. Vasek closed his eyes.

The girl must have thought that he was asleep, for she whispered: 'How is he?'

'Fine,' I answered, and then turned to my friend: 'Vasek! Miss Silver is here!'

Though Vasek was quite pale and tried hard to simulate faintness, he turned distinctly red. He opened his eyes and sat up.

'Lie down,' said Lenka Silver and put her hand on his shoulder.

'I have to thank you,' he mumbled. 'You saved my life ...'

'I did at that, didn't I.' The girl laughed.

Vasek kept on sputtering: 'Please, I don't know how to say this, but...'

She interrupted him: 'Can you walk?'

'He is supposed to rest,' I answered for him.

'Then take it easy. Would you like me to bring you something? A glass of water? Coffee?'

'Thanks very much,' said Vasek humbly. The girl's pupils, which had been avoiding me till then, met my gaze. Her bikini had dried off by now and yet it seemed even smaller than before. Her whole body, even the tenderest parts, had a strange, almost miraculous firmness. It was a mysterious anomaly. It occurred to me that if she were standing there naked she would look like a statue made of brown marble. A lithe, warm, kinetic statue.

'We'll be out in a little while,' I said. 'Will you be down by the river?'

She paused for a short moment, a moment which women can calculate with consummate precision even though they are proverbially weak in mathematics. Then she said in a voice that was as alluring as the call of a bird: 'I'll be waiting.'

Again, those damned glands of mine sent streams of tiny ants coursing through every nerve of my body.

As soon as she had left, Vasek jumped up so hard that the cot creaked.

'Ready to go?' I asked.

'Yeah, home!'

'Idiot!'

'I'll write her a letter.'

'Great idea.'

'To hell with everything.'

'How about getting drunk?'

'Maybe I will.' He held out his hand to say goodbye.

'Don't be a fool! I don't feel like leaving yet,' I said.

'I don't expect you to. You can stay.'

I knew it was safe for me now to play the devoted friend.

'Look,' I said. 'I'm the one that's going to get lost. You stick around and pick up where you left off before that stupid swim.'

'I can't, Karel. It's a fact. Maybe I'm an ass, but . . .'

'You're an ass, all right.'

'You writers are different. But how would you feel, if you . . .' Vasek was trying hard to think of an analogy. '. . . if you wrote her a poem and that poem turned out to be so dumb that all you'd want to do is burn it?'

I thought this over for a minute. A poem to Lenka Silver? For a long time now I had been writing poems about quite different matters, and when I did write about love it was not a personal emotion I was celebrating. I wasn't in the habit of modelling my love poems on flesh-and-blood women. Real women are too ephemeral, poetry is eternal. But, then, this girl with the iris-free eyes . . .

Vasek was developing his analogy further: 'It's the same thing with me. Except with me it's physical skill that's on the line. Sure, I know, you'd finesse your way out of it even if you'd written a lousy poem, but I'm not much good at bullshit . . .'

I wanted to tell him that just *because* he had failed today, *because* his biceps had written a lousy poem in the Moldau, it was important for him not to give up. Everything, everything in this world is only a matter of practice and training, no more, just like Vasek's stupid basketball. But I controlled myself and healthy egotism prevailed. I probably couldn't have managed to get that across to him, anyway. Yes, Vasek was a pal. But how many friendships had been betrayed because of women? As soon as this thought came to me – namely, that my duplicity was backed by massive precedent – my conscience cleared completely. Anyhow, I was sacrificing an abstract ethical principle to a living, passionate need, which is the most excusable sacrifice in the world. I said: 'Well, go then, if you really think you should. But don't forget, you said you'd take care of getting us all into that gymnastics meet.'

'Maybe,' answered Vasek. 'Be seeing you, and . . .' He hesitated: '. . . give her some excuse for me. Like I felt sick or something. Goodbye.'

Lenka Silver was sitting on a towel, hugging her knees. She was wearing her dark glasses again, which peered at me from a distance.

'What did you do with the professor?' she asked and moved over on the towel.

I sat down next to her. 'He went home.'

'Why?'

I hesitated for a moment. Should I say that he didn't feel well? To hell with it.

'You can figure that one out for yourself, can't you?'

She removed her dark glasses and looked at me with those mirroring black eyes. They gave no hint of what she was thinking, but an inexplicable shudder ran down my back.

'I don't know. What do you mean?' she asked.

'He feels embarrassed. He thinks that he failed.'

She kept looking at me for a while, at last saying pensively: 'Hmm.'

'He's dying to start something with you,' I continued in my treachery. 'That's why I'm here today.'

'I don't get it.' She put on her glasses again, quite unnecessarily.

'According to what he told me you're very cool towards him. He hasn't even managed to swing a date with you. So he engaged me as a go-between. I arranged a date for the three of us to go to the gymnastics meet with the understanding that I won't show up.'

The girl stretched out on her back. A flock of clouds was reflected in her glasses. 'Are you a friend of his?'

'Yes.'

'Then why are you telling me all this?'

'You mean you're not interested?'

Short pause.

'That doesn't matter,' she said at last.

'On the contrary. That's precisely what matters,' I answered.

She was silent. Then she said enigmatically: 'You forgot to say to whom, didn't you? You're telling me all this for the wrong reasons, aren't you?'

I laughed. She had seen right through me. Her face remained immobile, however. I said: 'Now, of course, I will certainly come.'

'But now, of course, I may not.'

'You don't have to ...' I gulped, '... see gymnastics, of course. That's still a week off, and a week has seven days. In the meantime I could meet you seven times somewhere else. What do you say?'

'I'd say that you are here and that Professor Zamberk has gone home. For the time being that should satisfy you.'

I lay on my side, propped on my elbow. I slowly examined Lenka Silver from head to foot. Short, raven-black hair, clean profile of an extremely beautiful face, well-rounded little shoulders as smooth as brown silk, breasts which, even now, when she was lying on her back, had not lost the triumphal, divine form of youth; hollow stomach dotted by the tiny dimple of a navel, fine black hairs at the rim of the bikini where the thighs slope towards the crotch; long, slender but not skinny legs, straight and bronzed and beautiful.

'Hmmm,' said the girl, while I continued my anatomical survey. 'Talk to me.'

'You haven't been in Prague long, have you?' I asked.

'No, only a month.'

'And where do you live? I've been here for ten years and still don't have my own apartment. Only a sublet.'

I looked into her dark glasses. She understood perfectly and her tanned face glinted with a smile.

'I have a small flat,' she said.

The joy of life stirred powerfully in me.

'That is,' she continued, 'a friend of mine put me up in her flat.' And as if that wasn't enough, she added: 'She's got the flu now, so she has to stay in bed.'

I frowned involuntarily. Behind the glasses, strange little sparks seemed to be dancing. 'Give me a cigarette,' she said.

Lenka Silver was turning out to be a very cool customer.

She asked: 'You write poetry, don't you?'

We were sitting on a bench under a willow tree, near the refreshment stand. I hadn't expected her to be aware of my literary glory. As I had already learned, she was an employee in one of those continually reorganized and reshuffled bureaux called Zoo-Export or Bio-Expo or something like that, and although I had not yet seen her fully dressed I had assumed that she was more interested in fashion magazines than in poetry.

'Well, yes, a little,' I answered modestly. 'Do you like my poems?'

'Not much.'

God knows, I wasn't conceited about the products of my muse. For a long time now my poems had been no more than pawns on the chessboard of my personal career and had little connection with the real meaning of my life. All the same, Lenka Silver's candour was hard to take.

'Why?'

'I get the impression that you don't take them seriously. They lack feeling. You're probably too interested in getting them published.'

Nobody had ever seen through me quite that painfully before.

Probably because few people ever read what I wrote, and those who did failed to evaluate it properly. The few letters I received from readers certainly revealed no such insight. I forced out a bitter laugh. 'You missed your profession. You should have been a critic. It's a lucky thing for me that you're not.'

She sucked green lemonade through a straw. 'I'm not an easy person to fool. Haven't you ever written a poem on the spur of the moment, just like that? A love poem to somebody, perhaps?'

Strange. A bit earlier I had thought about that very thing, in connection with this same bronzed girl. Actually, I had written love poems. A whole collection. When I was a highschool student.

'I have, yes. But that was long ago.'

'A boy once wrote poems to my sister,' said Lenka Silver. 'I was just a little girl then, but I like them better than anything I've read since. Not that I know anything about poetry,' she added quickly, 'and I don't remember too much of the actual poems. But something stayed in my head – a mood, you understand? And I remember one part. It went like this: "I am writing to you, Salina, from my window I see so far ... Mister Lustig sits on a wagon, strumming his guitar".'

'That was written by your sister's boyfriend? That's really funny! I should have thought he'd write about love.'

She interrupted me, gravely and firmly. 'He did write about love. And there's nothing funny about them. They were more tragic than you could possibly know.'

'What's funny about the part you recited is that it's stolen from Orten. That young Jewish poet, remember? He was killed by a Gestapo car back in 1941 or so. Your sister's boyfriend was plagiarizing one of his elegies: "I am writing to you, Karina, not knowing if you're alive ..." '

Lenka tossed the half-finished cup of lemonade into the trash can and got up. 'Let's go for one last dip, all right? "It is Sunday ... the sun knocks on the window panes." '

She took off her glasses and looked at me. It seemed to me that she was quoting that trite hit song with some sort of hidden sarcasm, as if she wanted to conceal an injured spot in her heart. I could just imagine the kind of heartaches girls like Lenka Silver were prone to have.

Coolly, deliberately, she lowered herself into the water. The surface reached her knees, her thighs, her gracefully modelled bun – as Vera daintily called it – her waist, until at last only the pretty little head was left above water. She flashed me a smile that could have come straight out of a toothpaste ad. In fact, her whole body looked like an ad. God can't create girls that beautiful, that's a job for advertising artists.

'I'm not swimming across the river with you, that's for sure,' I called out.

'Don't worry. I wasn't about to try that again,' she said, turning her back. 'One good deed a day is enough.' She plunged in and swam off at a good clip.

I jumped in and soon caught up with her. We swam close to the shore, past boats, children with inflatable toys, girls with rubber bathing caps, wide-eyed little boys gulping Moldau water. The water near the shore was almost warm now, especially close to the surface. Lenka turned on her back and floated. I stretched out to float beside her. Overhead, the July sun, though already dropping towards the west, still shone strong. Two long-legged girls on a raft were performing a striptease.

I turned my head towards Lenka. 'Where are you from?'

'Me?' she drawled with her eyes closed. 'From Bruenn.'

'Your parents live there now?'

'My parents are dead.'

'And your sister?'

She was silent for a moment. Then she said: 'She's dead, too.'

'I'm sorry.'

The bell of a trolley car tinkled from the shore. From the fleet of rubber rafts we had left behind us came the joyous din of children's voices.

'Excuse me, I wouldn't have mentioned your sister again,' I said. 'But for some reason that bit of verse you quoted stuck in my mind. "I am writing to you, Salina, from my window I see so far ... Mister Lustig sits on a wagon, strumming his guitar".' A shudder ran down my spine. Perhaps because it had been so long since I had written any poetry, or even had read any for my enjoyment. 'It's an obvious paraphrase, but all the same ... By the way, who is Mr Lustig?'

'The young man who wrote the poem was also a Jew, like the one you said had been killed by the Gestapo,' said Lenka, eyes still closed. 'He had smuggled the poem out of the Theresienstadt concentration camp.'

'I see,' I said. 'And ... did he survive?'

'No,' Lenka said. 'But Stana – that's my sister, he called her Salina – she died before he did, anyway. During the war, too. She got pneumonia.'

'Poor girl. How old was she?'

'Twenty-four,' Lenka replied. 'She was fourteen years older than me, but I loved her very much. You see, our mother died when I was born and Stana brought me up.'

She opened her eyes and threw me a glance, her eyes practically on the surface of the water; then suddenly she slipped under as smoothly as a watersnake. I quickly went under too.

The shadow of a slender, quickly moving body flickered through the greenish light. I tried to follow her, but she was too fast for me. Besides, I soon was out of breath and had to surface for air.

Lenka Silver was no longer there. I looked around and saw her suspended between the pontoons of a paddleboat. White foam churned up by the paddlewheel framed her body like a halo. A few strokes, and I was sharing the halo with her. She let herself be pulled by the invisible pedallers, her long legs trailing through the luminous green like the tail of a mermaid. Ah, sailor, sailor, you are lost for ever, I said to myself, and reached for her. As soon as I touched her bare hips I was seized by such a surge of delight that I almost drowned. I heard her muffled gasp. Then she writhed and twisted in my embrace until my hands slipped from her wet body. I had to come up for air. I found myself facing her laughing mouth and mocking eyes. I made another lunge for her.

'Easy does it! Don't tip us over!' somebody said from the paddleboat. The shadow of one of the boaters fell on Lenka's wet face.

'Vera! Not so wild, if you don't mind.' I recognized the voice of the Chief's wife. She quickly added – with that unmistakably fake tone of voice women use when they are ready to sink their claws – 'Oh, I beg your pardon! I thought you were Vera Kajetan! When I saw Mr Leden, I took it for granted that ...'

I snorted and introduced the mermaid. 'This is Miss Lenka Silver,' I said, turning to look at her. A thousand devils were dancing in her eyes. 'Comrade Prochazka, Mrs Comrade Prochazka.' Lenka glanced at the chubby figure of my superior silhouetted against the sun atop the metal framework of the boat.

'Pleased to meet you,' the boss pair sang in unison.

'It turned out to be a pretty decent Sunday, didn't it?' thundered the Chief.

'It certainly did,' I said with feeling.

'Who is he?' Lenka asked as we swam sedately back to shore, side by side.

'My Chief.'

'Chief?'

'Editor-in-chief of the *Our Book* publishing bureau.'

She said nothing but suddenly swam faster. She swam like a racer, keeping her mouth under the surface. Then she slowed down again.

'Wasn't he at one time ... ?'

Silence. I tried to catch my breath, winded by her tempo. She let her question hang in midair.

'What did you start to say?' I asked.

'Nothing. I just had the feeling I know his wife from somewhere.'

'That's possible. She is the daughter ... of Minister Snaider,' I stammered, breathless. 'The one who died last year ... had a state funeral.'

'Hmmm,' she said. 'Must be somebody else. I knew a Mrs Prochazka in Bruenn. Her husband was some kind of editor, too.'

'That must have been his first wife. He divorced her.'

'I see.'

'You see, after the Communists took over his wife began to age terribly – from a political viewpoint, of course. She was the daughter of a private publisher and she didn't properly understand the new era.'

I glanced at Lenka out of the corner of my eye. She didn't answer, but it seemed to me that her gentle profile had become sharper. I felt an unpleasant pang in my stomach. Was I being politically too irreverent? After all, I knew nothing about her. She sucked her beautiful full lips into her mouth, as if she wanted to bite them. We reached the steps.

Quickly and silently, Lenka climbed out of the water, and without turning around she ran to the spot where we had left our towels.

When I reached her I saw that she was trembling. 'What's the matter?' I asked. 'Are you cold?'

'N . . . n . . . o. It's n . . . n . . . othing. I overdid it a bit.'

'Overdid what?'

'Swim . . . m . . . ing.'

'But the water's not *that* cold.'

'I know. But I have a . . . a weak heart.'

Now was my turn to take charge. 'All right, into the shade with you! Let's go! You don't have much sense, carrying on like that with a weak heart! Put on some dry clothes. Give yourself a good rub with the towel, and I'll bring you some hot tea.'

'That's really n . . . n . . . ot n . . . n . . . ecessary,' she stammered.

'Let's go!' I took her under the arm and helped her to her feet. She got up obediently; suddenly she was as gentle as a lamb.

I led her down the narrow corridor between the cabins towards number seven, where I assured her – even though she hadn't asked for it – that I would meet her under the chestnuts with a cup of tea.

When I returned with a steaming teapot to the rendezvous, Lenka was no longer shivering like a wet poodle. Now, wearing a white dress with pink stripes and perched on the bench with her legs crossed, her tanned feet in pink sandals, she looked like an orchid.

'Such gallantry!' she said. 'But I'm feeling much better.'

I felt silly holding the steaming pot, especially in the heat of a July afternoon.

'A cup of tea will refresh you,' I said.

'I'll sweat,' she replied.

'No, you won't. Hot tea is a perfect summer beverage.'

'Yes. That's what Vladimir always used to say. But he himself always drank beer.'

Vladimir? My heart did a somersault. I sat down next to her and poured her a cup of tea.

'Which Vladimir?' I asked, trying to sound casual.

'My Vladimir.'

'And who is your Vladimir?'

'Why do you want to know?'

'Well, after all, I suppose it's none of my business. Anyway,' I said, resorting to an old trick, 'you used the past tense when you mentioned him.'

'But he's very much alive,' Lenka said. 'In spite of the past tense.'

'When you talk about a man in the past tense he might as well be dead.'

She laughed. 'And what about your friend Vera Kajetan? Does she belong in the present?'

'Definitely not.'

Lenka raised her eyebrows. 'I think you must be pretty ruthless.'

'What makes you say that?'

'You had a date with Vera Kajetan, didn't you?'

'Yes, but . . .'

'And, you're trying to take me over from your best friend, aren't you?'

'What do you mean? There's nothing between Vasek and you . . .'

'But he's interested in me,' she broke in. 'You said so yourself.'

'Sure he is. So what? So am I.'

'But I'm not.'

'No? Why?'

'Because I know your type. The typical unscrupulous male. I wasn't born yesterday.'

I was used to this sort of banter. I had loved it in the days of my youth. Now again, it gave me more pleasure than the collected works of our national prize winners.

'You're not being fair. I'm not betraying Vasek. I don't owe any loyalty to anybody.'

'And what about your friend Vera?'

Damn Vera! I recited darkly: '"It is not good for a man to live alone."'

'This is getting better all the time. So you're playing around with that poor, helpless thing just because you're bored?'

'I'm not bored. I am lonely.'

For some reason, Lenka's allusion to my girlfriend as a thing excited me sexually. But she changed her tone: 'What will she feel like, when you ...'

Pause.

'When I what?'

'Well, when you do what you're obviously planning to do?'

'Which is?'

'You know very well. The answer's written all over your face.' Lenka looked stern.

I winced. 'I won't break off with her ...'

'Oh?'

'... until I find somebody else,' I said with just a dash of the sort of cynicism women like. It seemed to work on the mermaid.

'Hmm.' Her eyebrows went up a notch. 'And when will that be?'

'I don't know,' I replied. 'But I'm hoping it will be very soon.'

It was becoming pretty clear that Lenka Silver was falling for me – or that she was one hell of a tease. It was hard to tell which.

She steered me into a tavern where we had supper and where she grilled me about my past. It felt queer, sitting in that tavern with her. Vera lived only two blocks away and we had often come here together.

Lenka led me to confess to a number of crimes – among others, that my poetic career was mainly based on political expediency. Once, long ago, I had earned a name as an innovator, because I slipped lyrical poems in between the conventional odes and effusions about building socialism. The critics had got all worked up, of course, and the resultant publicity had served to distinguish me in the readers' vague consciousness from the general mob of hacks and scribblers.

Lenka asked me to recite one of those lyrics.

'I've forgotten them,' I said. 'It's been a good seven or eight years since I wrote those poems.'

'I thought poets remembered their poems for ever.'

'They do, when the poems contain real feelings,' I said. 'But you said yourself that mine don't.'

'Not the ones you're publishing now. But I thought that perhaps in those days ...'

'Then or now, they are all the same,' I said. 'The only difference is that then it didn't matter.'

'And now it does?'

'It's beginning to. Not to me. To the critics.' I confessed. 'That's why I now publish them only in newspapers. Nobody pays any attention to things that appear in newspapers, and I don't have to feel like a cheat when I show my Writers' Union card.'

'But you are a bit of a cheat all the same, aren't you?'

I shrugged. 'I am only one of many,' I said elegiacally. 'How many poets do you think there are among poets?'

She was silent.

'Besides – you won't believe it – I still get a letter now and then from some reader. Just the other day, I had a poem called "Alabama Children" in the paper and ...'

Lenka's cheeks flushed. 'That's the biggest fraud of all!' she said, her eyes flashing. 'Do you really care about the children of Alabama?'

I shrugged again. Anger heightened her beauty. I decided to make her even angrier. 'My poems harm nobody,' I said, 'and what's going on in Alabama certainly is not very pleasant.'

'But do you really care? Are you really concerned about those black children?'

I grinned, delighted at being able to shock Miss Silver. 'Racism is disgusting. My poem won't hurt anybody. I got paid for it, and money won't hurt me. That pretty much sums up my aesthetics.'

'If you really mean that, you're a cynic,' Lenka said acidly. 'And, frankly, I do not like cynics.'

No? Well, in that case, I thought, it's time for evasive tactics. 'I was kidding, of course. But unless a person is morbidly sensitive, he won't be moved by anything that doesn't directly concern him.'

Lenka looked at her plate of anchovies. A tiny vein pulsed on her temple. It seemed to be telling me what a fragile and complicated instrument this young lady was, what a pleasure it was to be with her and near her. She blinked as if she had something in her eye, and said softly: 'Well, you may be right.'

'There you are. And is this any reason for me to stop writing?'

She slowly returned from her reverie, got out a mirror, and performed a few ritual motions with her slightly tousled hair. 'Perhaps you should. Yes, I think you should stop.'

I smiled. 'Aren't you a bit too exacting? There would be very little left of literature if it had to pass such strict tests.'

'In certain things I am very exacting,' she answered, completely recovered from her meditation over the anchovies.

'Aside from literature, what do you have in mind?'

'Think about it,' she snapped.

She speared an anchovy with a toothpick and popped it in her mouth.

I did the same. Then I said: 'You can certainly get into a passion over poetry!'

'I am simply trying to warn you. I really can't stand ...'

'What?'

Fixing her gaze on a massive plush-covered chandelier which hung from the ceiling, she began to count on her fingers: 'Cheaters, hypocrites, literature dabblers, cynics ...'

'You really think I'm a cynic?'

Lenka stopped counting and closed her eyes. When she opened them, she rewarded me with such a radiant smile that my heart almost stopped.

'I don't know yet,' she said as she pulled a red carnation out of the vase on the table and stuck it in her décolletage. 'You probably are. Like all people whose life is too easy.'

She said this in a voice that made it sound as if she loved a cynic more than anyone else in the world.

As the evening progressed, however, I became less and less certain just where I stood with Lenka Silver. At times it seemed as if everything was going forward smoothly, but just as I reached out she eluded me. I put superhuman effort into the contest. And she encouraged me. Any other girl who would have given me so much encouragement would have been wrapped up long ago. But Lenka was a pink and white enigma. In the end, I was standing, completely wilted, on the sidewalk in front of the tavern, blinking at the stars.

'Where do you live?' I asked so gloomily that Lenka laughed and, for the first time that evening, took me by the hand.

'Just around the corner,' she said. 'You can see me home.'

I came quickly to life. 'And you'll ask me up for a cup of coffee?'

'I'll think that over on the way.'

I took her by the arm. We walked side by side. We turned the corner and found ourselves in bright moonlight. The street was as broad and deserted as a Paris boulevard. It seemed as if we were the only people left in the city. Our images faintly appeared in the window of a dark shop. In the moonlight, Lenka seemed like a fairytale princess. Our eyes met somewhere in the dark behind the window.

'You are so beautiful,' I sighed. 'You are absolutely the most beautiful girl in Prague, Czechoslovakia, and Europe.'

'Mr Leden,' she said. 'You talk as if you were serious.'

I fell to my knees and lifted my arm towards the moon. 'I swear that I am serious! Have pity on me, Lenka!'

Lenka looked around cautiously. Then she reached out her hand. 'Editor Leden,' she said, 'you are a clown – and probably a hypocrite too.'

I moaned.

'But I don't want you on my conscience, so I'll let you in on a secret.'

My heart skipped. She was a secret incarnate, and now ...

But before Lenka had a chance to confide in me the clack of high heels sounded. I was still kneeling on the pavement when Vera turned the corner. She was carrying a large bag out of which stuck a blue towel and a mournful pair of knitting needles.

It was like a scene from a farce. Vera stopped dead in her tracks and her normally ruddy face took on a ghastly, lunar pallor. I got down on all fours and said casually: 'Hi, Vera.'

Lenka sighed. I started to crawl around diligently and for a moment I even thought that maybe I should sniff like a hound. Then I looked up at Lenka and said: 'I can't find it.'

Her reply stunned me. She said: 'What are you looking for?'

I was furious. I knew she wasn't that stupid, that she knew perfectly well what was going on, but had decided not to help out. Her eyes, mirroring nothing but the moon's mockery, confirmed my worst suspicions.

In the meantime, Vera had come to her senses.

'What in the world are you doing, Kaja?'

'I'm looking . . .' for a painfully long time I couldn't think of anything to say. 'Miss Silver lost an earring somewhere around here.' This was, of course, the dumbest idea I could have possibly come up with.

'Here?' asked Vera incredulously.

'Somewhere along the way,' Lenka chimed in.

For God's sake, why, then, was I crawling around in this particular spot, on the corner of the Avenue of November Nineteenth?

Vera was just about to ask that obvious question when Lenka extended her hand and said sweetly: 'I am Lenka Silver.'

'Kajetan,' said Vera, taken aback. Tears tinkled in her voice.

I knew that sound. I got to my feet, at a loss what to do next. I dusted off my knees. Vera turned to me. 'Are you coming . . . are you coming with me?'

I cleared my throat.

'Are you coming?' Vera repeated, with a somewhat different intonation and with more than a tinkle of tears

An embarrassing pause followed. Lenka finally broke the silence: 'Time for me to go. I live just across the street. It was a pleasure to meet you. Goodnight.'

For the second time in five seconds she reached out her hand to Vera. Vera shook it mechanically, totally preoccupied with the effort of holding back her tears.

'Thanks for seeing me home,' Miss Silver said to me. Then she crossed into the darkness on the other side of the street. The entrance of a tile-covered apartment house glowed with a greenish light. Lenka's striped-carnation figure flashed in the door. A lock clicked shut. There was a glint of chrome and the pink apparition vanished.

Her vanishing act took only a few seconds. I returned to meet Vera's gaze. Her forget-me-not eyes were brimming with tears. In my dazed condition I could think of nothing more witty than to mumble: 'Let's go.'

She set out obediently. Neither of us said anything for a time. My head was still full of the striped carnation, the mermaid. Then, in a wavering voice, Vera said: 'Who is she?'

Who? Her very name, the melodious combination of Lenka and Silver, seemed perfection. The quintessence of lyrical nostalgia. I was perfectly aware that I was succumbing to an illusion – after all, I wasn't exactly an adolescent. But I didn't care. Illusion – how beautiful you are! Linger yet a while! I had completely forgotten about Vera.

Plaintively, she reminded me of her presence: 'Will you answer me or not?' she cried, her voice revealing everything about that good, trusting soul.

And I heard my own voice, sounding strange and lifeless, reply: 'She's a friend of Vasek Zamberk. I was at his house this afternoon, as I told you. She came to pick him up. The three of us went for a swim.'

After a moment's silence, she said in a voice that she tried to make sound harsh: 'Why didn't Vasek take her home if she's his friend?'

'He got sick. He had to go home.'

Again she lapsed into silence. I didn't say anything, either. Rather than explaining further, I kept as still as a tomb – a tomb in which, slowly but surely, I was burying my little Vera. Being buried like that isn't really all that bad. Most people manage to come back resurrected. Vera, who was a solo dancer on the professional stage, was fading fast into the chorus as the spotlight turned to the beautiful Lenka Silver.

Vera broke into my reverie: 'So she lost an earring?'

'Yes.'

'Just one? Then why wasn't she wearing the other one?' the little detective blurted out between sobs. Women see everything! Like all murderers, I had slipped up.

'I don't know. Maybe she took it off and put it in her purse.'

More silence. Vera's heels tapped out a mournful tattoo on the pavement. I glanced at her; a tear was trembling on the end of her lashes. All it would take to start her crying, I knew, was for me to hold her arm or murmur something reassuring, anything at all. With just a little effort, her tears would have washed away the calamity, and when the flood was over she would have thrown her arms around my neck and everything would have been back to normal. Which is precisely why I did not take her by the arm or whisper anything consoling.

She stopped at the corner.

'Kaja.'

'Yes?'

'Why are you lying to me again?'

I didn't give any reason. It wasn't my style to offer lengthy explanations, though usually I at least admitted my guilt. I was counting on my silence to infuriate her.

'You think I don't know what you were up to?' she shouted hysterically. 'You think I'm *that* stupid? I'm pretty stupid, all right, but not that stupid.'

Again I said nothing. I didn't want to get caught up in a debate about how bright she was.

'Maybe you have forgotten now,' she said, self-pity replacing hysteria, 'but you used to fall down on your knees in front of me, too. And in the same spot! That's a little act you use on all of them, right?'

I shrugged my shoulders and started walking on ahead towards her house. Yes, that is my act, Vera dear. Everybody has his own time-tested routine. So don't be angry at me. The high heels clipclopped after me.

'Kaja!' she implored. 'Don't you ... don't I mean anything at all to you any more?'

Again, I neither confirmed nor denied. A cigarette butt lay on the sidewalk, glowing in the moonlit dusk. I automatically lengthened my stride and crushed it underfoot.

Vera sighed. 'Why did you do that?'

'What?'

'Why did you step on that cigarette?'

'I don't know. Because it was there, I guess.'

'Oh no! You had something in mind!'

I looked into her eyes with indifference, but – God knows why – I started to feel sorry for her. Poor girl. If it had been possible I would have patched things up – if, that is, it wouldn't interfere with the Silver affair. But girls are selfish. They want everything for themselves alone. And the perfect Miss Silver would certainly turn out to be a perfect egotist. Vera would have to go. Under the circumstances, the kindest thing I could do would be to give her a quick *coup de grâce.*

'It's pointless,' I said.

'What's pointless?'

'For you and me to go on this way.'

'But Kaja . . .'

'It's no use.'

'Kaja! Don't say that!'

'Goodbye, Vera! It's best for both of us to end it. And the sooner the better.'

Vera was already weeping bitterly as I intoned this traditional adieu. Fortunately the entrance of her building was quite near.

'Kaja, please!'

'Goodbye, Vera dear. Don't be angry with me.' I turned and tried to make a quick getaway. But the high heels tapped after me.

Vera caught up with me and grabbed my arm. After a brief struggle I freed myself. 'Go home, Vera. Stop following me!'

'But you can't leave me like this . . . Kaja! Kajik!'

I smiled at her, a benevolent, officious smile straight out of a May Day poster.

'Go home, Vera!'

As I was leaving, I saw her turn and rest her forehead against the wall of a house. She was sobbing violently. I quickly rounded the corner, and, to be on the safe side, began jogging towards the Nulse ramp. But she was no longer following me. Tomorrow the telephoning would begin, and the letters, the demands, the pleas. But the worst was over.

Only after I began to descend the moonlit staircase to Nulse did I feel a pang – a slight pang – of remorse. The thought of Lenka Silver, the reward for my Judas-like behaviour, acted as a soothing balm. I stopped. The belly of the moon was almost touching the city spread out beneath me, and I recalled that it was here, on this romantic staircase, that my affair with Vera began. Or was it somewhere else? Possibly. I was no longer sure. Perhaps it was only the association with moonlight, perhaps it was another girl, another place. But I had certainly passed this way with Vera that night as we walked to her apartment, where she proceeded to ask me foolishly whether I thought her a loose woman.

Our love reached its fulfilment after an acquaintance of only two days, this despite the fact that she suffered from a peculiarly delicious complex – she was morbidly afraid that because she was a dancer, men would take her virtue lightly. She told me about the event that marked the beginning of this *idée fixe*. We were having breakfast; I was stuffing myself with eggs fried by Vera's housewifely hands. She was wearing a turquoise dressing gown she had brought back from Paris, not realizing it looked just like the ones cheap Parisian prostitutes wear, hardly in keeping with her rather puritanical attitude towards sex. Poor Vera was not too bright. She told me the story with deadly seriousness, showing no appreciation whatsoever of its comical aspects. The point of the anecdote was, of course, that Vera Kajetan was no tramp, but a decent young woman who had gone to bed with a man two days after meeting him only because she sincerely loved him.

The story concerned our Czechoslovak diplomats in Paris. One of those cultural attachés or first secretaries or similar pinstriped characters had waited for her after the performance in his Peugeot and offered to take her to a cultural event at some embassy. As soon as she got in the car he began to fumble around under her skirt. Vera was dumbfounded, not having the slightest idea what one was supposed to do with one of our honoured diplomats under such circumstances. After brief deliberation she gave him an old-fashioned Czech slap in the face. The cultural attaché was as dumbfounded as she had been. 'Excuse me, Miss,' he sputtered, 'but you *are* a dancer, aren't you?' He was probably terrified that he had mistakenly tickled the privates of a member of the Ministry of the Interior.

This incident was a shock for Vera. The shock developed into trauma. After that, whenever she was asked to fill out any form that asked for *occupation*, she wrote 'theatrical artist'. She also confided to me that since the unfortunate episode in the Peugeot she had refused to let any man touch her. The chaste interval wasn't all that long, but considering the ephemeral lifespan of young dancers, it was long enough. Later, she confessed further that even before the Incident, her sex life hadn't been especially colourful. She was something of a drudge and she took her work with deadly seriousness, completely ignoring the non-artistic aspects of the profession that so intrigued the cultural attaché. Instead of practising the art of turning lovers' heads, she practised pirouettes and various steps with French names from morning to night.

She finally admitted that before me she had only had one real lover. It happened while she was still at the conservatory. And because Vera was Vera, he naturally turned out to be a tuba player from the Philharmonic. A tuba player and a dancer. I laughed so hard that Vera was offended. She had no sense of humour and saw nothing funny in this alliance. But her sulks never lasted long. She needed gentleness as much as other people need air, which is why she moved through the world like a half-suffocated puppy.

Even the affair with the tuba player ended in a traumatic shock, and though the *dénouement* came straight out of a two-reel comedy, she saw nothing funny about it. The tuba player worked now and then in a vaudeville band, and he took up with a lady chimpanzee trainer. One day he was teasing the chimp and the animal bit him so severely that his leg had to be amputated below the knee. Vera, who had character, intended to stay faithful to her cripple. Fortunately, somebody took pity on her and wrote her an anonymous note about all the other women in her lover's life. The tuba player confessed everything, and this proved too much even for Vera's character. Or perhaps she just couldn't take another shock. Thus, I was the third in a series of burlesque shocks administered by life to my faithful ballerina.

But what could I do? I couldn't give up an experience that attracted me so powerfully just for Vera's sake. Perhaps more shock therapy would finally cure her. I heaved a deep sigh for my sentimental *danseuse*; then, in a mellow mood, I scampered down to Nulse to meet a future called Lenka Silver. At that point, of course, I still had no idea what I was letting myself in for.

2 *Publishing*

That night I dreamed that I was discussing poems with Lenka. The devil knows what mechanism is responsible for annoying us with dreams that trouble our consciences. In any case, instead of enjoying mermaid kisses, a stupid discussion of the essence of poetry filled my dreams that night.

In the morning I was sitting at my uncluttered editorial desk. The motto 'Hurry slowly' under the glass desktop was nicely balanced by Lenin's exhortation 'Learn! Learn! Learn!' hung on the wall during an earlier, more enthusiastic era. I had long ago solved the problem of the essence of poetry. I knew that poetry was a temporary manifestation of psychophysiologic development, characteristic of the borderline between puberty and adulthood. Normal people bother about poetry only as long as they are virgins, in a sexual as well as a general sense of the term. When a person is young and green, he resents the fact that the world is full of injustice and hypocrisy, and he longs for beautiful girls, adventure, and all sorts of nonsense. Eventually all of this passes, the longing for girls is cooled by taking St Paul's advice (better to marry than burn) and by going to the movies; the longing for adventure is satisfied by detective stories and football. The handful of individuals who remain virgins in the non-sexual sense turn into real poets. And a certain number of others, whom the world has deprived of all forms of virginity, turn into male or female whores. It had long been clear to me, without undue bitterness, that I belonged to this last group, though not to its extreme wing, perhaps.

My Chief certainly belonged there, too. In the days of his youth he had written poems about the loveliness of the Virgin Mary and inveighed against the moral depravity of the times. Later, like myself, he stopped appraising the world and its wickedness from the viewpoint of moral ideas and began to regard it from the viewpoint of personal safety. I had just reached this point in my sour early-morning ruminations when that eminent personage called up and requested my presence.

I therefore postponed my first telephonic attack on Miss Silver, and trotted into the Chief's office.

It was a big office whose most important piece of furniture was a long conference table around which important discussions were held.

In the old days, these conferences used to be fairly placid affairs. We would slowly sip our coffee and discuss such questions as: should the immortal nineteenth-century classic *Grandma* be published once again next year with full-colour illustrations by Adolf Kaspar as part of the 'Classical Heritage' series, while simultaneously appearing without illustrations in the 'Roots of the Past' series or else with pen-and-ink drawings in the 'Primrose' library edition line, or, alternatively, the deluxe edition could be postponed one year (the author, Bozena Nemcova, was safely dead) and replaced by a new edition of the novel *Onward, Mountaineers!* by the eminent writer Marie Burdych (still dangerously alive), taking into account that *Onward* had been adapted for the theatre last year, was currently being made into a film, and would soon come out in a special 'Young Readers' edition under the aegis of the Children's Publishing House, with a concurrent braille edition prepared by the Pedagogical Institute for blind readers.

Such problems were rather easy to solve to everyone's satisfaction (with the possible exception of the readers), and only rarely led to any unpleasantness. The delay in bringing out an illustrated edition of *Grandma* might perhaps have occasioned a complaint to the Ministry of Culture by some doddering art historian, such as Trejlibenovsky. His plaintive nostalgia would be transmuted by the watchful zealots of the Ministry into a sharp attack on the negative attitude of our publishing industry towards national classics. However, only a bit of attention to strategy was needed to avoid such mishaps, and once they occurred they were easily rectified: in planning for next year, an illustrated edition of *Grandma* would be supplemented by two other beloved classics.

A much greater danger lurged in apparently trivial matters which ultimately turned out to be like icebergs – harmless-looking to the superficial observer, but capable of sinking giant ships. For example, not long ago we were faced with the dilemma of whether, in the new edition of *Grandpa Bezousek*, the other seemingly safe classic, the first letter of the word 'God' should be capitalized or not. This was not an easy nut to crack, nor was the problem merely an abstract one. Marxist science had conclusively demonstrated the non-existence of a higher power, and using an upper-case G could be interpreted as a blasphemy against the founder of socialism. The wrong decision could lead to a major *contretemps*, a political *malheur* – in short, a fuckup. And while one of my Chief's outstanding qualities was his uncanny and widely admired knack for getting out of fuckups, on several occasions even he barely escaped.

In trying to solve the painful dilemma posed by the capitalization of God, my Chief drew on related experience connected with the publication of *Uncle Tom's Cabin*. We had planned to reissue this classic in celebration of some African jubilee, and the Chief almost paid dearly for Uncle Tom's profound religious feelings. At a meeting of the editorial board, young Hartman attacked the book's anti-Marxist religiosity. My superior at once grasped the potential peril and gravity of the situation, and the indefensible nature of his own position. He cut off any further discussion of the matter by proposing that we would not publish the book in its original version, but in the form of a so-called 'adaptation'. At my suggestion, this job was turned over to Melisek, an indigent Latin translator, who adapted the work in such a masterly fashion that Uncle Tom talked like a trade unionist and all references to the non-existent deity were eliminated.

Of course, it was impossible to adapt *Grandpa Bezousek* in this way, since it was a part of the classical heritage of our own national literature. Furthermore, the hero of the book invoked the Lord too many times to make radical blue pencilling a practical possibility. The author's status as a classic master, of course, afforded some protection, and in the end my Chief decided that consistent downgrading of the divinity to lower-case initial would be sufficient to ensure our safety. And, indeed, the book went through without a hitch.

An extremely clever operator, my Chief. Now, sitting with a half-finished cup of coffee beside a huge bust of Marx, he was holding a manuscript at arm's length, as if it turned his stomach; and he looked unhappy.

'Sit down. Had your coffee?' he said, in lieu of a greeting.

'Yes, thanks,' I answered and made myself comfortable in an armchair that faced the Chief's chair and was meant for visitors.

'The reason I called you,' he continued in a mournful tone, which signalled the slow emergence of a new iceberg, 'is this manuscript. It was recommended by Blumenfeld,' he added with distaste.

I knew right off that a Titanic-sized iceberg was on the way, and that we were in for it. Miss Blumenfeld was the most recent addition to our staff. As it soon turned out, taking her on proved to be a strategic mistake, despite the fact that she had brought with her academic recommendations that abounded with superlatives. In an unguarded moment the Chief once hinted to me that these recommendations had more to do with Miss Blumenfeld's personal charms than her professional abilities. And certainly her escapades during the short time she had been with us tended to confirm the Chief's uneasiness. In the course of her short career as editor she had already set afloat five icebergs, which only the greatest exertion on all our parts had kept from wrecking our office. In fact, two of these cases required private intervention on the highest levels of government.

Now, the Chief was disgustedly telling me of the latest incipient fuckup.

'It's called *Between Us Girls*. A novella. Written by Jarmila Cibulka. You know the name?'

'It sounds familiar. Didn't she have a story in *The Torch*?'

'She did,' said the Chief tersely. 'And because of that story, Pepik Hajny got called all the way up to Comrade Kaiser. They had to yank it out in the page-proof stage and the whole damn magazine had to be reset.' He looked at me with a martyred expression.

'And this is the writer that Blumenfeld is recommending?' I asked indignantly.

'Yes. I read it myself. It is ... just awful. If I print this they'll think I'm out of my mind.'

'Send it back to Blumenfeld, then.'

'That's the rub. She got three positive opinions for this thing,' the Chief said, completely dejected.

'From whom?'

'That's just it,' he sighed. 'One is from Kobliha. That would be no problem. After the way Kobliha got flattened upstairs, on account of that preface to Karel Čapek, we don't have to pay any attention to him. The second is from Ferda Hezky. That's no big deal either. But the third one, Karel – the third one is from Academician Brat, no less!'

I stared at the boss incredulously.

'Brat approves it?'

'With qualifications,' said the Chief, and I detected a flicker of hope in his voice. 'With qualifications, but ... let me read you the conclusion of his report,' he said and picked up a few sheets from his desk. He cleared his throat and began to read. The opinion was written in classical style:

In general and with appropriate qualifications it may thus be said that in spite of a number of shortcomings – notably substandard expressions and lack of ideological clarity – the manuscript reveals signs of epic talent. In principle, and assuming that the editors are willing to collaborate with the author in revising the manuscript, I am not opposed to possible publication, after appropriate discussion with the editorial board, providing that sufficient time is given to mature deliberation and providing that publication is not at the expense of worthier material.

The text left us so many escape clauses that it didn't seem like a mortal threat. I said: 'That gives us an out. We simply return the manuscript to be rewritten ...'

'Blumenfeld has already done that. And it's as bad as ever.'

'Then send it back again.'

The Chief sighed. 'That woman rewrote every single passage Brat marked for revision. But now it's worse than before.'

'Did Brat see the revised version?'

'No. That's the whole trouble,' moaned the boss. 'He's gone off on a trip abroad.'

'Let's send it to him.'

'We can't. His secretary says that he explicitly instructed her not to send him anything.'

The Chief was in hot water, all right.

'And you say the rewrite only made it worse?'

'Blumenfeld maintains that it's greatly improved. And Hezky agrees with her.'

'That's strange.'

'I'll say it is,' said the Chief. He gulped down the last drops of coffee and added despondently: 'You can be sure of one thing – none of the higherups are going to congratulate us for publishing stuff like this.'

In the ensuing silence I gazed at him. His high forehead, framed by greying sideburns, was furrowed with wrinkles; his black-rimmed glasses sat askew on his nose. His tropical jacket was unbuttoned; his sober but expensive necktie hung at halfmast. I could still vividly recall the golden age when he had come to the office dressed in proletarian denims and coarse, open-necked shirt. But that had been long ago. The Chief always mirrored the historical context down to the last detail.

Now, however, he was clearly on the brink of disaster.

'What are you planning to do?' I asked.

'Karel,' he said in a confidential tone, 'in the old days, when things got rough we could always count on the editorial board. But now ... I don't have to tell you.' He paused significantly, 'Between you and me, Blumenfeld knows how to exploit the situation.' He leaned towards me across the desk and continued in a lowered voice: 'Look, you know me. I understand Blumenfeld. She's a young woman and she's green. To her, life is just one big lark. If the situation wasn't so risky I'd wash my hands of the whole thing and let Blumenfeld find out for herself what it's like to be called on the carpet. When you're young a couple of little catastrophes aren't the end of the world. At least she'd learn her lesson, grow up, and stop trying to fight the system.' He tried to coax one more drop of coffee from the bottom of the cup. It was empty. 'But you know the situation. Blumenfeld seems to be obsessed by that stupid book. Even if the other reports turn out negative – and since I'm picking the readers myself I'm pretty sure they will – the vote will still be three for and three against and we'll have to pass it on to the editorial board. And she's a demon. She'll buttonhole everybody and half the board will be on her side even before the meeting begins. And the timing couldn't be worse – just before the Writers' Congress convenes, you understand? We'll need every voice and every argument we can muster.' And again he tilted his head back in one final attempt to suck coffee from the upturned cup. Then he scraped some sediment with his spoon, licked it off, looked me in the eye, and said: 'That's why I wanted to ask you to read it for yourself. Just so you could help in the discussion later on and perhaps talk to one or two people on the editorial board, to explain the situation. I know this falls outside your area, but . . .'

'I'll be very glad to read it,' I lied. I was one of his men and I couldn't refuse. As soon as I touched the manuscript I felt a slight shiver, and for some reason thought of Doctor Faustus and his pact with the devil.

'I'm very grateful,' said the Chief warmly. 'You know, I've decided to introduce a new system – that is, if it meets with your approval. From now on questionable manuscripts will be given to six outside readers and three inside readers, plus three other people from other bureaux. When it comes to prose, as is the case here, the manuscript will be read by one person from the prose fiction department, one from translation and one from poetry and criticism. That's why I'm giving this to you. And you'll pass it on to Pecakova.'

I felt a lot better. In the old days Pecakova had had the reputation of being a cliché-monger, but recently her stock had gone up because Academician Brat had praised her in an exhaustive, private report as an exemplary worker who was not disconcerted by de-Stalinization but always kept a clear head. Pecakova was a simple soul. She had publicly described her utopian dream in a great socialist novel which, with the dramatic force of an *Anna Karenina*, depicted the tragic yet happily resolved conflict between new and outmoded production methods. Her mere existence cast doubt on the theory of life as a continuous development, and her clearheadedness during the de-Stalinization was indistinguishable from her clearheadedness during the Stalin era. But if she was going to speak at a meeting of the editorial board – and she was inordinately fond of addressing such meetings – everything would be all right. I would have my say after hers, and by the law of dialects I would be spared from making a fool of myself. It will probably take mankind a few more centuries to realize that clichés are not a matter of form but of content, not the products of fuzzy tongues but the products of fuzzy beliefs.

'You're absolutely right,' I said. 'A specialist sometimes can't see the wood for the trees. A person who normally works in an entirely different area brings a fresh eye to bear on the subject and can spot things the specialist would be likely to miss.'

The Chief grinned at me.

'I knew I could depend on you, Karel. I had that in mind when I drew up my new system. By the way,' he said, switching to an entirely different tone and half-closing his rather weary looking eyes. 'Who was that nymph I saw you with yesterday? I hope I'm not being indiscreet.'

The glum problems we had to deal with to earn our daily bread magically vanished, and the scent of pink violets seemed to permeate the Chief's office. I smiled. 'Not at all She's a girlfriend of one of my friends, Vasek Zamberk. He was there, too, but he didn't feel well and had to get out of the water.'

'Of course, of course. I didn't mean to pry into your private life.' Then, in a carnal voice, he said, 'Her name was something like Silver, wasn't it?'

'Lenka Silver. She works for Bio-Ex.'

The Chief got up. 'Watch your heart, my friend. You're still young, but you're approaching the age when it can be dangerous. Take care!'

He squeezed my hand energetically and rewarded me with the yellowish glint of his friendly smile.

'You, too,' I answered, and briskly left the room.

When I returned to my own office, Annie wasn't there. Instead, there was a note on my desk written in her repulsive, microscopic handwriting which said, *'I am at Comrade Bukovsky's.'* This meant that she was in the beauty parlour and poet Bukovsky was serving as her alibi, which, in turn, meant that the telephone was free and that I could talk without fear of being overheard. I could call Lenka.

I found the number for Bio-Ex in the phone book and reached for the phone. But before I could dial, the phone rang.

'Hello,' I said in a voice meant to show that I was overworked and that my nerves were on edge.

'Karel?' said the small voice in the receiver.

I frowned. 'Hello, Vera.'

Silence. I never enjoyed hurting people. After a long pause there was a feeble call for help: 'Don't you have anything to say to me, Kaja?'

'No.'

More silence.

'What have I ever done to you?'

I got the vague but highly unpleasant feeling that I was a swine. But over the years I had got so used to that feeling that I stuck to my principle of making a clean surgical break.

'You haven't done anything, Vera, but don't call me any more.'

'I'll kill myself!' she announced.

'I'm telling you, Vera, this way is best. You'll get over it and then you'll be grateful to me that we broke up as friends.'

'I'll kill myself!' she repeated.

'Goodbye, then, Vera.' I hung up.

Then I lifted the receiver again and dialled the number for Bio-Ex. The line was busy. Irritated, I put the receiver back on the hook and picked up the manuscript. Jarmila Cibulka: *Between Us Girls. A Novel of Our Time*. It was written on an ancient Underwood. In the righthand corner there was a quotation from Walt Whitman:

Womanhood and all that is a woman, and the man that comes
from woman.
The womb, the teats, nipples, breast-milk, tears, laughter,
weeping, love-looks, love-perturbations and risings ...
Poise on the hips, leaping, reclining, embracing, arm-curving
and tightening,
The continual changes of the flex of the mouth, and around the
eyes.
The skin, the sunburnt shade, freckles, hair,
The curious sympathy one feels when feeling with the hand the
naked meat of the body ...

Next to the quotation the energetic hand of Academician Brat added: 'Torn out of context, not appropriate.' This remark was followed by the proofreader's symbol for 'delete'. Somebody else, with an equally energetic hand, had crossed out the Whitman poem and replaced it with a citation from Robinson Jeffers:

... the present time is not pastoral, but founded on violence, pointed for more passive violence: perhaps it is not perversity but need ...

I winced and turned the page. The very first sentence hit me in the eye: 'Now Hanka knew it for sure: she was knocked up.'

Brother! The sentence was underscored with a forceful, wavy line, and another, equally familiar and forceful hand had written in the margin: 'Now Hanka knew it for sure: fucking with Franta had had unfortunate consequences, and she was in a jam.'

I was fascinated by the author and her methods of revision. I thumbed through the manuscript, looking for Brat's comments and the girl's responses to them. She certainly had lots of imagination. Her lexicon of obscene terms was enormous; for every expression questioned by the academician she substituted an equally pungent synonym, sometimes even adding two or three variant forms in parentheses. It was either a manifestation of her innocently passionate dedication to the text or of her impertinent sense of humour. Did she really think that Brat, who had underlined the sentence 'I will kick you in the ass!' would accept as aesthetically valid either one of the suggested alternatives: 'I will kick you in the anus (shithole)'?

As I leafed through page after page covered by Brat's wavy lines, I began to feel that the writer must be a graduate of some school for morally disturbed girls, and I decided, then and there, to look her up.

Then I remembered Lenka. The phone was right next to me. Once again I dialled her number.

The phone rang several times; then Lenka Silver's unmistakable voice sang out: 'Hello, Bio-Ex.'

The sound was made even more seductive by the parrot-like cawing in the background. 'Good morning,' I said. 'Please be kind enough to repeat that a few more times.'

'Is your phone out of order or are you hard of hearing?'

'Neither. But I love music. And your voice sounds like an oboe.'

'Ah,' said the voice in the receiver. Just then my office door opened and Dasha Blumenfeld strode in.

'Hi,' blared Dasha, sounding like a trumpet. The voice in the phone kept repeating: 'Bio-Ex, Bio-Ex, Bio-Ex ...' I covered the receiver with my palm and barked at Blumenfeld: 'One moment!' Anybody else would have taken the hint and left. Not Blumenfeld. She ambled up to my desk and sat down on one corner. 'Bio-Ex, Bio-Ex, Bio-Ex. Will that do?' Lenka asked.

'No,' I said. 'I have to hear it with my own ears.'

'Why? Are you listening with someone else's?'

'What I wanted to say was, are you free this evening?'

'Yes, but I have no intention of repeating Bio-Ex all afternoon.'

Blumenfeld was listening without even pretending not to.

'Can I call you back in a little while, Lenka?'

'Sure, but Comrade Benesova will be taking over in a few minutes.'

'Where are you going?'

'To the zoo.'

'I'll meet you there, then.'

'I am going there for a professional consultation. Bozo has hiccups.'

'Bozo?'

'The chimp,' Lenka explained. Good Lord! A tuba player with an amputated leg appeared before me and the icy finger of God touched my conscience. What a strange coincidence! Perhaps the nonexistent creator of my soul was preparing to punish me for Vera?

'Well, then ...' tinkled the voice in the receiver.

'How about after the consultation?'

'I'll be busy.' There was a brief pause and then she said unexpectedly: 'Until this evening. I'll be at Manes at around seven.'

'I'll be there half an hour early.'

'Bio-Ex, Bio-Ex,' Lenka said and hung up. So did I.

'Can I interrupt your conversation for a moment?' Blumenfeld asked, crossing her tight-skirted thighs and leaning her stupendous bosom towards me.

'What do you want?' I asked.

'Look here – his highness gave you the Cibulka stuff, right?'

'Right.'

'And you'll be nice and let it go through, right? It is awfully important to me.' Her pudgy hand stroked my hair.

'Why shouldn't I?'

'Well, the stuff isn't exactly kosher.'

'I am not a prude.'

'I know. But you're awfully cautious.'

'What makes you say that?' I asked.

'Oh, I know who I'm dealing with,' Dasha purred in an affected way. Clearly, even though she had joined our staff only recently, she had got wind of my reputation as the boss's man. She slid off the desk, her impressive breasts bouncing resiliently. 'But underneath it all you're all right and I trust you. Look, I admit the stuff is a little raunchy in parts, but this half-assed outfit could use some of that.' Her vocabulary was no less expressive than her gargantuan breasts.

'Of course, of course, if she's really talented ...'

'Talented? You'll be amazed. She's a teacher in a home for morally disturbed girls, and she knows what she is writing about.'

I opened the manuscript, trying to recall whether we had ever published anything about morally disturbed girls. I could only remember the *Satyricon*, from which the Chief, acting on the advice of higher-ups, had removed all the objectionable episodes. The book had shrunk so drastically that it could only be used in our house organ. It is hard to imagine a manuscript about morally disturbed girls without erotic scenes. Just the very first sentence – I looked at it again: 'Now Hanka knew it for sure: fucking with Franta had had unfortunate consequences, and she was in a jam.'

'Sure, the stuff is naturalistic.' My musing was interrupted by Blumenfeld, who had been watching me as I scanned the manuscript. 'But everything she writes is true.'

'What was that stink in *The Torch* all about?'

'There was one sentence they didn't like, and they clobbered her with it.'

'Why didn't she change it?'

'She's stubborn.'

'Well, you know ...'

'That's just what I like about her,' she interrupted.

'So do I. But the trouble is that neither you nor I have the last word and ...'

'But if we keep sending up good stuff, in the end they'll have to swallow it,' said Dasha, and then she repeated her basic credo, though in a somewhat laundered form: 'Sooner or later, there'll be an end to that crap and better stuff will prevail.'

Prevail! Nostalgically, I remembered the paradise lost when we said either yes or no, and that was that. In those days there was no question of 'prevailing'.

'Well, we'll see. I understand you have a positive report from Brat?'

Blumenfeld lit up. 'That's right! And Cibulka has mellowed since *The Torch* affair. She followed his recommendations ...'

'So I see,' I said, citing one underlined passage: '"Pressing her body against his in the dark, she took his hand and placed it on her breast." This has been changed to read "and placed it on her tit." Is she kidding? Doesn't she know who Brat is?'

'No problem. Brat's out of the country and he left orders not to be disturbed, so he'll never see it.'

'Why did he go on that trip, anyway?'

'To wait to find out which way the wind is blowing,' answered Blumenfeld. 'And when he finds out, he'll let Cibulka go scot free because the wind is blowing our way.'

She said this with absolute certainty, with that brash confidence which I had admired from the first and which she manifested in all aspects of her work. I didn't have that kind of certainty. I glanced at the manuscript, without really concentrating on the letters. Blumenfeld. What was it the Chief said? 'A young woman ... green ... she acts like she's obsessed ... she'll buttonhole everybody.' What makes her do it? Damn it, what does she get out of battling for manuscripts about morally disturbed girls? She's become the champion of an inexperienced young writer as if the fate of the world depended on it! One writer more or less, what difference does it make? The world is rushing towards extinction anyway; life is short, so why court danger? I shivered. What will this new era be like, this era of dangerous freedom, dangerously free of the old restraints?

And what was it, I wondered, that drove Blumenfeld? She herself didn't write – something of a rarity these days. Not even prefaces. Her literary abilities found their only outlet in dust-jacket copy, and in making those quixotic books of hers 'prevail'.

She looked a bit like a female Sancho Panza: petite, pudgy, not beautiful, but attractive, with lovely Jewish eyes. She stood, bending over me, the enchanting tips of her vast breasts pointing arrogantly, her tanned arm propped on my desk. The serial number 8394771283 was tattooed near her elbow. As the Chief said, 'she was a girl with no real experience, a green young thing.' After the war she had spent three years in Norway in a sort of pension for Jewish children who had survived the holocaust. There she had learned perfect Norwegian – which, of course, was useless in our office – and had been unofficially adopted by a childless Norwegian Jewish couple, who ultimately became a source of endless gift parcels. Dasha recklessly traded this bounty on the black market and managed to live quite well. A green girl, Dasha.

'I'll read it,' I promised. 'And if it's as good as you say it is, I'll recommend it for publication.'

She smiled at me. 'You're a darling.'

'You are right, I am cautious,' I said. 'But sometimes it's better to go slow, one step at a time, and not to be too . . .'

'I know. It's written on your desk,' she pointed an ink-stained finger at the motto under the glass top: *Hurry slowly*. 'But a new era is beginning,' she said, turning at the door and smiling at me again. 'By the way, I'm celebrating . . . well, let's just say I am celebrating a birthday. It doesn't matter how old I am. Come on over. It should be a great party. Bring your friend who consults with chimpanzees if you want to.'

She slammed the door. Lenka Silver. Ah, Lenka Silver, you have entered my life just as furious storms are about to break. But perhaps you're a good omen, a sign that all will end well.

I reached for Cibulka and began reading.

After about ten pages I was no longer reading the book as an editor. I was simply reading. Period. The book wasn't fit for publication, wind or no wind. Brat must have been out of his mind to have given it a favourable report. All the same, the book wormed its way into my heart. This can't be literature, I told myself, this story of a model factory worker's daughter left on her own by her super-politicized parents. I had run across this theme before, of course. In fact, our resident laureate Zluva had recently belaboured it. Zluva's version had a happy end, with the heroine ultimately saved by the regenerating power of the collective. In Cibulka's story, the heroine was ultimately saved by an abortionist. But it wasn't so much the story that counted here as the way it was told. Zluva's book was full of endless conversations, of prefabricated wisdom thinly disguised by fake-folksy slang. Cibulka's story was a tapestry of memories, a gallery of heroes and heroines and places that nobody ever heard about but which nevertheless bore the stamp of complete authenticity. The story of a guy named Vozejk, rocking and rolling with his girl Majda – until she was locked up for petty larceny and prostitution. The story of Bejk, who achieved lasting fame by sleeping off a wild binge in the Soviet tank parked in Smichov square as a war memorial. Trying to make himself comfortable inside, he practically ruined the tank – and was locked up, too.

As I read on, I became aware that my youthful ambitions, which I had long considered dead and buried, were stirring. Damn it, this was how I had wanted to write, long ago. And about the very same subject. Before safely settling down in the comfortable armchair of literature, I had known a guy just like Bejk. His name was Risa and he kept alive by selling what he stole from department stores. And there was Majda, only her name was Kvetuse, and she was a whore who had gone off to Germany during the war. I had wanted to write about these people, and I had tried, but failed. Then it was no longer possible, socrealism had replaced plain realism, so I said to myself that it was no longer possible, and turned to writing poems about our native soil, our heroic generals and stoic generalissimos, labour's proudly beating heart, revolution's fetters sundered. That sort of thing.

I put down the manuscript and glanced at the bust of Lenin standing on the bookshelf. Nonsense! Blumenfeld is completely crazy. We're not living on the moon. On the other hand, I can't help it. Cibulka is a beautiful writer, unbelievably beautiful. But there were many beautiful things in this world, and now they're gone and we are still here. I *refuse* to succumb to the siren song of somebody's beautiful talent. Comrade Kaiser won't fall for it, that's for sure. And if I give in to that girl's talent, Comrade Kaiser will let me fall. And I can't afford that, especially not now when all I want is for Lenka Silver to succumb to me.

The door flew open and Annie floated in, sporting a new permanent.

'Anybody ask for me?'

'Yes. The boss.'

'What did you tell him?'

'That you had gone to the beauty parlour with Bukovsky.'

'You're awful!' Annie sat down at her desk. 'Has the Chief read the preface yet?'

'There's something on your desk.'

'Thanks.' Annie reached for a reader's memo which had been dropped on her desk earlier in the day by the editorial secretary, and began studying it.

I returned to my deliberations. No. No, sir. If this bomb were to go off, it would ruin literature for all of us. All of us who are now living off literature would look ridiculous by comparison. What was it Lenka had said about my poems? Well, whatever it was that she couldn't find in my poems was there in full tone in this beautiful horror script. I had never been able to write like that, and I never would be able to. Our kindly era, though, forgave me my lack of talent, and rewarded me for my suppleness. If I were to write a favourable opinion of this book, I would be betraying that era. Yes, of course, everything comes to an end. I never had any illusions, like some people. But life is short. Our only hope lies in delaying the inevitable, and every delay is worth its weight in gold. Life is short.

'For Heaven's sake!' called out Annie.

'What is it?'

'Look. He took out Paustovsky!'

She handed me the Chief's memo accompanying Bukovsky's preface to the anthology of Russian poetry. The Chief had written: 'The preface is good, correctly oriented from a political viewpoint, artistically sensitive. I suggest, however, that the quote from Paustovsky on page 3 be deleted. It is not necessary, the explanation stands on its own without it, and Paustovsky has recently come under negative criticism!'

Farewell, Cibulka! We cannot permit you to come under negative criticism! Excuse us, but you'll have to wait for the next era.

I got up and carried the half-read novel to Pecakova's office.

3 Manes

It was already half past seven and Lenka had still not appeared. The sun, perched on top of the Petrin observation tower, looked like a huge joke played on the city by a drunken sculptor. Blondes and brunettes paraded in pastel dresses around the Manes balustrade. None of them even came close to being as beautiful as Lenka. She was unique.

She jumped off a passing trolley, her pink-and-white-striped skirt fluttering above her knees.

'Have you been waiting long?' she asked pleasantly.

'Oh, only an hour,' I said. 'Without you, time has no meaning for me. Don't you need an assistant at Bio-Ex?'

She laughed as I kissed her hand. Then I floated at her side towards the Manes terrace.

As soon as we had sat down on the terrace, Lenka steered our conversation away from her eyes – which was all I wanted to talk about – to literature.

'Why are you so interested in that stuff,' I finally asked. 'I thought you said you didn't care for literati.'

'I said that?'

'Try to remember,' I began to count on my fingers, just as she did the day before: 'Hypocrites, cheats, literary dabblers . . .'

She laughed. 'Well, actually, I *don't* like them.'

'Why not?'

She gazed out over the railing towards the river. A memory passed over the beautiful profile.

'Because I've had experiences with them. One of them played a rotten trick on me.' Lenka took a sip of lemonade. Bubbles floated up from the tip of the straw like lost souls.

'What did he do?'

She was silent, but I wouldn't be put off.

'Hell, he couldn't have jilted you, that's for certain. He would have died of a broken heart.'

'You think so?'

'I know so. You are like Naples, only in reverse. Not to see you again after having seen you once means death.'

But Lenka refused to be melted by the warmth of my flattery. I began to feel like Vasek Zamberk.

'He did not die, though,' she said. 'Instead . . .'

On a small podium in the corner of the terrace a saxophone began to play. It sounded forlorn, like a lone elephant abandoned by the herd. A ruby ball flamed up in the girl's emerald lemonade. It was the sinking sun focusing its rays on the green glass.

'Instead?'

'Forget it. He simply used the whole thing as a subject for a story. A stupid story at that. Just listen to that music!'

'I'd like to read it. Will you lend it to me?'

'Just listen,' she urged me, and placed her pink-nailed fingers on the back of my hand. The electric charge shook my whole body.

'You like jazz?'

'I do,' she said forcefully. 'I like saxophones. Especially baritone sax.'

I followed the direction of the opaque gaze until my eyes came to rest on the sax man. I think his name was Konopasek. His neck was swollen, the veins on his forehead bulged. He was blowing a strange, raw, nostalgic tone. Lenka listened in a trance. He was blowing like the wind, like the wind that wafted old Professor Lev Ilyich Shubatov from Moscow to Prague for a conference on current socialistic music. Grandpa Shubatov listened to Konopasek and his band, listened and when the music stopped he said to everybody's amazement: 'They play beautifully, the youngsters!' And when one of the comrades whispered the word '*Kosmopolitism*' . . . Grandpa Shubatov shook his head: '*Nyet, eto nye kosmopolitism. Eto musikalnyi experiment*,' and added that the real enemy was mechanical traditionalism. Comrade Pechacek, who was supposed to deliver the final address the following day, quickly disappeared and spent the whole night revising his speech. Instead of accusing Konopasek of reactionary diversionism, the revised version bristled with indignation against a group known as the Society for the Study of Traditional Jazz for falsely glorifying pseudo-nationalistic folk music.

Lenka came out of her trance, removed her hand and thus broke the electric circuit. The saxophonist stepped down. A bespectacled fellow started pounding on vibes. The resonant, neurotic sound brought Miss Silver back to normal. She blinked her black eyelashes at me and smiled as if by way of apology.

'Why are you so partial to saxophones?' I asked.

'I don't know. They almost seem to talk, don't they? They are like human voices.'

'I guess I'd better learn to play the saxophone, then. My own voice doesn't seem to interest you nearly as much.'

She laughed again, and again placed her fingers on the back of my hand, quite intimately. I tried to cover them with my other hand, but she abruptly slipped her hand away and stared off towards the Petrin observation tower.

'Tell me about your Chief. He interests me,' she said.

'What's so fascinating about him?'

'As I told you, I don't like intellectual phonies. But I like to listen to stories about them, to hear what phonies they really are.'

'Couldn't I talk about myself, then?'

'Modesty is becoming to a man,' she said, rewarding me with a goodnatured laugh. 'Your story can wait till later. Now tell me all about your Chief.'

'Very well.' I leaned against the back of the chair, and for an instant the dying rays of the sun blinded me. 'Well then: Emil Prochazka, age forty-nine, editor-in-chief of *Our Book*. Profession: writer. Political attitude: positive.'

Encouraged by a warm smile, I went on: 'Since early childhood he had exhibited a poetic talent, which, in the years 1930 to 1938, was enlisted in the service of the Masaryk ideology; in the years 1939 to 1945 in the service of our Lord Jesus Christ; in the years 1945 to the present in the service of the philosophy of Marx, Engels and Lenin; until the Twentieth Party Congress, also in the service of Stalin. His work, characterized by a deep love for his native land and a hatred of social injustice and imperialism, was accorded the 1953 Poet Pioneer Prize. Critically acclaimed as one of the foremost representatives of socialist realism, tempered by profound understanding of the Czech spirit.'

As I continued, Lenka's smile faded.

'Aren't you bored by this?'

'Not at all,' she replied hastily. 'You put it very well.'

'Really? And yet when I told you yesterday that my Chief's private life was a political act, you looked so forbidding that I thought I had made a political *faux pas*.'

She grinned. 'I felt a bit faint at that point, but not because of what you were telling me. What really happened with those wives of his, anyway?'

'You really want to know?'

Lenka sucked up the last drops of lemonade. Her face was now obscured by the lengthening shadow of the Petrin observatory.

'Of course I do. Women are always dying to know about marital affairs. There is nothing personal about it, you understand.' She looked me in the eye, holding her straw in her teeth like a cigar.

'I see,' I said. 'All right. The first one was the daughter of the publisher Vana. He married her around the start of the war and he stuck it out with her until the Communists took over in 1948. Her dad went the way of all millionaires. Then he married . . .'

'And there was no woman in his life before that?' she interrupted. A waiter flew by, noticed the empty glass, stopped, and asked: 'Another one, Miss?'

She looked flustered, as if the waiter had startled her. She stared at him vacantly, then shook her head: 'No. Bring me a vodka.'

'One vodka. And the gentleman?'

'Make that two vodkas,' I said gleefully.

'Two vodkas!' the waiter announced to the world and flew off. A bass trumpet started screaming from the podium.

'You like to drink?'

Lenka looked bewildered. Her face was flushed as pink as the stripes of her white dress. Then suddenly she turned white. 'What? No. Well, yes, sometimes.'

'Why did you order a drink just now?'

'Why did you?'

I stared into her eyes, in vain. What was the meaning of that vodka? Did she want to recover from some shock, à la Vera? To drown her distaste for hypocrites and literati?

I sighed. 'Because you're driving me to distraction. It's a beautiful terrace by the river, and we're discussing my boss. Why aren't we talking about you?'

She smiled. 'We'll get to that. Patience brings roses. First answer my question.'

'What question was that?'

'About your Chief.'

'I refuse to talk any further about my Chief. If you're so interested, I'll introduce you to him. He's very fond of attractive young comrades.' I was really getting fed up.

'I'll take you up on that,' she said.

'It will be a pleasure. It might be interesting to see you get burned. Let me warn you, on the average he starts up a new affair every three months. He's got about fifteen illegitimate children.'

'I noticed his sex appeal right away,' sighed Miss Silver. 'Who was he involved with before his first marriage?'

'With President Benes's wife,' I answered. 'Of course, it was a secret liaison. The Munich crisis put an end to it. She had to clear out of the country.'

The waiter brought us our vodkas, and after letting his eyes rove over Lenka, hurried off towards less pleasant duties. Lenka immediately grasped the glass, lifted it avidly towards her mouth, then paused at the last moment and looked at me. 'May your wishes come true,' she said.

'You know what my wishes are, don't you?'

She affected a mysterious expression. I noticed that the lovely little vein was again pulsing on her temple. 'I think so, yes.'

'And you hope my wishes come true?'

Uncertainly, she lifted the glass to her eye and peered through the transparent liquid at the last blood-red patches in the sky over Petrin.

'I am a kindhearted person,' she said. 'I wish you success in all your undertakings. But I cannot guarantee it.'

'I don't want a guarantee,' I grinned. My good mood was returning. 'I am satisfied with hope.' I lifted my glass.

'Hope is something nobody can take from you,' said Lenka as she clinked her glass against mine. 'But all too often ... too often hope is all we've got left.'

I wanted to add some seductively witty remark, but Lenka gulped down her vodka like a parched sailor. I downed mine in one gulp, too. Then I changed the subject; I thought maybe it would be wiser for now to leave this matter of my wishes coming true pleasantly ambiguous. 'Won't you tell me why my Chief fascinates you so much?'

She opened her eyes wide. 'As I told you, it's sheer female curiosity. I have a weakness for gossip. By the way, how is your girlfriend? Where did you tell her you were going this time?'

'You promised we would talk about you.'

'Later,' Lenka said. She looked around for the waiter.

His black form materialized at our table so fast she didn't even have to call him.

Later that evening she told me a little (much too little) about herself: she had always liked animals, and she had worked in Bruenn in some biological institute taking care of laboratory guinea pigs.

'You gave them food and ...'

'I cleaned their cages, checked on their condition, and so on,' she said. 'Then I worked as an assistant to a veterinarian, helping him during operations.'

'What kind of operations?'

'Mainly on cats and dogs. Once we operated on a parakeet.'

'I had no idea that sort of thing still existed,' I said in amazement.

It was her turn to be amazed. 'Why shouldn't it?'

Actually, why not? Somehow or other poodle parlours and cat sanatoria were fixed in my mind as major symptoms of a corrupt, capitalist world. Societies where neurotic dogs are treated for stomach ailments while unemployed workers are dying of starvation. A corollary of this syllogism implied that fondness for poodles was equivalent to contempt for the proletariat.

'Well, so, in other words ...' I stammered, taken aback by my discovery that some people obviously didn't connect kindness to animals with reactionary political convictions. 'In other words, these animals are anaesthetized – or do they operate on animals without anaesthesia?'

'Of course they're anaesthetized! Otherwise they could suffer psychic shock and die. They are cared for, just like human beings.'

I regained my composure and attempted a witticism: 'And the animals have to count to ten, too?'

'You're a hundred years behind the monkeys, if you don't mind my saying so,' said Lenka. 'Nobody counts to ten any more, not even people. You just put a cat into a kind of metal box with a glass window and you turn on the gas.'

'So it's actually a small gas chamber.'

'Yes,' she said, and fell silent. The disc of the sun had climbed down the observation tower and disappeared behind the Petrin hill; a huge moon had taken its place. It was hanging so low over the city that it almost seemed as if I could pluck it from the sky and set it on the table in front of Lenka. By her side, anything seemed possible, and I was almost on the verge of reaching for the moon – when I noticed that she was shivering.

'Are you cold?'

'A little.'

'Let's have another vodka, all right?'

'No thanks. I've already had three. Let's go home.'

'To your place? Will you ask me up for coffee?'

She shook her head.

'But you practically promised!'

'I'm all out of coffee.'

'I don't care. A glass of water will do.'

'You can walk me home,' she said. Then she asked me if I could please pay for her drinks.

Ah! For three vodkas, not to mention emerald-green lemonade, I deserved more than walk home. But what the hell! I'd buy a hundred vodkas for the pleasure of walking beside her through the magic moonlit streets. Will you sleep with me some day? I mentally asked her. And she replied: Later. All right, then, later. Just as long as the answer is not 'never'.

I had some doubts on that score, but I paid the bill.

And so we were back again on the Avenue of November Nineteenth, and I wasn't one step closer towards possessing the mermaid. True, along the way I managed to compose a fairly impressive prose poem about her slender legs, her eyes, lips, and ears, in short about all those parts of the body which decent girls like to hear celebrated. After I had exhausted all the permissible topics, she said: 'You certainly know how to put things attractively, my dear editor. You are obviously a professional.'

I wilted like an overwatered cactus. She burst out laughing, took me by the hand, and allowed me to walk with her arm-in-arm down the quiet Avenue of November Nineteenth. A fat, overstuffed moon hurried after us to see what would happen next.

Nothing was happening. We reached the corner and stopped at the glistening abyss of the dark shop window. Lenka looked into the black mirror. Again, she seemed like a carnation. No, like a moonlit water-lily leaning on an ugly, dark tree – me.

'You are absolutely the most beautiful girl in all Czechoslovakia,' I muttered stubbornly.

She laughed. 'Couldn't you kneel down again for me? Yesterday you knelt so romantically!'

'For you I would even crawl on all fours and search for non-existent earrings.' I let go of her hand and got down on my knees.

As the cliché goes – life is stranger than fiction. No sooner had my knees touched the sidewalk than steps clacked around the corner and Vera appeared. At first I was sure that it was all a dream. But it was Vera all right, in the flesh. She stared at me in the light of the pudgy moon, her moist eyes shining. Then she squeezed her way between us and ran off. I stared at her with my mouth wide open, watching her slim yet muscular legs flicker down the ghostly street and disappear in the darkness.

I couldn't believe my eyes. Lenka's voice brought me back to reality.

'I'm afraid I've got you in a mess,' she said.

'Vera . . .' I blurted out stupidly.

'I knew it wasn't your grandmother,' she said. 'Get up and run after her!'

'But . . .'

'Quickly! You've got to catch up with her!'

I got up and dusted off my knees. 'That's just great,' I said bitterly. 'And who ordered me to kneel down, anyway?'

'I know. It's my fault. Don't be angry. It was stupid of me. But now you must explain to her.'

'You're a monster to send me after her.'

'You are a monster if you don't go.'

I looked Lenka up and down from head to toe. She blinked at me with those black eyes and couldn't seem to decide what to say.

'That's just great,' I repeated.

'I beg you, go to her, really!' And then she added, almost pleading: 'You've no idea how painful this can be. I'm sure she's feeling awful. I don't mind if you go.'

Don't mind? Ah, Lenka, that's the cruellest thing you could say!

'I'll go up with you first. I'll stop by at her place on my way back,' I said.

'You can't come up. My room mate is home.'

'Couldn't you have told me that sooner?'

'I didn't make any promises to you. I only told you that you could see me home.'

Lenka, Lenka, what game are you playing with me? 'I don't believe you,' I said.

She shrugged her shoulders impatiently. 'Don't then. But you can't come up.'

'So let's go somewhere for a nightcap,' I offered in desperation. By then it was clear that whatever she was after, I wasn't it. It was a terrible feeling, one that I hadn't experienced for years.

'I'm a working girl,' she said, 'and I have to get up early.'

I hung my head dejectedly. She took pity on me: 'Another time,' she said in a warm voice.

Really? Was it worth the struggle? I had certainly struck out this evening. Yet I knew that she was worth a million tries, even if they all failed.

'You will get tickets for that gymnastics meet, won't you?'

'I will!'

We stood there under a moon that seemed to have spread across the entire sky.

'Well, goodnight,' she said.

I took her hand and kissed it. She got a key out of her pocketbook and opened the door. I stared at her, with what must have been dog-like supplication. Her eyes seemed to shine out of the darkness with a black light. It was unbelievable. And then I heard the soft, oboe tone of her voice: 'Go to her, please!'

The door clicked shut.

Damn it all! Aching all over, I turned to the moon.

I didn't feel like going home. I sat down on a bench overlooking the Nusle hillside, stretched out my legs, and surrendered myself to sorrow. The world was as young as it had been ten thousand years ago. My heart ached. The thought that I might never possess Lenka Silver, that I might never come any closer to her, was unbearable. I was being sacrificed before the god of love, on the green altar of holy, naïve youthfulness, being slowly roasted over the hellish flames. My fate lay in the hands of the slim, long-legged girl in the blue bikini.

The Nusle valley dissolved in tears, the moon broke up into long silver slivers. Everything within me melted. I moaned as Lenka – grimacing like a lovely Jezebel – twisted red-hot irons in my wounds. And then, illogically and unexpectedly, out of the infernal shadows stepped forth the image of Vera, and the torments of love were deepened by pangs of conscience. I tried to banish her from my mind; I couldn't. Vera was standing behind Lenka, looking over her shoulder, that good soul in whose apartment I had so often warmed myself when winter winds were blowing and I didn't feel like carting coal up four flights of stairs to my sublet. Vera, the girl who expended all her spiritual energy on gaining graceful control over her body; she had no spiritual strength left, that betrayed ballerina, crushed – as I was – on the cruel wheel of love. 'Light as a feather are burdens borne for others ...' – a poem which I was currently editing rang in my mind, an old-fashioned *fin de siècle* poet's naïve, obsolete verse. I had heard the verses declaimed at a recent recital, with exaggerated bathos, and at the top of the voice as our era demanded. This kind of attitude was passé, like Lenka's reserve.

Suddenly I had the absurd feeling that at last I understood Lenka Silver's enigmatic essence: in spite of her daring bikini, in spite of her painted fingernails, she was actually living at the turn of the century, at a time before all values had become relative. 'Only the wrongs that you have done your brothers ...' – I imagined Lenka reciting these lines, and on her lips they didn't sound the least bit obsolete or ridiculous. In the midst of these meditations, in the midst of my painfully sweet love sickness, a flash of anxiety about Vera shot through me. Suppose ... suppose she was really on the verge of some desperate act?

I jumped off the bench and started running towards the Avenue of November Nineteenth. Terror drove me through the quiet streets, the houses dark at that early hour of the morning except for an occasional yellowish light oozing through a drawn curtain. A frightful image – the little ballerina with her absurdly small experience of life, her pathetic little erotic escapades, tying the sash of that vulgar dressing gown around her neck! I turned the corner and on a dead run pulled the keys out of my pocket, the keys which she had had made for me and which she had personally brought to my office because I was too lazy to pick them up myself. In the nameplate on the door on the fifth floor was a familiar card: VERA KAJETAN, MEMBER OF THE BALLET THEATRE. Now that ridiculous card had turned into a reproach: a pathetic little memorial of glory, a symbol of the successful completion of years of drudgery which had begun when this country girl was five years old, when she first started going to a dreadful hole in southern Bohemia. The card was now the last pitiful outcry, a weak, prematurely silenced voice calling into the immense, indifferent emptiness of the universe. I shivered with terror – on the other side of the door there was deathly silence. Carefully I put the key in the lock, and ever so quietly – quietly for no good reason – I opened the door.

Vera's light blue raincoat was hanging in the hall. Beneath it stood a pair of white pumps: a light was on in the bedroom; the bedroom door was slightly ajar.

I tiptoed in. Not a trace of Vera. The convertible couch in the corner had been pulled out and made up. A white dress was draped over the armchair.

I shuddered with a new, terrible thought and turned towards the bathroom door. A sliver of light escaped from the crack in the door, but all was silent. I closed my eyes and saw Vera floating like a good erotic angel through blood-red clouds towards the gates of purgatory.

But when with wildly beating heart I pushed open the bathroom door and looked in, there she was, lying in the tub, reading a book.

I walked in and stood over the tub. Vera glanced at me and then nonchalantly went on reading.

I sat down on the rim of the tub. Crystal clear under the water's smooth surface lay the girlish body of my ballerina, with its wavy little tuft below the belly, delicate breasts, and hips which only hinted at the curves of a female pelvis.

'Vera,' I said, my heart still thumping like mad.

She went on reading.

'Vera, damn it . . .'

At last she glanced at me over the book. 'Yes?'

'I thought . . . I was afraid . . .'

'Afraid?'

'Well, yes, afraid. Afraid you might be up to some stupid trick,' I said, infuriated. 'Right away, you start bawling like . . .'

'What was I supposed to do?' she interrupted me. 'Laugh my head off? Not that you didn't look ridiculous, kneeling on the ground in front of that woman . . .' She was losing her self-control. Traditional tears sprang out of her forget-me-not eyes. She threw the book down on the rubber mat; then she started to sob painfully into the tub.

I picked the book off the floor. *Metaphysics of Love*. Schopenhauer. Property of the Municipal Library. So that's where she was hoping to find the answer to her problems. I put my hand on her wet shoulder.

'Don't cry.'

She quivered.

'That's better.'

She stopped sobbing and lifted her head. Her tear-filled eyes looked up imploringly.

'Kaja . . . please . . .' she sat up in the tub. 'Kaja dear.'

I sighed. She flung her arms around me and pressed her mouth firmly against mine. Through my shirt I felt the moist warmth of her body.

All kinds of ideas were racing through my head. Vera was lying next to me, her head on my chest. She was breathing deeply, but I knew that she wasn't asleep. As if she was reading my thoughts, she said mournfully: 'You don't like me any more, do you?'

'Of course I do.'

'No you don't. You know what I mean.'

'I like you. The same as I always did.'

She sighed, and laughed bitterly. 'That's just the trouble. I like you, too – the same as always.'

I didn't answer. I was looking at the ceiling, across which a stripe of moonlight lay like the hand of some giant illuminated clock.

'And that other one – do you like her as much as me?'

'No, no,' I sighed. 'Vasek likes her.'

'Then why do you keep going with her all the time?'

The white dress shimmered on the chair. The alabaster nude on the dresser stood in the shadow except for its head, which was touched by the hand of the moon clock and glowed with a pale light.

'I was supposed to help Vasek get fixed up with her. The idea was that we'd buy three tickets for a movie and then I wouldn't show up.'

'But why were you with her?'

'Because Vasek didn't come.'

'Did you know that he wasn't going to come?'

'No.'

'Then why did you go when you were not supposed to show up?'

Lies have short legs, they don't get very far. The white glow was slowly climbing down the statuette's neck.

'Well, you know me, Vera,' I said. 'It doesn't really mean anything, but I like her.'

Vera's head slipped from my chest to the pillow, and I heard a strange sound – perhaps a sob, perhaps the hiss of love's furious anger.

'What can I do, Vera?' I said. 'That's how I am.'

She turned her moist face towards me. 'And what can I do? That's how I am!' Pale, unhappy, tear-stained face.

We lapsed again into silence.

I said: 'Let's break up.'

She jerked her body, almost shouted: 'No! Not that, Kaja! Please! Please!'

'It would be better that way.'

'No it wouldn't. She doesn't love you – *I* love you!'

You're absolutely right, Vera dear, I thought to myself, but what good does it do? There's a lot you know, and a lot you don't know: What good is your love to me if Lenka doesn't care for me?

'I know. But ...'

'I will always love you! Be quiet!' she said when I tried to interrupt. 'You have no idea how a woman can love.' Yes, I do, Vera, I felt like saying. 'You only had a bunch of ...' tramps, say it, Vera, but you're wrong if you think that tramps are incapable of love. She didn't say it. 'But I really love you, Kaja, you know that?'

She kissed me. Tenaciously she tried to suck reassurance from me, but I had none to give. Then she laid her head on my chest, the scent of her shampooed hair tickling my nose. But I was empty. Empty except for a little pity. 'You'll get over it, Kaja. I don't hold it against you. I am a modern person,' said the girl from the backwoods who didn't understand the real meaning of a single abstract expression and whose tiny library contained a well-thumbed dictionary of foreign words. 'I am not the kind of person who makes scenes. I will be patient, and you'll get over it.'

'I have never loved you, Vera,' I said huskily.

She quickly covered my mouth with her hand. 'Don't say that! But you like me, don't you? Tell me.'

'Yes.'

'That's enough. I love you. You can even beat me, as long as ...' She stopped. Then, after a while, my modern, progressive artiste added in a small voice: '... as long as you stay with me.'

The alabaster nude was now shining from the waist up. The moon had stripped off its dark robe and the nipples of the breasts stood out like black eyes.

'I couldn't stand it if you left me. I'd do something terrible . . .'

The unhappy little voice trailed off into space.

Something terrible. Like reading Schopenhauer and seducing me with your pretty, wet body. But I am not going to fall for it again. Next time not even Goethe will help you. The white hand of the moon caressed the alabaster loins. I came to my senses. I regained my cool wisdom, the rigorous wisdom of modern logic: *x* wants to sleep with *y*; *z* is in the way; ergo, *x* must get rid of *z*.

4 *Birthday*

Blumenfeld lost no time in celebrating her birthday. As I approached her lair in the morning I heard an explosion of laughter. I opened the door and stepped into an office packed with people and blue with smoke. Colleague Salajka was just reading aloud something amusing from a thick manuscript, and Blumenfeld was choking with laughter.

They all froze when the door opened, but when they saw me the laughter picked up again.

'Happy birthday, Dasha,' I said to Blumenfeld and kissed her on the lips. Her mouth smelled of imported tobacco. 'I wish you at least half as many more years as you have already lived through.'

'You want me to die so young?'

' "Whom the gods love . . ." '

'The gods don't love me. Especially not God the Father.'

'Who?' asked the writer Kopanec.

'Comrade Prochazka, of course,' said Dasha. 'He didn't invite me to celebrate his birthday, even though we were born on the same day.' Then something occurred to her and she raised her voice: 'Comrades, did any of you get invited to the boss's party? Just so we know who is who around here.'

It turned out that nobody in the room had been invited to the party the Chief was giving that night. Blumenfeld made a toast to celebrate the founding of an office shitlist club – and furtively glanced in my direction as she lifted her glass. Actually I was a bit mystified by the Chief's not inviting me this year, and under normal circumstances I would have worried about it. But the new life that had begun for me this week had rather drastically changed the way I reacted to things. I thought no more about this little mystery and joined the others in poring over Salajka's manuscript, which was apparently the source of great amusement.

It was the manuscript of a Czech classic – or, rather, of an edition which had resulted from an exhaustive study conducted by the Institute for National Literature. The Institute's aim had been to produce a definitive text on the basis of comparative examination of all previous versions of the work. As the introduction pointed out, the new version embodied the totality of the author's original aesthetic and idealogic intent; it had been cleansed of editorial distortions on the part of bourgeois publishers, and was free of typographical errors and factual mistakes. Thereafter (this was not mentioned in the introduction) Academician Brat had replaced all references of Christian nature by their appropriate materialistic counterparts, with the result that the manuscript now fully reflected correct literary-historical-linguistic principles as well as the most advanced Marxist-Leninist thinking of the time. Colleague Salajka, who had been assigned to copyedit the manuscript, was now declaiming some of Academician Brat's particularly pungent revisions.

Brat's changes made some people furious. 'Somebody should send this to the newspapers!' fumed the well-known literary critic Kobliha, who had recently been attacked in the daily press. 'This is disgusting! How can anybody lend himself to such cultural barbarism!'

To the amazement of all, the writer Kopanec rose to Brat's defence. Kopanec's latest novel, *Battle for Brnirov*, had recently earned him the esteemed title of Master Fuckup. Essentially a classic work about the building of socialism, Kopanec's *Battle* contained more jousting in bed than was considered proper, and the publishing house that had brought it out had nearly had to close up shop. Lately Kopanec had been trailing after Blumenfeld – mainly for professional reasons, I suspected. He had evidently discovered the weakest point in the great wall which our Chief had erected against the incursions of troublesome talents.

'How can you defend that butchery?' asked Annie, bewildered. 'You of all people – such an apostle of the truth!'

'Oh well, I have my weak spots,' said the apostle, and adjusted his dark glasses on his buttonlike nose. 'That's why I have compassion for everybody. After the Victory of the People in 1948 I became a ghost writer for Karel Starec when he received the title People's Artist from the Party . . .'

'So you're the one responsible for all that garbage,' squealed Blumenfeld.

'No, not all of it. The books he wrote as a People's Artist are all his own doing. My job was to make Marxist revisions of his earlier novels – the ones he wrote as a bourgeois artist. And there all I did was sharpen the class characteristics of the main figures, add some cosmopolitan touches to intellectuals, and so on.'

A new wave of laughter swept through the company. Blumenfeld broke out another bottle of Scotch and handed out Lucky Strikes. Kopanec gulped down his Scotch with the urgency of a man about to commit suicide, and immediately held out his glass for a refill.

'Save yourself for tonight's party,' cautioned Blumenfeld. Salajka, resuming his reading from the Academician's work, read a passage in which two seventeenth-century priests meet in front of a firehouse (rather than chapel), shake hands (rather than crossing themselves), and greet each other with the words '*Pax tecum*, comrade.'

'You know how I got into the good graces of our leader?' said Blumenfeld after two more drinks. I, for one, knew very well – she held the record for having been in the Chief's good graces for the shortest interval ever recorded in the annals of our office's history.

'At last things are getting interesting,' remarked Kopanec.

'If you're expecting an erotic adventure you will be disappointed. It has nothing to do with sex. I'd give up literature before I'd climb into bed with the Chief.'

'I'm surprised to hear you say that,' said Salajka. 'After all, that new girl in the secretariat is even younger than you – no reflection on your tender youth – and yet it seems that she . . .'

'Which one?' broke in Annie. 'How come I don't know about it? You mean the blonde?'

For a while the discussion centred on the new blonde whom Salajka said he often saw in the Chief's company long after office hours. Annie, eager to update her mental file of scandals and gossip, was eager for every last detail, and everyone joined in to help her out.

'So as I say,' said Blumenfeld, picking up her story where she had left off, 'it had nothing to do with sex. It had to do with Karel Čapek. In his *War with the Newts*, I caught an error that had been passed from one edition to the next: the English expression "wel-come" was spelled with two "ll"s. I should have kept my trap shut.'

You should have, Dasha, I thought to myself, recalling how she turned the idyllic debate into a nightmare. At first nobody could believe his ears; we were all sure that we were suffering the effects of some collective hallucination. But there was Dasha's strident voice asserting that now we had the first correctly spelled version of *War of the Newts*, the well known science-fiction novel and anti-Nazi political satire, we should go further, and in accord with the spirit of the Twentieth Party Congress we should reinstate the section entitled 'Molokov's Manifesto'. The 'Manifesto' had been included in all editions that had appeared in the author's lifetime but had been deleted from all the postwar editions, since the name of the leader of the belligerent bugeyed monsters was a pun on Stalin's Minister of Foreign Affairs.

I remembered how painfully far the Chief's chin had dropped, the deathly silence around the conference table, the deep, deep sighs.

The Chief had pulled himself together and showed himself worthy of his responsible position. Karel Čapek, he had informed us, was a bourgeois democrat and an idealistic humanist and so on and so forth, who had correctly analysed the role of fascism and so on and so forth, but who had never managed to transcend his bourgeois origin and upbringing and to rid himself of his prejudices against the Soviet Union, and so on and so forth. Furthermore, recent disclosures concerned the cult of personality, whereas the chapter in question did not deal with a specific person but was instead an abstract invective against the USSR, which would only offend the modern reader.

We were further instructed that Comrade Blumenfeld was an extremely young and inexperienced comrade who had learned a great deal in school and had shown good ability in her work so far, and so on and so forth, but who still lacked that proper political outlook which can only be achieved through experience. The Chief's sermon on this topic had run on and on, and he had preached so beautifully and persuasively, with such an air of authority, that even Blumenfeld had been awed. The new edition of Čapek designed for the 'modern reader' subsequently came out with one 'l' in 'welcome' and no Molokov.

Nothing could daunt Dasha for long, however. Now she was sitting on the edge of a desk, grinning into the clouds of smoke. Whisky glasses stood scattered among the dwindling pile of sandwiches and the heaps of mimeographed instructions concerning approved ways of deleting objectionable material. Kopanec put his arm around Dasha's waist. She slid off the desk top, raised a glass high in the air, and shouted: 'Here's hoping that on his study trip to the Soviet Union, Academician Brat will be exposed as an enemy of the people!'

Everyone raised their glasses. The door opened. In walked the Chief, his flushed face creased by a yellowish smile.

'Your health,' he said. The only sound was a loud laugh let out by the Master of Fuckups. The assembled editors quickly regained their composure, however, thanks to years of training in handling similar situations. The Chief, grinning broadly, strode up to Blumenfeld and shook her hand. 'Dasha dear, all the best, good health, and a handsome boyfriend!' He kissed her forehead.

Smiling sweetly, Blumenfeld replied: 'The same to you, Comrade Prochazka. Except for the boyfriend.'

'But we wish you a pretty girlfriend,' shouted Annie and embraced the Chief.

'Now, now!' protested the boss, who proceeded to kiss Annie on the mouth with great gusto. It seemed pretty clear from the way the two of them acted that Annie had worked for him in that capacity somewhere along the line. One after another we congratulated the Chief on his birthday.

'Ah well,' sighed the Chief, after he had taken a drink, 'to reach fifty is really nothing to be congratulated about. Your birthdays are still happy occasions, Dasha.'

'I'm not exactly a baby myself,' said Blumenfeld. 'I'm nineteen and a half. I celebrate my birthdays every six months, to make the most of them. That's why some people think that I'm too old for my age.'

The telephone rang. Salajka answered the call, then nodded to me. I picked up the receiver, and stuck a finger into my left ear to keep out the racket. 'Hello?'

'Hi,' said the faroff voice of Vasek Zamberk. His voice promptly transported me into the world of Lenka Silver. Away from the smoke and unreality of these offices into the beautiful, aquatic unreality of love.

'Is there a party going on over there?' asked Vasek.

'Yes. One of my colleagues has a birthday.'

'I'm just calling to tell you ... I tried to call you yesterday but there was no answer.'

'I was out. What's up?'

'Nothing, really. I don't want to bother you if you're in the midst of a party.'

I could tell, though, that he was dying to find out what had happened with Lenka. 'That's all right. We can talk.'

'I just wanted to know ... what did she say? I mean on Sunday.'

'Miss Silver?' I asked, as if I were trying to recall who he was talking about.

'Yes. Didn't she say anything ... I mean, did she make fun of me or anything like that?'

'You fool, you should have stayed. She said very nice things about you.'

'You're joking.'

'No, she said sometimes she has the same trouble swimming long distances. She has a weak heart, just like you.'

'There's nothing wrong with my heart. It happened because ...'

'Because you were nervous, sure But as far as she's concerned, you have a weak heart – get it?'

'Stop making fun of me!'

Vasek's sense of humour was rather limited. It stopped at horseplay. He tickled girls during gymnastic exercises and swapped jokes with muscular buddies in the locker room, but in matters of love he was as solemn as a bureaucrat.

'I am serious. And by the way, you're supposed to get those tickets for the gymnastics meet.'

'I am? Really?'

'Really.'

'All right, I'll get them. But do you think ...'

'What?'

'Well, do you think ...'

'Do I think what?'

'That there's any point to all this?'

'Of course there is, you idiot. Call me up when you have them.'

'I can get them right away. We can meet for lunch, if you're free.'

'All right. At half past one in the fish place. Bye.'

I hung up. I took the finger out of my ear, but it took me a while before I grasped what was going on in the office. My mind lingered in the world of Lenka Silver. After a while, though, I became aware of the Chief's voice. 'Well, yes, satire,' the Chief was saying. 'You're right, Dasha, there is a place for satire. But you know what I always say? Good satire criticizes conditions only after they have improved.'

Salajka laughed dutifully. The Chief looked at him, puzzled. Obviously he had not intended his remark as a joke. During my brief mental lapse the conversation had drifted into treacherous waters: the topic was Jarmila Cibulka. The Chief continued: 'I always try to read every manuscript with the eyes of Comrade Kaiser. Up till now, this principle has paid off for every editor I know.' He cast a significant glance at Blumenfeld.

Blumenfeld perched on top of her desk again, showing off her knees. Her head was cocked to one side; her forehead was creased by a wrinkle of dissatisfaction. In the heat of the discussion she appeared to be oblivious to the fact that Kopanec was holding her hand.

'I know, Emil,' she said. 'But I believe that if a piece of writing is really good we should do all we can to get it published, even if that involves some trouble.'

She stated her naïve credo, then she blushed. For a moment her rather ordinary face became truly beautiful.

The Chief took refuge in dialectics: 'It all depends, however, on what you mean by "doing all we can". Sometimes, for instance, a little delay is in the author's best interests. If you let your enthusiasm run away with you, if you rush into things, you can stir up a lot of trouble – and then the author is in hot water for years. Just ask Comrade Kopanec.' The Chief pointed a nicotine-stained index finger at the Master Fuckup, who guiltily let go of Blumenfeld's hand. 'He could tell you volumes, Dasha,' the Chief went on. 'Comrade Kopanec is a talent. A great talent. And what happens? He submits a story to *The Torch* and the story goes straight up to Comrade Kaiser. Why? Just because the author is Comrade Kopanec.'

Comrade Kopanec, embarrassed, nodded his head: 'It's a fact.' Blumenfeld threw him a dirty look.

'That whole affair that blew up over his *Battle for Brnirov* was very unfortunate. If they had taken their time instead of rushing the book into print, Comrade Kopanec would be sitting pretty. Instead ... now, even if he submits a story that has absolutely no significance, it is regarded in a special light by the people on top.'

The Chief cast a fatherly glance over the gathering. Salajka lost his nerve and energetically nodded his head in agreement. Kobliha wrapped himself in cigarette smoke and met the Chief's gaze with an ironic smile. He was fortunate to have been the only critic who had written an ambiguous review of *The Battle for Brnirov*. He had written the review in a hurry, and by the time Comrade Kaiser had decided to reject the book the piece had already been set in type. Kobliha had tried to yank it out at the last minute, but the presses had already printed 50,000 copies of the newspaper – half the total edition. He had bribed a few key people and they had let him change the title of the review on the rest of the press run from 'Significant New Prose' to 'Significant New Problems'. These hectic goings-on had earned Kobliha the reputation of being a courageous and unorthodox theoretician.

The Chief avoided the critic's mocking eyes and looked at Annie, who was munching on a sandwich.

'Or take Comrade Houska. Annie, here, is the one who could tell you that story. Houska brought us a preface. Intelligent, well written, thoughtful – there's no denying that. But all I had to do was thumb through it and I knew what Comrade Kaiser's attitude would be. Remember, Annie?'

Annie frowned and went on munching.

'You took Comrade Houska's side, as I recall. And I know why, too. Don't blush!'

'That's not true!' protested Annie, whose affair with Houska had ended in a celebrated fight which had left him with a black eye, and her black and blue for days.

'Never mind,' said the Chief. 'It was a good preface, an interesting preface, I read it through at one sitting. But what was my reaction? I said: "Annie, there are some ideas in this preface which smack of revisionism." And what happened? Comrade Houska wouldn't listen. We returned the preface to him, he turned it into an article, had it printed – and we all know the consequences.'

We knew the consequences, all right. Revisionist tendencies were uncovered in Houska's article. The same tendencies became retrospectively evident in all of Houska's activity to date at the Institute for National Literature, a post from which he was ousted so fast that it made his head swim. The Chief neglected to mention that Houska's dismissal followed not only the disclosure of revisionist tendencies, but also a negative review of the Chief's own collection of poems which had up till then stood unchallenged as models of rhymed patriotic sentiment. It was, of course, difficult to prove a causal connection, and perhaps none existed.

'As publishers, we have the duty to protect talents. Talented people are generally impetuous young persons, full of uncritical enthusiasm, and they are eager to plunge headfirst into any project without really knowing what's at the bottom of it. For their own good we've got to lead them by the hand.'

'But where are we leading them?' shouted Dasha Blumenfeld, her face flushed with anger.

'To prudence,' answered the Chief. 'Recklessness never yet earned anybody a State prize.'

Somehow or other, the conversation gradually shifted from literature to the safer ground of sex. Blumenfeld did her stubborn best to keep the discussion about literary policy going, but Salajka launched into a dirty story and the Chief gratefully followed it up with a *double entendre* Jewish anecdote. It was a masterly psychological move on his part because Dasha promptly succumbed to the storytelling passion of her people and proceeded to display her encyclopaedic knowledge of Jewish jokes, each one dirtier than the one before.

When her voice grew hoarse, Kobliha courageously told his anecdote about Comrade Khrushchev. Then the Chief threw caution to the winds and recited the old joke about the four main problems of our socio-economic system (summer, winter, spring, and autumn). Comrade Kaiser had recently told the joke at a writers' conference as a ploy to win over restive intellectuals, so to some extent it had been officially sanctioned. Still, for the Chief to tell it was an act that bordered on audacity.

As we were all going back to our own offices, he took me aside.

'Listen, Karel,' he said, 'would you like to drop over this evening? I'm throwing a little party, and I'm expecting Minister Perla to come by.'

Naturally, I didn't feel like telling him that I had already been invited by Blumenfeld, so I lied. 'I'd love to, but ... well, I have a kind of date.'

He shook a playful finger at me. 'Oh, with that brunette, eh? Miss ...'

'Silver.'

'Bring her along, then. The party starts at eight, but come by any time.'

He patted me on the back and disappeared. He had been acting curiously paternal of late. Was he trying to make sure of his allies – or, it just occurred to me, was it Lenka he was after? But why not go to his party this evening, anyhow? Lenka was a zoologist – she might find our human zoo interesting.

'Oh, it's you again!' said her melodious voice over the telephone.

'It's only my second time. Can I see you this afternoon?'

'I don't think so. If you see me too often you might become disenchanted.'

'I'm glad to know you care. But if you really care, don't torment me by your absence.'

'Hmm.' There was a moment of silence. Two serious official voices could be weakly overheard from another line.

'Did you go last night to Miss Kajetan?' she said at last.

'No.'

'Goodbye, then.'

She hung up.

I immediately dialled her number again.

'Bio-Ex.'

'They cut us off.'

'I'm sorry, you must have the wrong number. This is Bio-Ex.'

It was some other woman's voice. 'I was just talking to Miss Silver and we were cut off.'

'Comrade Silver just left. She'll be back this afternoon.'

'Where did she go?'

'I'm sorry. I don't know.'

I banged down the receiver. What game was she playing now?

'I've got to go out for a while. Be back after lunch,' I barked at Annie.

She flashed me a conspiratorial smile as I rushed out of the room.

Lenka was in her office, just as I had expected. I spotted her all the way down the hall and through the glass doors. She was wearing a bright yellow summer dress, and she was sitting behind a desk on which a green parrot was strutting back and forth with a fountain pen in its beak. A grey-haired lady with glasses sat behind the other desk.

I opened the door.

'Good morning,' I said.

They both looked at me. Lenka sighed and made an unhappy face.

'Good morning,' I repeated humbly and approached her desk. 'I'm from the agricultural collective at Kunratice. I've come about those snails you sent us for breeding. In your last shipment there were only males.'

Lenka still looked unhappy but she went along with the joke. 'Are you the biologist in charge there?'

'Yes.'

'And what was your mark in zoology on the State exam?'

'It was "satisfactory", Miss.'

'Then I will write to your chairman and tell him to send you back to school again.'

'Why?'

'My dear Comrade, ever since God started making snails they've come in only one model. They're hermaphrodites.'

'You don't think that maybe a few slipped by God's control department?'

The grey-haired lady guffawed. Lenka smiled wanly. The vaudeville act was over.

'Can you come to lunch with me?' I asked. Lenka glanced at her watch. The green parrot waddled to the edge of the desk and offered me his fountain pen. I took it and wrote on a pad lying on the desk: 'If you don't come, I'll make a declaration of love to you right here and now.'

'A charming parrot,' I said. 'What's his name?'

'William,' Lenka said in a murderous tone, and turned to her grey-haired colleague. 'Mrs Benes, is it all right if I go to lunch now?'

The woman peered at me over her glasses. I smiled at her. 'Certainly, dear,' she said. 'Did you make a note about those turtles?'

'Not yet.'

'I'll do it for you, then.'

'Thank you, Mrs Benes.'

As Lenka got up, the parrot croaked in protest. 'Don't be jealous, William,' said Lenka. The bird cackled contentedly; then it started to sing, or cackle a marching song. Lenka glanced into the tall mirror on the wall, ran her hand through her short hair, and set out at a quick step.

'You certainly know how to make a nuisance of yourself,' she said on the stairs.

'Don't blame me. I've lost all control over myself. You attract – and I am drawn.'

'Look here,' she said. 'If there's one thing I hate it's breaking up other people's relationships.'

'This was no relationship. At least, not for me.'

'So much the worse. If there's one thing I hate even more it's men who want all the pleasures and none of the responsibilities.'

We turned into Wenceslas Square. Yesterday's baritone sax reverberated from a record store. I said:

'May I ask you something?'

'Go ahead.'

'Why did you go out with me last night?' The only reply was the stubborn staccato of her heels on the pavement. 'If you hate breaking up relationships.'

My devious question apparently touched her conscience. She shrugged her shoulders. One of her shoulder straps slipped, revealing the sleek, light-brown velvet of her breast.

'It was sheer stupidity. I had no idea you'd carry on like this.'

'You know better than that.'

'I am only human. I do things without thinking, now and then.'

'Me too. Like my affair with Vera.'

'All right, then,' she said. 'But if you no longer love her the least you can do is to end your affair as gently as possible. You have to give her time to get over it.'

'I don't think so. The best thing is a quick *coup de grâce*.'

Lenka frowned. 'A what?'

'A *coup de grâce*.'

'I'm sorry, I don't speak French.'

'A merciful blow.'

Black malice flashed from her eyes. 'And how would *you* like a merciful blow?'

'No. Not that! Please!'

'There you are!'

I stared at her black eyes, then looked at the ground and said in my most pitiable voice: 'Judging by the way you're treating me, I suppose I'll have to hang myself anyway.'

She laughed. 'You're quite a clown, Comrade Editor. But we are discussing very serious matters.'

'I will reform. I will abandon my evil ways,' I said. 'But I'll need your help. Would you come with me this evening to an interesting party?'

'I think you should take Miss Kajetan.'

'She has a performance.'

'Poor ballerinas,' said Lenka. 'Their boyfriends have so much time for intrigues . . .'

'It's my Chief's birthday party,' I said slyly.

'Your Chief's birthday party?'

'That's right. The man you find so sexy.'

Lenka was thinking it over. I could practically see sparks of curiosity in her eyes.

'And, if you thought he was sexy the day you saw him, you should see him in a tuxedo. He's a real . . .'

'When is the party?'

'I'll pick you up at around five in front of the museum,' I said suavely.

Then, all at once, Lenka waved and shouted: 'Professor! Professor Zamberk!'

I spotted Vasek, who was just starting to cross the street. He was sporting the same kind of stylish cap I had seen my Chief wearing on Sunday. He looked miserable. The sound of Lenka's magic voice made his face turn suddenly crimson. He came towards us and took off his cap.

'Hello, Lenka,' he croaked.

'Quite a coincidence, isn't it?' I said. 'I was having lunch and who should I meet but your star pupil. I asked her if she'd like to go to the meet with us. And the answer is yes.'

'I'm g-g-glad,' stuttered Vasek, as Lenka glared at me. For a minute she looked ready to tell Vasek what a liar I was. Instead, she asked him if he was feeling better.

Vasek's red face turned practically purple. 'Yes, it was nothing, really. Just a kind of . . . a painful moment . . .'

Vasek's tongue-tied awkwardness seemed to inspire Lenka to flights of eloquence. I had never heard her so chatty and gay, and by the time we sat down at our table in the restaurant I was doing nothing but listening. The two of them talked about gymnastics as if it was the most exciting subject in the world.

Then, at last, fate smiled on me. Vasek was just explaining something he called double reverse jackknife spin – or something like that – and he was using his hands to show how to execute it. In front of him stood a bowl of creamed carp roe soup. What happened next was a bit of slapstick on a par with the rest of this athlete's classic mishaps. He pressed down on the table to demonstrate the double reverse. His hands slipped, the bowl tipped, and the milky roe splashed over Lenka.

'My new dress!' she moaned beautifully.

Vasek sat there stiff as a stone. Then he pulled a dirty handkerchief out of his pocket and reached out to wipe the soup off the top of Lenka's dress. His hand wavered in front of her bosom. Frantically, he smeared the roe around in her lap.

'Wait! Don't! Leave it alone!'

Lenka got up. There were tears in her eyes. A waiter ran up. 'Kindly follow me to the kitchen,' he said. 'It will come out with warm water.'

Amid a hum of talk, he led the mermaid off. Another waiter came over to our table. 'May I?' he asked, with mock respect; then he transferred the soup plates to a serving table and deftly changed the tablecloth.

When we sat down again Vasek was pale and completely crushed. 'This is getting ridiculous,' he said.

'True. I just hope you can take it as a joke.'

'I'm leaving!' he said. 'Please tell Miss Silver that I'll pay for her dress. Here ...' Vasek pulled a large bill from his wallet. 'Here, take care of the lunch ... and take her home in a cab. She'll have to change her clothes. I'm going.'

'Wait a minute. Wait till she gets back, and make your apologies. And take her in a taxi yourself. You can patch things up in the cab.'

I egged him on, knowing very well that he wouldn't listen to me.

'Goodbye,' he said in a voice that sounded as if he was going to cry any minute.

'What about the tickets?'

He stopped and pulled out his wallet again. 'Here. Take all three. After this I couldn't possibly face her.'

It was then that the fateful idea occurred to me. 'No. Don't worry. You can go. She won't be there. She said she had to visit some relatives. So if you don't mind, I'll bring Vera.'

'Why ... yes, certainly!'

I handed him one of the tickets. 'Keep it and come, you nut. Vera likes you. And in the meantime I'll smooth things over with Miss Silver.'

Vasek waved his arm in despair but he took the ticket and disappeared through the revolving door.

I sat back comfortably.

I liked my plan. It was really a devious variant on our old trick: I would send Vera to the meet in my place, telling Lenka that the date was off. Vasek was longing for female sympathy, and Vera was a very sympathetic girl. Also, when Vera realized what a trick I had played on her she would probably be only too eager to get even with me. There was one rub: there was always the chance that Vasek might refuse to take advantage of our friendship. But knowing this world as I did, that seemed highly unlikely.

Lenka returned wearing a borrowed polka-dot dress. Her eyes were still tearing. I told her how sorry Vasek had been and that he had had to leave. To my pleasant surprise this didn't bother her in the least. 'A brand new dress!' she wailed. 'And today was the first time I wore it.'

'I'll buy you another one!'

'No, thank you,' she snapped. 'But Professor Zamberk will pay the cleaning bill.'

Lenka was plainly irritated. For a time the silence between us was so complete that I could hear the clack of silverware at other tables. When our waiter brought us the fish course I broke the silence. 'Will you take me to the zoo sometime? The next time you go for a consultation with a chimpanzee?'

'No,' she said firmly. 'But I will go with you to that gymnastics meet. Not for your sake, though. For the sake of Professor Zamberk. I don't want him to get an inferiority complex just because of what happened to my dress.'

Her normal mood – including her sense of humour – seemed to be coming back.

'I'll bring you a ticket this evening. First row.'

'First row?'

'Of course. We think very highly of you, you know.'

'We? Don't you mean Professor Zamberk?'

'I think a lot more of you than he does.'

'But your thoughts are of a special kind, my friend. Anyway, don't talk so much. There are bones in this fish. I'll go with you to that party tonight – and you can bring me the ticket. We'll meet at five in front of the museum.'

That's where we left it. The pike had slowly turned resistant, cold and unappetizing. Knives clinked metallically. Lenka ate daintily and sipped her cider. The polka-dot dress was so horrible that her black head appeared like a lovely orchid sticking out of an ugly flower pot.

5 *An underground party*

The apparition of Lenka Silver in a white cocktail dress created a stir when we arrived near the end of Dasha Blumenfeld's birthday party. Black & White Scotch was flowing like water, thanks to the gift coupons Blumenfeld received from her international patrons; and the conversation was already drifting into the ethereal world halfway between reality and fantasy. Dasha's squeaky voice rose above the din; she was in the process of revealing various carefully kept office secrets.

We sat down in oddly shaped chairs, evidently foreign made, and heard about a recent incident that concerned revisions in the novel of a well known woman author. In two sentences the author's choice of words revealed undue sympathy for a character who had become a 'non-person' for political reasons. Fifty thousand copies of the book had already been printed and bound, but the Chief ordered the two sentences revised and the pages in question reprinted and stitched by hand into the book. The costs incurred by the State on account of this operation ran into six figures. But, as usual, the Chief had made the right decision: had the offensive sentences gone through, no amount of money would have undone the damage.

Lenka, who was more familiar with zoology than problems of cultural policy, listened in amazement.

She drew men like flies. I knew most of them. They knew me. They didn't think much of me, but they did more or less trust me. In the old days I had been one of them; more recently I had become so circumspect and cautious that I was accepted as part of the normal background. Moreover, I had helped to support several of them, and in some cases I had helped them to land really lucrative assignments. Take Brejcha, for example, who had been drinking heavily before our arrival and now sat slumped in a bamboo chair: I helped him get the job of designing a huge outdoor portrait of a well known State minister. Brejcha had started out as a surrealist and had gone on to paint pictures that looked like peeling plaster walls. He had painted the official in a realistic style, though. With the help of a horde of assistants, he finished the job in two months: the result was a superman, with coat buttons the size of truck tyres. Brejcha was delighted with the outcome and so was the minister. His future looked promising. Shortly thereafter, however, the minister fell into official disgrace. As a result, so did Brejcha, only he didn't end up on the gallows. To protect himself politically, I advised him to paint a portrait of Marshal Stalin and suggested that he should use the old court painters' trick of making Stalin's eyes seem to follow the spectator all around the room. He dedicated the painting to Comrade Krpata (also at my suggestion), who was in charge of decorations related to official holidays. Knowing this comrade's aesthetic tastes, I was certain that he would be greatly pleased by a Stalin with hypnotically moving eyes. As luck would have it, no sooner had the portrait been hung in Krpata's office than the Marshal fell into disrepute, and Brejcha was once again out in the cold. He realized, though, that I had no control over historical processes, and he remained grateful to me.

Long ago, we had all been members of an artistic group that had signed a manifesto greeting the advent of the new era – we solemnly pledged our support to our new leaders, expressing the conviction that they would free the arts from the tyranny of money and private patrons. Our new leaders promptly freed a number of us from any connection with money. Among those liberated were the ultramodernist Kocour, the surrealist Brejcha, and the twelve-tone composer Rebus. Kocour and Brejcha sank into cultural limbo. Kocour even spent half a year in jail on suspicion of having been the author (he was) of a brutally frank story about the mental capabilities of a certain high-placed comrade's wife. Rebus escaped such a harsh fate. He landed a job as an arranger for a leading dance band, and, after the denunciation of its musical director, went on to play in a circus band. But with the easing of restrictions in the realm of music – the most abstract of the arts and thus the one least vulnerable to political regimentation – he regained to some extent his stature as a serious composer, simultaneously with my losing the status of a serious poet. Oh, damn, *panta rei!* I looked at Lenka Silver.

She was still a bit sulky. She had accused me of luring her out under false pretences when she discovered that my Chief wasn't there and we weren't going to his party until much later that evening. In the meantime, however, the fun part of such parties had begun, namely the gossip, and Lenka found it fascinating. Perched like a beautiful white swan on the edge of Blumenfeld's curious armchair, she was listening to Rebus. The cut of her dress showed off her splendid breasts to perfection. They welled up like beautiful dusky slopes of an inviting valley.

Rebus, surpassing himself in the spotlight of her eyes, was telling a story about the difficulties he had encountered in connection with his book *A Nutshell History of Jazz*.

The *History* was a brief compilation from American sources, meant to serve as a basic introductory guidebook for jazz buffs. It had been given to editor Hymler of our music department, who had been instructed to make it acceptable to Comrade Kaiser, or, if he couldn't, to junk the whole project. Hymler had written a long, negative report; somebody in our office had secretly made a copy of it and given it to Rebus, who was now reading the summation:

In general, the work of Jan Rebus may be categorized as an uncritical admiration of jazz personalities, creating a cult which distracts our youth from performing more important tasks and from preparing themselves for the performing of other tasks. It is also characteristic of Jan Rebus' bourgeois viewpoint and ideologically questionable orientation that throughout the chapter devoted to the origin of jazz he consistently uses the expression 'Creoles' rather than 'Negroes', and that he fails to stress the utter poverty of these Creoles. On the contrary, he refers to some of them as affluent. He also suggests that jazz came into being through the interplay of various musical influences, following the etiologic approach favoured by bourgeois musicologists, rather than stressing the suffering of the Negroes in slavery, which is the source of jazz. Furthermore, the book is burdened by a large number of irrelevant names (e.g. Bunk Johnson, Trixie Smith, Pee Wee Russell, Jelly Roll Morton, Bix Beiderbecke, 'Tricky Sam' Nanton) which are totally unfamiliar to our readers. These names are an unnecessary burden and I recommend that they be deleted. It is a serious failing of the book that Comrade Paul Robeson is nowhere mentioned, even though as a Negro he has a close connection with jazz. This oversight should be corrected.

'Did you correct the oversight? And did you cross out those names?' interrupted Kocour.

'Yes,' answered Rebus. 'But in the meantime Hymler was fired.'

That gave me an opening – and a chance to prove to them, and especially to Lenka, that I was a real insider.

'He was fired, all right,' I said. 'He was fooling around with one of the girls from the secretariat. One of her brothers was in jail and Hymler threatened to use his connections to get her brother worked over unless she agreed to sleep with him. Then he got tired of her and used the same tactics on another girl from the director's secretarial pool. She had a husband in jail. But she was no pushover. She went straight to the party chairman and Hymler got the boot.'

'A boot that kicked him upstairs,' Rebus interposed. 'He's in the Composers' Union now. They were telling me in the office yesterday that he's still interested in my book – and has drawn up a whole new list of objections.'

'Is he that fat sorehead who always walks around the swimming club with a pair of cameras swinging on his belly?' Kocour asked.

'That's the one. Only lately he's switched over to making movies. He's rented a cabana, and shoots through knotholes – makes pictures of girls taking their clothes off. He . . .'

'So your history of jazz will come out without any names?' broke in Kocour, who was interested in the politics of culture rather than in the political methods of laying women.

'It will contain Armstrong, Bessie Smith – whose presence is justified by her having bled to death outside the doors of a white hospital – and Paul Robeson. I tried to save Duke Ellington, but it was hopeless,' Rebus sighed. 'It seems that there's a strict ban against praising aristocrats.'

The stories droned on. Lenka began to glance anxiously at her watch. Obviously, for her own mysterious reasons, she preferred meeting my Chief to an education in folklore. I lost my good mood which had come when I saw the mermaid amused by the Chiefless underground. But the amusement was over. The baldheaded stag had apparently not been forgotten.

'Shall we go?' she asked me in a casual tone.

'Let's,' I said, trying to get up, but my head was spinning. 'One mo-moment,' I said. 'I'll be back . . . just a moment . . .'

Blumenfeld jumped up and took me by the arm.

'Come, I'll show you where it is.'

But I didn't want to go to the bathroom. As soon as we reached the tiny hall, I asked her to fix me a strong cup of coffee.

In the kitchen she looked at me intently: 'Who's the mysterious brunette?'

'A monster.'

'She won't let you, right?'

She thought that I was drunk and that she could be fresh. But I wasn't that drunk. Just a little under the weather. I said gruffly: 'What business is that of yours?'

'Sorry.'

She was a little insulted. For a while she watched the water heating then she asked: 'You finished the Cibulka book yet?'

'Yes.'

'What do you think?'

'Comrade Kaiser won't praise us for that one.'

'No, seriously! What do you think?'

I looked her straight in the eye. Shop talk snapped me out of my daze.

'Look here, Dasha,' I said. 'What did you do to Hezky to make him write a favourable report?'

Blumenfeld mimicked me: 'What business is that of yours?'

'Oh, I see, it was one of those things!'

'What do you mean?'

I made an obscene gesture, and the next minute – wham! When I recovered from her slap, a redfaced Dasha asked me: 'You want another one?'

I shook my head.

'I thought not.'

She poured boiling water over the instant coffee. I rubbed my face.

'Don't be mad,' said Dasha. 'But you just don't do things like that in front of a lady.'

Still rubbing my face, I looked at her. Her behaviour seemed absurd; at the same time my respect for her increased. She glanced at me uneasily and said: 'I talked him into it.' First she countered my suspicion with a slap; now she was using logic. Naturally, that only made me all the more suspicious. 'I went to dinner with him twice and I talked him into it. It's true that he tried to take advantage of me – but you know yourself that it's hard to pull something on me.'

Mentally, I agreed that it was. Aloud, I said: 'Well, that's all academic now. The Chief is giving the book to a bunch of flunkies outside the office. He gave one copy to Pecakova and another to young Hartman.'

'You know that for sure?'

'For sure. Straight from our leader. And you can just imagine what kind of review young Hartman is going to turn in.'

The chubby girl bit her lip. Then she said: 'We'll see about that. Finish your coffee so that you're in shape for your beauty.'

I drank up. It was hot and very strong. Blumenfeld had a good heart and a generous hand. But would either help her soften up young Hartman?

6 *A party in the clouds*

We took a taxi out to the Chief's villa. That imposing house, which had previously belonged to his father-in-law, the late minister, shone into the starry night like an immense chandelier. It was close to ten when the mermaid and I entered the grand *salon*. The entertainment, or what passed for entertainment, was already in full swing.

The Chief bounded across an endless Persian rug to greet us with the usual shouts of welcome and delight. I looked around. Like so many other manifestations of our time, this gathering demonstrated that the advent of the new society predicted by nineteenth-century social scientists was a utopian dream. The dazzling smiles, roving eyes, and mindless conversation came right out of some English novel depicting the life of high society. Almost everyone there was a prominent personage.

Normally, gatherings like this were interesting only because of the women. But in this respect the Chief's soirée left a lot to be desired. Most of the women on hand belonged to the older generation. The only real beauty was the wife of the film director Binder, who had managed to snap her up when she was working as a script girl. Unfortunately, she was as dumb as she was attractive, and Minister Perla, to whom she was introduced in the hope of enlivening his evening, had already given up trying to talk to her. The minister was now sitting next to the poet Vrchcolab, trying to look interested in the poet's analysis of the youth movement. The rejected beauty was resting under a huge rubber tree, a Mona Lisa smile on her lips. My colleague Andres, who was sitting beside her, was sweating profusely.

Lenka's entrance had created a ripple of excitement. As soon as my Chief introduced her to the minister that eminent statesman lost all interest in Vrchcolab. He cut him off so abruptly that the poet was left speechless. Unfortunately, Lenka seemed suddenly

speechless, too. Perhaps she wasn't used to such exalted company.
I noticed that her eyes were constantly roving the room. I followed the direction of her gaze and made a puzzling discovery: she was following my Chief's movements as he left the minister's circle, chatted for a while with a prominent tragedian, and finally arrived at the chaise-longue supporting the lonely Mona Lisa. The mermaid's enigmatic concentration on my Chief's wanderings worried me. But there was nothing to be done at the moment. The poor minister, stymied by Lenka's continuing silence, became increasingly morose. At the same time, the poet Vrchcolab was regaining his spirits.

'One very encouraging sign in regard to today's youth,' he was saying, as the minister retired completely into his shell, 'is that the number of participants in this year's young people's cultural competition was fifteen per cent higher than last year. Still, we must not be complacent. In certain areas the competition seems to be a purely formal affair. In Jenikov, for example, the principal of a public school enrolled all of his pupils in the recitation contest, without bothering to tell them. Five of them were chronic stammerers ...'

'Did you ever take part in this contest, Miss?' the minister said, in a desperate bid to draw Lenka into the conversation. The concentrated gaze of the black irises had been directed towards the chaise-longue, filling me with an almost insane fury. Now, she turned politely towards the minister. 'Me? No, I am afraid I am too old.'

The minister gallantly waved his arm: 'Go on. You're in the bloom of youth!'

'The youth organization welcomes citizens up to the age of thirty-five,' explained the poet Vrchcolab. 'Incidentally, before I forget, the teachers in Houbovo Tyn have introduced an interesting novelty. They judge individual classes on the power and sincerity of their jubilation. For example, classes get points for waving in May Day parades ...'

The Chief moved from the chaise-longue to the liquor cabinet. Lenka's eyes followed him. Unable to bear it any longer, I got up and walked over to the liquor cabinet myself. At least that way I'd be in her line of vision.

'Kaja, tell him to leave me in peace,' the Chief greeted me, his arm around Kopanec's shoulders. He poured me a drink with a shaky hand.

I took a gulp. The vodka coursed through my veins, and for a moment let me forget Lenka's treacherous behaviour. The Chief had been drinking a lot; obviously he was trying to drown his problems in booze. He released Kopanec, hugged me instead, and babbled again: 'Tell him to leave me in peace.'

'Who? Comrade Kopanec?'

'Yes. Comrade Kopanec. Do you know what they call you, Comrade?'

Kopanec shook his head, knowing that the Chief would be upset if he couldn't make his little joke.

'Master Fuckup, that's what they call him,' announced the Chief, turning to me. 'And he'd love to fuck me up, too, which isn't very nice of him. Me, you, all of us – he'd love to fuck up all of us!'

'Really? And how is he planning to do that?'

'He keeps on rec-recommending that Cibulka book,' the Chief said. He downed another shot of vodka. 'But you'll help me, won't you? You'll talk him out of it, right?'

'I am sure Comrade Kopanec has plenty of experience.'

'But he has no official position. He has no responsibilities to worry about,' moaned the Chief. 'But I can count on you to reject the book, can't I? You won't recommend it, will you? Tell me you won't!'

'I will recommend it,' I said with a grin. When the Chief winced, I added in a stage whisper, 'For thorough rewriting!'

The Chief roared with laughter. I felt Lenka's black eyes beaming in on him. What did she see in him, anyway? I examined his face. His two most striking features were his yellow teeth and blotched bald head. I was mad with jealousy. The Chief took my scrutiny as a sign of admiration, or else the vodka had got to him, because suddenly he said: 'You're a man in a million, Karel. I knew I could count on you. You're a man one can trust. You have no idea how rare that is nowadays.' He leaned towards me and lowered his voice: 'Even Pecakova, even Comrade Pecakova stabbed me in the back! She *liked* that book! She says it shows talent. Talent!' lamented the boss. 'What the hell do we need talent for!'

'To create fuckups,' said Kopanec. The Chief turned to him with perfect seriousness: 'Right, Pepa. You've put your finger on it. We need talents like a hole in the head. Let's have another drink, boys, we'll live longer that way.'

We quickly finished off the bottle, and the Chief got another one from the cabinet and expertly opened it.

'It's all the work of that Blumenfeld woman,' he went on. 'Her and her damned Jewish need to show off all the time. I'm no racist – you know me better than that. But Jews – I'm not very fond of Jews. They're all a bunch of modernists and Zionists – it's an international conspiracy! If I was running this country, I'd let them all move to Israel.'

'Maybe some of them don't want to go,' I said.

'They damn well would if I had my way – every last one of them!' the Chief shouted in a fury. Apparently nobody had got around to telling him that Kopanec was chasing after Blumenfeld. 'They'd clear out of here so fast their heads would spin.'

This anti-Semitic outburst – especially with a cabinet minister standing just across the room – was making me very nervous. To get the Chief off the subject, I said matter-of-factly: 'What are we going to do about that book?'

'Andres is going to read it, and he can be trusted. Young Hartman, too. We'll see who's got talent!' Then the Chief whispered in my ear: 'I had a meeting with Comrade Kaiser today. You know what he told me, Karel?'

I shook my head.

'He said that anybody who defends modernism will find himself six feet under!' The Chief's eyes were bulging with terror. 'Six feet under, Karel! And when Comrade Kaiser says six feet under that's exactly what he means!'

A loud peal of laughter rang out from across the room. The Chief lifted his head, like a dog picking up the scent. Then he grabbed a bottle of vodka and rushed over to the minister, his head deferentially tilted to one side. I caught sight of his face reflected in a Venetian mirror on the wall behind the minister; the Chief was grinning like a slave.

Kopanec got up, too. He ambled over to the Mona Lisa, who had been abandoned by the exhausted Andres. I remained alone on the sofa next to the liquor cabinet.

Lenka seemed to be having the time of her life. I watched gloomily as she gestured, chatted, and gazed lovingly at the Chief's splotchy dome. I gave in to melancholy which I nourished on vodka. Somebody put a hand on my shoulder from behind. It was the Chief's wife. 'Are you drowning your sorrows, my friend?'

I nodded.

'What is it?'

I shrugged my shoulders. She sat down beside me. 'When young men like you drown their sorrows, it usually means only one thing.'

She was wearing a strapless silk gown. The skin on her shoulders revealed her unpublicized age.

I said nothing.

'Who is it?'

I slowly looked over at the mermaid. She had turned her back on the minister and was giving her full attention to the Chief. The Chief was playing the role of the middle-aged lady killer to the hilt. His wife poured me a drink. 'Tell me about her.'

'I don't know a thing about her.'

'Nothing? You can't be serious.'

'Not a thing.'

'And you're not interested, either, I suppose.'

I shook my head.

She laid her hand on my arm. 'You have sad eyes,' she said. 'I don't like seeing people look sad. Why don't you call me sometime?'

'I will.'

'You certainly don't sound very convincing.'

I compelled myself to turn away from the scene surrounding Lenka. I frowned.

'I have a good job and I don't want to lose it.'

'Then stick with me, friend. Emil does what I tell him to do. In case you didn't know.'

I looked at her carefully. Her little eyes, sunk into her puffy cheeks, had an evil glitter. It would be foolhardy to antagonize a woman like her. I sighed. 'That Emil of yours is making my life miserable!'

'Ah! I must give him a good talking-to. What is he doing to you?'

'He hands me insoluble problems.'

'Cibulka, right?' she said in a knowing tone. The story of the supervisor of morally disturbed girls had obviously spread far beyond our office walls. 'But that shouldn't make much difference to you, should it?'

I grimaced. 'He wants me to scuttle the book.'

'So?'

I paused. The minister's entourage, so awkward and glum a few minutes before, had grown very lively. The Chief had his arm around Lenka's waist and she was laughing her head off. She didn't seem to mind having the Chief hold her like that. In fact, from the way she stroked what was left of his hair, she seemed to be enjoying it. Once again jealousy swept over me – jealousy and rage. So that's what you're like? What is it you're after? Money? Bald heads? *Roués* with political connections?

I looked at the liquor cabinet only to find that I still had half a drink in my hand. The Chief's wife, who had long since outgrown jealousy, nevertheless showed understanding for my predicament. I gulped down my drink.

'So?' she repeated. It took me a moment to remember what we had been talking about. Ah, yes. Cibulka.

'I'm not sure this is the right moment to scuttle this particular manuscript.'

'Doesn't Emil know that?'

'My situation is more delicate. He is more . . .' I was about to say 'compromised', but I changed my mind, and said instead: 'He's the boss. It's a lot easier for him to ignore opinion around the office than it is for me.'

She x-rayed me with those evil little eyes. 'And he can kick you out if you cross him, is that it?'

Yes, she sees right through me, I thought. Then, suddenly, I saw in her eyes a possible solution. To the devil with caution.

'He certainly can kick me out. And on my part, I have no power over him, you understand?' I looked straight in her face.

She lowered her lids. 'You don't need to worry,' she whispered.

'Attractive young men like you have nothing to worry about. As long as they're agreeable.'

She pressed her breasts against me. 'Come over tomorrow afternoon. Emil has a municipal council meeting.'

I was drifting in a perfumed alcoholic haze. The Chief's arm was still hugging the waist of my deceitful companion. My little rose, I'll kill you!

'Will you come?' whispered the Chief's wife.

'Maybe,' I mumbled. The last shot of vodka started a rock-and-roll pounding in my veins. The room swayed.

Midnight witnessed the utter degeneration of the party. It found me sitting on a sofa behind the rubber tree, on the other side of which was parked the minister, surrounded by Vrchcolab, Andres, and Binder. The minister's eyes stuck out of his boredom-stiffened face like a pair of monocles. The Chief, always eager to be of service, for once managed to do as he pleased – he had the mermaid all to himself. They moved to the remotest corner of the room, where they sat intimately *tête-à-tête*. Lenka's lips were moving quickly, silently, tirelessly; I was desperate. The Chief's wife had left me. The minister momentarily emerged from his lethargy to glance longingly at Lenka, but this only goaded Andres and Vrchcolab to talk even more loquaciously than before. In spite of the late hour, these two continued to propound the problems and challenges of the youth movement. I almost felt sorry for the minister, who was always and everywhere destined to fall victim to some Vrchcolab, to always be denied the pleasant banter of some dusky rose for the sake of listening to inane, gratuitous reports and proposals. But soon I concentrated all my pity on myself.

It was 12:30, and Andres was still babbling: 'Some people underestimate the guerrilla movement in central Bohemia. But my book will open their eyes. I am trying to collect village chronicles in counties around Prague. And you'd be amazed, Comrade Minister, at the kinds of things that come out!'

'Is that so?' answered the hollow voice of the minister. He picked up an empty vodka bottle and tried to shake out a few last drops. Andres paid no attention.

'There were at least twice as many guerrillas than is officially recorded. After the war many of them refused to acknowledge that they took part in the movement, out of modesty. And, of course, many of them unfortunately died in battle.'

'I see,' said the minister and put the bottle back on the table. Binder, the director, made one of the last observations in the evening's conversation: 'This would make a good film. I am sure that in going through these chronicles you come across a lot of interesting material.'

'Definitely. It would be a great film about the heroes of our time.'

'I see,' repeated the minister and glanced at his watch. 'But I must go now. In the morning I'm off to Bruenn to address a beekeepers' convention.' He cast a mournful look at the mermaid and got to his feet. We all followed suit.

'I'll take the liberty of sending you a copy,' Andres managed to get in.

'Please do that,' said the minister, and hesitated. The Chief's wife left the lifeless Kopanec and strode towards him. The minister, obviously still loath to go, gazed into the far corner.

But there the Chief was holding Lenka's hand, totally oblivious that his guest of honour was about to leave the party.

At long last the dusky rose belonged to me. I was carrying her off in a taxi. We drove along the Moldau and the moist midnight air of the beautiful summer night caressed our faces. But she was present only physically. Her spirit hovered in some mysterious realm from which I was excluded. Lost in her secret thoughts, she gazed silently out at the river which was fragmenting the moon into a collage of tin foil. Her breasts shone in the moonlight. I was mad with desire, furious with jealousy.

'Did you have a good time?' I asked, each word dipped in poison.

She slowly emerged from the land of mystery, and turned her opaque gaze on me. Her eyes only reflected the outer world – the procession of dark villas silhouetted against the Milky Way, a bathhouse with white clouds on a black sky, a ruby ball over the castle as seen from the terrace of the Manes restaurant. It was the world around Lenka Silver, not the world inside her. What was that other world like? I wondered.

She did not reply.

'Did you have a good time?' I repeated.

'Yes, thank you.'

'The big man treated you well?'

'Yes,' she replied. 'You saw for yourself, didn't you?'

'I certainly did.' Overcome by anger, I hissed stupidly: 'But if you want to play with somebody's hair, I've got more than he has.'

She noticed my anger – she couldn't help but notice – and snapped: 'I am particular about whose hair I play with.'

'I should hope so,' I answered, almost sobbing. 'Prague is full of baldheaded men.'

For the first time since I met her she mimicked my poisonous tone: 'I like the feeling, you know? A bald head is pleasantly smooth, like warm marble.'

'Perhaps I could shave my head.'

'It wouldn't do you any good. You'd have a scalp like a cheese grater.'

Up front, the taxi driver giggled. Such non-professional behaviour only added fuel to my fire.

'You want us to talk a little louder?'

'Sorry. No offence meant. They don't give us earplugs, you know.'

'Then stick your foot in your ear!'

'No hard feelings,' he said soothingly, and I fell silent.

Lenka, too, lapsed into silence. We were speeding down the quay and after a while the taxi driver turned on the radio. Some all-night West European station was broadcasting jazz. Wild bebop saxophones, the kind Lenka liked. We zigzagged through the sleeping city until we reached the Avenue of November Nineteenth.

She got out on the corner. I paid the driver, without giving him a tip. But he took it with good humour: 'No hard feelings.'

I turned around. Lenka was standing like a white statue right in front of the shop window so that I saw her from all sides. Her low-cut dress revealed the shallow ridge of her spine reaching almost all the way to the small of her back.

I drew closer to her. 'Today,' my voice broke with excitement, 'today I have no intention of kneeling down.'

'No?'

'No.'

I took her by the bare shoulders.

'Lenka,' I said abruptly, imploringly. 'Damn it, I love you! I'm not myself any more!'

I embraced her. Through my thin shirt I felt the firm thrust of her young breasts. Experience, wisdom – everything was rudely shoved aside by desire. I pressed her close to me and tried to kiss her. It was our third moonlit night.

But she slipped out of my grasp. One of her shoulders was completely bare, a smooth, hot, velvety shoulder. I lunged for her again.

'Stop it!' she hissed. 'You're drunk!'

She braced herself and pushed hard. I staggered back. She turned and started clipclopping off. I ran after her and grabbed her by the hand. She pulled it free. I caught her again and started pulling her towards me.

'Stop it, for heaven's sake! You want to rape me in the middle of the street?'

I noticed how heavily I was breathing. That restored me to my senses a bit, but I couldn't think of anything more intelligent than: 'Take me upstairs!'

'And what do you want me to do with my room mate at one in the morning?'

'Then come to my place!'

'Like this? You're drunk.'

One blow after another. I felt like crying. 'Lenka, I love you!'

'But I don't love you.'

I let her go. I had a tremendous desire to punch her ruby mouth.

I croaked furiously: 'You're in love with my boss, aren't you?'

'How perceptive you are!'

'You're a monster!'

'And you're as naïve as a schoolboy.'

'At least I have some pride!' I shouted. 'I don't go for lecherous old bags!'

Suddenly I felt scared. Had I gone too far? I glanced at Lenka. She was standing in the middle of the Avenue of November Nineteenth, bathed in moonlight, and as proof that I totally misunderstood everything she seemed to be smiling. She made me feel like a drooling degenerate who attacks young girls in the park. And her next remark did nothing to raise my self-esteem: 'You don't know much about life, my dear editor.'

We walked slowly side by side towards the green vestibule.

'Please forgive me,' I said. 'I didn't mean that last remark. But I am terribly jealous.'

'Of your boss? Are you crazy?'

'Why did you let him put his arms around you?'

'Don't you think it was a slightly different situation than your pawing me in the middle of the street like a drunken truckdriver?'

'At Blumenfeld's party I only wanted to take your hand and you wouldn't even let me do that.'

'Because I didn't want to.'

'Why not?'

'Let's just say I had my reasons.'

I laughed bitterly. She said: 'It makes more sense than you think.'

We reached the doorway.

'With him, it's an entirely different situation,' she continued.

'He's older and he's got more money.'

'He's also married, in case you haven't noticed.'

'It's something he often seems to overlook himself.'

She sighed. 'Look here, let's put our cards on the table. You want to get me, and you think it's possible.'

'And it isn't?'

'It isn't,' she said firmly. 'In his case it's only a polite flirt. He isn't thinking about anything else.'

She adjusted the top of her dress with her thumbs. Sorrow flowed through the Avenue of November Nineteenth like a thick soup.

'You don't seem to know much about life yourself,' I said.

'I know enough.' She turned and stepped towards the door.

'Maybe you'll still learn a thing or two.'

'A good lesson won't do me any harm. Nor you.'

I didn't answer. We stopped in front of the door and Lenka looked up, as if to see whether there was a light in her window. I didn't even know what floor she lived on with that damned room mate of hers.

'I'll give you the same advice as last time,' she said. 'Go to Vera. You might think about somebody else for once, instead of thinking only about yourself.'

'I think about you.'

'Not about me,' she shook her head. 'About yourself.'

'I no longer think about anything but you.'

'Only about yourself,' she repeated.

I got her point. I dropped my eyes to her white shoes, then lifted them to her infernal black eyes.

'Then why did you go out with me, if you knew that you didn't care for me at all?'

'I was interested in the people who were going to be at the party.'

'But you knew I wasn't taking you there just to have you meet my Chief.'

She thought that over. 'No. That's true.'

'Then, wasn't it cruel and selfish of you, according to your principles, to hold out false hopes for me just for the sake of your own amusement?'

'I suppose so,' she admitted. 'None of us are perfect.'

'You are.'

'Perfectly imperfect,' she sighed.

'If you're serious about that, then I'm still hoping.'

'Don't,' she said, pulling a key out of her handbag.

'You can't stop me from hoping,' I said. 'Are you coming to the gymnastics meet tomorrow?'

'With the Professor?'

'No. He won't be there. With me.'

'Why isn't he coming?'

'Because he spilled fish soup over your new dress.'

'But he is going to pay the cleaning bill, isn't he?'

'I assume your affection is not for sale.'

She gave me a black glare. 'No, that's true.'

I stared right back at her. My muscles were once again under my control. I didn't lunge for her. Not that I no longer felt like it. Quite the contrary. The sharp claws of her rejection pierced my heart like a skewered rabbit. But we were living in a civilized country. I didn't pounce, but I did try to wound her.

'You're talking so prettily that I almost believe you.' I paused meaningfully. 'But for a socialist functionary my Chief, seriously, is quite a rich man.'

'Goodnight,' she said briskly and opened the door.

'Lenka,' I called softly but quickly. 'At least give me your hand.'

She hesitated inside the door, then stretched out her hand. Long, slender, dusky. As fragrant as youth itself. Made of brown velvet. Bathed by the moonlight. I turned the small pink palm towards the moon and pressed my lips against it. Then I noticed the pink tattoo mark near her elbow. Quickly, I kissed the little smooth rectangle. But already she was pulling back her arm into the glassy darkness of the vestibule, and she disappeared like lost hope.

'Are you coming tomorrow?' I whispered into the darkness.

I heard a cruel, erotic, maddeningly unapproachable voice say: 'Of course not.'

The chrome door snapped shut, leaving me alone once again, under that sardonic, silvery old libertine that glowed high in the Nusle sky.

7 *Telephones*

The next day, a day full of life's little ironies, the grey-haired lady answered the telephone. At eight-thirty, at nine, at nine-thirty. At eight-thirty she asked who was calling, and when I told her, she informed me that Miss Silver was visiting the biological department of the university and that she had no idea when she would return. At nine and nine-thirty she no longer asked my name; she recognized my voice.

I dropped in on Blumenfeld. Fortunately she was alone in her office. She burst out jubilantly with the hard-to-believe news that Pecakova was on our side. She said 'our side', so I celebrated with her for a while. Then I exploited her good mood and asked her to dial Bio-Ex and to ask for Miss Silver.

Bewildered, she asked why. I wasn't afraid to tell the truth to a seasoned skirmisher like Dasha.

'Some old bag keeps picking up the phone and won't let me get through.'

Blumenfeld at once grasped the situation. 'What did you do to her?'

'Nothing. I hardly know her.'

'I'm not talking about the old lady. I mean the girl.'

'Can't you guess?'

'What?'

'We had a fight.'

'All right, dial the number.' She picked up the receiver. 'Auntie Blumenfeld will fix everything up.'

She handled it skilfully. In a few moments Lenka's velvet voice was caressing my ears.

'Silver here.'

'It's me,' I said.

'That's a dirty trick,' she said angrily. Blumenfeld made a grimace and tiptoed theatrically out of the office. As soon as I was alone, I took a deep breath: 'You're not playing fair with me, either.'

'Yes I am. But you're not.'

'What can I do if I love you?'

'Forget it. A person can't have everything.'

'I don't want everything. Only a certain young lady.'

'I am sure you will find one. There are millions of them.'

I seemed to recognize a slight shade of coquetry in Lenka's melodious, ironic voice. We were interrupted by the repulsive, nasal singsong of the switchboard operator: 'Hang up, please. We have a long distance call.'

'I'll call you in a little while, all right?'

She hesitated slightly, then said: 'All right.'

I had broken through the barrier!

As soon as I hung up, the phone rang.

'Hello?'

'Is Comrade Blumenfeld there?'

'She just stepped out. Who's calling, please?'

'This is Hartman. She called me this morning about . . . about one of Dad's stories. It has to do with permission to quote.'

'Just a moment, Comrade. I'll see where she is.'

She was certainly a quick worker. The Chief was right when he predicted that Blumenfeld would buttonhole the entire editorial board; he deserved credit for clairvoyance. And one had to admire Blumenfeld's relentless energy. Permission to quote! My foot!

'Blumenfeld!' I shouted down the hall. A door opened at the far end and Dasha stuck out her head.

'Comrade Hartman is on the phone.'

She broke into a typical feminine trot, knees close together, her curves bouncing up and down under her imported blouse. She looked as radiant as if a long-gone lover were on the other end of the phone.

Indiscreetly, I remained in her office. There was no need for discretion. This was a question of political tactics, not amorous dalliance.

Dasha greedily picked up the receiver and cooed: 'Hi, Jara dear!'

The literary voice of young Hartman droned monotonously.

'Just a moment, dear!' Dasha said. 'I'll get a pencil.' But she did nothing of the kind. Hartman was dictating something which Dasha repeated word for word without making any note of it whatever. A comedy routine. 'Listen, you're a darling, Jara. Incidentally, there is one other thing I need from you, but I'd better drop in at your place . . .'

Annie stuck her head in and called me back into my office, just as the conversation was getting most interesting.

I had a call, a most inconvenient one. The Chief's wife.

'I thought you were going to get in touch with me,' she said, reproachfully.

'I'm sorry, but I was all tied up.'

'Oh, I have forgotten what a model worker you are. Will you come to see me?'

'Well, tonight's out, I'm afraid.'

'For me, too. How about this afternoon?'

I was vaguely aware of yesterday's alcohol-dimmed conversation. Annie was pricking up her ears.

'All right. Around four o'clock. If anything should happen I'll call you.'

'I'll be waiting. By the way, what's happening with Cibulka?'

'Headaches.'

She laughed. 'Ciao!' she said.

I banged down the receiver and rushed back to Blumenfeld.

Blumenfeld was no longer cooing with Hartman. She was just getting ready to leave, holding a powder-spattered compact in front of her pudgy face.

'Can I make another call?'

'Be my guest.' She put the mirror back in her pocketbook, adjusted her blouse like a soldier checking his equipment, and said: 'If anybody is looking for me, I am with young Hartman.'

I winked at her conspiratorially. She winked back.

'Cibulka's going to make it. I can see that,' I said.

'Stop it,' she snapped back and left.

I quickly sat down behind her desk and dialled. The mermaid answered the phone.

'It's me again. How about coming to the gymnastics meet with me?'

'Is Professor Zamberk coming?'

'No.'

'I want him to come.'

'Good Lord,' I moaned. 'Maybe I should ask the Chief, too? Then you'd surely come!'

'No,' she answered. 'I'm getting tired of him.'

'You are a monster.'

'Then we're even. Wouldn't you like to see if you can change the professor's mind?'

I didn't answer and there was a long pause. She said at last: 'Hello? Are you still there?'

'Yes. I am thinking.'

'About what?'

'I am trying to figure things out. Either you love gymnastics but are afraid that I would molest you, and in that case . . .'

'Yes?'

'. . . in that case Zamberk is supposed to act as your chaperon . . .'

I paused again.

'Or?'

'Or you are terribly fond of Zamberk, but because he's afraid to speak for himself, I am supposed to act as a go-between.'

A lilting laugh pealed out of the receiver. 'You seem to consider only extremes.'

'What's the real answer, then?'

'I feel sorry for the professor. I don't want him to feel sad.'

'Call him up yourself, then.'

'I don't want to do that.'

'Why not?'

'Don't be so nosy,' she said gently. I was again convinced that the whole thing was a game in which I was destined to score an impressive goal.

'And if I talk him into coming, will you come, too?'

'Well, I guess so. Yes.'

I heard a male voice in the background; Lenka was talking to someone in her office. Then she said into the receiver: 'I have to see the director. Let me know how you made out with Professor Zamberk. Goodbye.' She hung up abruptly.

I made myself comfortable in Blumenfeld's chair, using the foam rubber pillow which she always stuck under her rear end. I could just see myself urging Vasek to come. And I could see Lenka playing hard to get when Vasek failed to show up. And he wouldn't show up. Only I would. She wouldn't walk out on me, either, because, I thought to myself, she didn't really want to get rid of me.

I returned to my office and waited half an hour – just long enough to pretend that I was trying to convince Vasek to come. In the meantime, I amused myself by reading a letter from some retired person who was desperately offering his services as a *perfect translator into and from German, English, Spanish, French, and Italian*, a skill acquired in the course of many years of experience as an executive with Schicht-Unilever, which is a *high recommendation from a linguistic point of view*. Yes. The applicant did not mention that it was hardly a recommendation from a political point of view. I wrote him the usual rejection to the effect that there were at present no openings, etc., that we would keep his name on file, etc. Then I looked at my watch and returned to Blumenfeld's office.

I was still walking down the hall when I again heard Annie calling: 'Karel, telephone!'

'Who is it?'

'Some woman named Silver.'

Oh? What was up?

Annie remained standing in the door. I asked her maliciously: 'Would you please transfer this to Blumenfeld's office?'

After a call is transferred it is impossible to listen in from a second receiver. Annie was hurt. With her nose in the air, she disappeared behind the door. But she did transfer the call.

'This is me, for a change,' said Lenka.

'Help!'

'What's the matter?'

'I can't believe it! *You* calling *me*?'

'Well, I just wanted to tell you ...'

'All by yourself?'

'Please calm down. You are getting too excited, and you'll soon see there is no reason for it. I can't go to the meet with you tonight.'

That brought me down to earth in a hurry. I couldn't think of anything to say.

'I have to go to Liberec on business. I'm supposed to be there early tomorrow morning, and the only way I can make it is to leave tonight.'

'I'll come with you.'

'Comrade director is coming with me.'

My heart sank. The evening began to turn into a desert.

'You disappoint me, my little rose.'

'What did you say?'

'I say, you disappoint me.'

'No – I mean what did you call me? Rose or something?'

'Yes. That's what I call you secretly.'

'My name is Silver.'

'You don't allow me any pleasure at all.'

'You allow yourself enough. Goodbye, then ...' she said, tactfully adding '... for now.'

I promptly lunged for those lifesaving words: 'Wait a minute! When will you be back?'

'Saturday night.'

'I'll meet you at the station.'

'I don't want you to.'

'I'll carry your suitcases.'

'I'm not taking any.'

'Your handbag, then. Or your newspaper. Anything.'

'I don't want you there at all. If you really want to make me angry, then come to meet me.'

'I want to come, but not if it will make you angry.'

'Then stay home and examine your conscience.'

'It was never as pure as it is now.'

'And what about your young ballerina?'

'But ...'

'I'm serious, just as I was the last time.' Her words again had the old hard edge. 'I am really not interested in you, so please stop trying.'

She sounded as if she really meant it. Her banter at the start of our conversation had given me high hopes. They were all gone now.

'Really?'

'Really.'

I felt suddenly furious. She said: 'We can be friends, if you like.'

'Thank you very much,' I answered ironically.

'Well, goodbye then.'

I said nothing.

'Goodbye,' she repeated.

'Your servant.'

The receiver clicked. She had hung up.

And once again I didn't have the faintest idea where I stood. I couldn't make her out at all. She was like an evershifting kaleidoscope, like April weather. She was a detective story in the flesh. Does she care for me? Doesn't she? Does she detest me as much as she puts on? Is it perhaps all a game, a way of postponing the inevitable capitulation, an exquisite prolongation of torture to make the ultimate pleasure almost unbearably sweet? Or is she quite serious? And why is she so interested in my Chief? And why the concern for Vasek?

Nothing but questions, and I was feeling too glum to try to puzzle out the answers. I dialled the executive office of Bio-Ex and announced myself as Comrade Novak. I said I had been trying to reach Comrade Silver. She was supposed to leave tonight for Liberec. Had she left yet? No, Comrade. They are leaving later this evening. Call extension thirteen. Thirteen! No wonder! What? No, no, never mind. I was talking to myself. I'll try to call again. Thank you.

She hadn't been lying. We're back where we started. Except that now I'm worse off than I was when we first got to know each other. As far as Lenka's concerned, I'm not even in the running.

8 *Three theatres*

The doorman at the ballet theatre let me in. I took the back staircase, which always gave me the pleasant feeling of being a big shot, an insider in this illusion factory. In reality, of course, I was only a shareholder in one small ballerina.

The theatre was dark, except for the stage which was lit by two spotlights. They were rehearsing some kind of modern ballet. Slender girls, one like the other, uniformly appealing, dressed in black leotards. Leotards always made them look so tiny. The musical director was banging on a piano in one corner of the stage, and the girls twisted their bodies into the same odd shape and kicked their black legs. The choreographer barked orders in an exasperated tone; the leotard-clad figures obediently stopped, then obediently resumed their twisting and hopping. They looked like a bunch of trained dwarfs.

Vera was in the front row. Her long blond hair was done up in a bun and she was working hard. I sat in the middle of the theatre and watched her. I was in a tender mood; I almost felt sorry for the little ballerina whom I intended to betray so cruelly. She, as always, knew nothing and went right on working. It was that way with everything she did – she threw heart and soul into it. They liked her in the theatre. That is to say, the directors liked her. That's why, at a tender age, she had already become a soloist. She was obviously dancing a solo part now, because, while everyone else hopped one way, Vera hopped towards the other side of the stage.

And yet, what was the point? What kind of career was this which all these obsessed, pretty girls were pursuing? It lasts some ten or fifteen years; then the best ones leave to teach a new generation of starry-eyed fools, while the others are left with their memories. I scowled at the brightly lit rectangle in front of me. What nonsense!

Ten, fifteen years, or forty, fifty years, what's the difference? It's all a painful experience, painfully brief, one way or the other.

But strange forces drive us over the surface of the earth. Lenka Silver. This ridiculous hopping before the lecherous eyes of art lovers. The director clapped his hands. A rest period.

I left my seat and made for the dressing rooms. I caught Vera outside in the hall, a sandwich in her hand. Her forget-me-not eyes lit up. There was a sweaty, gymnast smell about her.

'Kaja! You came to see me!'

'Yes. A magic trolley brought me here.'

'Come to my room. Lida is out today.'

She led me into her solo dancers' dressing room, which she shared with another girl.

'Listen,' I said, 'you want to go to a gymnastics meet with me tonight? You like gymnastics, don't you? That's why I thought ... It's Czechoslovakia versus the Soviet Union.'

She understood, as I had hoped she would. That everything was all right. Which made her all the more vexed that anything should keep her from going out with me.

'I have a performance tonight, Kaja!'

'Damn. I thought this was your night off.'

'It usually is, but Lida asked me to take over for her.'

'Well, I guess there's nothing we can do about it, then.'

I could see that she was thinking hard about a solution. When was the last time I had asked her out, anyway? I couldn't remember. She probably remembered, though. I could tell that she was desperate not to miss out this time.

'And what's Lida doing that's so important?'

'Her brother is celebrating. He just got his doctorate.'

'I see. Well, I suppose that's that.' I glanced at Vera. She was gazing at me intently. 'Too bad.'

Then she made a decision. She jumped up. 'Wait here!'

The black figure disappeared out the door.

I stepped outside and looked down the hall. Vera was running towards the phone at the far end of the corridor. I saw her dial a number, tapping her foot nervously. Then she leaned forward and talked rapidly in a low, urgent tone. I couldn't make out the words.

I returned to the dressing room and sat down to wait in an armchair. The chair faced Vera's dressing table with its huge mirror, its frame lined with pictures. A photograph of me was wedged into one corner. I scrutinized the two faces, the one in the photograph, the other in the mirror. Ordinary faces of an average comrade. The history of the last ten years was reflected in them, in that faintly sneering mouth, those grey eyes, those undistinguished features which you saw by the thousands at meetings, in offices, in apartments of girlfriends, in dressing rooms of ballerinas.

It was not a particularly pleasant history, nor a particularly disgusting one either. Just rather nonsensical. Who can tell a man's worth from a face, anyway? And who is right? The young lady who has just made that face look foolish or she who would do anything to win that face, and the man, for herself?

Teatrum mundi.

Vera burst into the room. 'Lida will take my place!'

She was exuding foolish female happiness. She sat down on a stool and tilted her face close to mine. I again smelled the aroma of strenuous exertion.

'Kaja!'

'What?'

'I am delighted you came.'

'So am I.'

She hugged me. A male voice sounded from the hall: 'Everybody on stage!'

Fate was niggardly in measuring out Vera's moments of happiness.

I pressed the kiss of Judas on her forehead. Then I handed her a ticket, explaining I might be a bit late since I was going to be tied up in a meeting. And, finally, from the phonebooth in front of the theatre I called Vasek Zamberk.

'Young man, you're about as hotblooded as an icicle,' said the Chief's wife, pushing me away. We were sitting on her salon sofa, where

Comrades Andres and Vrchcolab had worked hard to entertain the minister the previous night, and where Lenka had practically seduced the Chief. Now, with the help of Hungarian burgundy, the Chief's wife was trying to seduce me – in vain.

'Excuse me, Ella. I've got a lot of things on my mind.'

'So I see,' she said. 'What sort of things? The office? An affair?'

'Just about everything, I guess.'

'Ah! A victim of melancholy!'

She poured herself a glass of burgundy and downed it as if it were water.

'I wish I had your troubles,' she said.

A red cuckoo popped out of an old-fashioned carved clock that once must have adorned somebody's hunting lodge, and duly cuckooed six times.

'What's your problem, anyway?' she said. 'A young bachelor with a good job ...'

'What's yours?' I retorted.

The Chief's wife – an overweight, forty-year-old woman – gazed vacantly at the bull's head on the label of the bottle. Her little eyes no longer looked evil at all. She bolted down another glass of red wine.

'My problem?' she said. 'Age, husband, children, work, everything.'

'Why don't you get a job?'

'You really think that would help?'

'Why not? Work is a good opiate.'

'Does it help you?'

I shrugged. 'I'm in the wrong line of work.'

'And what kind of job would you recommend for me?' The wine bottle was empty. She reached behind the sofa, pulled out a bottle of Marie Brizard cognac, and poured some into her wine glass.

'I had the right kind of job once,' she said. 'I worked in the Youth Federation, you know.'

Then, waving the bottle in the air, she started to sing:

Fresh winds are blowing
All across our land –

No more fascist crosses
No more fascist bosses!

'You bet!' she said bitterly. 'My father was appointed Minister and Mr Prochazka became Comrade Prochazka. A model socialist marriage. Except that they found I couldn't have children.'

'That's sad,' I said. 'But – hell – this is no world to bring children into!'

The Chief's wife laughed – a laugh full of despair. 'You put that well, Kaja. It's no world for children. And you only know the half of it!'

Hadn't Lenka said something similar recently?

'I know that life is no picnic,' I answered.

'There you are. So how can you believe that a little work will chase my depression away? Work! I used to think that my work helped to achieve a noble goal. But I should have been born in a different kind of family. I should have been the daughter of some idealistic little official.'

She looked around the room. Everything in it had been owned by somebody else once. The collection of objects was the product of the old minister's antiquarian passion and his excellent connections. Some of the pieces were normally sold only to museums, like the rococo silverware in which our two faces were reflected.

She sang the next stanza:

The end of hunger, the end of need,
The end of thievery and greed!

She burst out laughing. 'They cured me of my idealism in a hurry,' she said. 'My father, that well known unmasker of the enemies of the people. And my comrade husband. That poet. That engineer of human souls.' She laughed and tears came to her eyes. 'And I was mad about Mayakovsky. "Let socialism built in the course of hard battles rise like a memorial over us all." Battles! What kind of battles is my husband involved in? I don't have to tell you.'

'No,' I answered. 'Cibulka battles.'

She grasped my hand. 'Kaja – if you really think that book is good, fight him! Goddammit, be reckless for once and fight for a cause with all you've got!'

I smiled sardonically. 'I am not a fighter,' I answered. 'Your husband has already assured himself of a majority. And the idea of getting clobbered doesn't appeal to me.'

'Yes.' Her voice broke. She almost sobbed. She slugged down another shot of Marie Brizard. 'Nobody wants to take a chance. I only hope that in the end we don't all get clobbered to death.'

'Don't you believe it,' I said. 'This is the age of prudence. Only careless people get hurt. Fools. Idealists.'

'But what happens in the end?'

'Life is short,' I replied. 'There are no posthumous punishments. With the help of prudence we may live to enjoy our pensions.'

She turned away and glanced out of the wide french window. It looked out on a neglected garden with a fountain, in the middle of which stood a headless marble cupid.

'I've known both kinds – the careful and the careless. And before they knew it, their spirits left this earth. Something left this earth, anyway. I don't know what, do you?'

I shrugged. 'I once skimmed through a satirical novel, written by an old, careless anti-Communist – what was his name, Zak? It was called *The Spirit of Matter*.'

'Anyway, they are dead. Or in jail. And some of them were so careful! And so loyal – they worked their heads off for the cause!'

'Life is risky,' I said.

'And they believed in what they were doing. The noble goal, you understand?' She looked at me with brandy-bleared eyes. 'Like me. But that's a long time ago. They've cured me of that spiritual disease.' She looked dully at the bottle of Marie Brizard.

'Now I am a spiritually healthy alcoholic. And I seduce young men.'

A grey pigeon perched on top of the headless cupid. He lifted his tail, relieved himself on the empty fountain, and rose again towards the sky, which was beginning to turn pink.

'Ella,' I said. 'Do you believe in anything?'

Pinkish light shone through the french window into this warehouse of antiques, like the gaudy spotlight that sets the mood before a belly dancer steps out on the stage. But here it was only glinting on alabaster figurines, old paintings, a bottle of Marie Brizard, the Chief's wife, and me.

She stared at me. Her pupils reflected the light like a cat's eyes, and flared up pink. 'Are you crazy? Or do you think that I haven't lived through enough to know better?'

'I was just curious.'

'Do *you* believe in anything?'

Did I? I had stopped thinking about such matters a long time ago. Until recently I had believed in certain rather intangible feelings, but a certain young woman ... No, I didn't really believe in anything.

Belief, disbelief – those are big words. I never burned for anything or anyone, my dear lady. I was always as cold as a dog's snout. And I was good at sniffing the prevailing winds. I just thought that some things were true and others were lies.

'I don't believe in anything, on principle,' I said. 'But I think. I think that we are sitting in the right boat, after all.'

'You do?' she scoffed.

'Yes, I think so. Personally, we're the same swine as the others, but we placed our bets on the right boat.'

'Are you referring to socialism?'

'You can call it that.'

The pink light in her eyes went out. 'Darling, are you a politician or something, that you divide the world into capitalists and socialists?'

'How else? That's an objective fact, isn't it?'

'It's a geographic fact But I thought you were a poet. You *are* a poet, aren't you?'

I smiled bitterly. 'Let's say so anyway. But a poet living to the east of the demarcation line. It behoves him to live accordingly.'

She burst into a hiccupy laugh. 'That line is not fixed by meridians – at least not for real poets. For real poets, those two worlds are not geographical concepts at all.'

'What are they, then?'

She poured out another glassful of Marie. 'It's ridiculous, my talking to you this way, drunk as I am. But we educated people; even when we're half-crocked we make more sense than washerwomen. Capitalism and socialism, you say?'

'If we leave out pockets of feudalism somewhere in the Orient.'

'Both of those,' she said, 'are just two variations on the same theme. The idiotic theme which that old madman Gorky talked about so proudly. Humanity, you understand, darling? Human beings. And the line of demarcation goes straight through that damned mammal. Either he is a man, or he is a swine.'

She went into a fit of coughing.

'And usually ... usually ...' she hiccupped, 'you can't even tell the two apart.'

About an hour later I was experiencing a living parable of our conversation. I was sitting alone under a cloud of cigarette smoke, trying to kill the evening at a boxing match. The wooden roof of the Winter Stadium kept the smoke from trailing up to the moon. Down below, in the nasty glare of the klieg lights, two human beings played out variations on Gorky's theme of humanity. One was a Russian who looked like a gorilla. The other, an Englishman, was bleeding profusely from the nose; his chest was red with blood. All around surged the din of the crowd. The Russian missed with a wicked hook; his glove lashed through empty space and a few drops of blood landed on the referee's white shirt.

Behind me, Comrade Andres was playing his part. He was screaming himself hoarse: 'Kill him! Kill him! Kill him!'

He didn't see me. I hunched low between a pockmarked, beefy giant and a mercurial girl who had to be forcibly held down by her young escort during attacks of bloodthirstiness. Comrade Andres, without realizing the symbolic role he was playing, represented another facet of the parable of humanity.

I was in a strange mood – had been from the moment I turned my back on the decapitated cupid and left the Chief's wife to her cataleptic tryst with Marie Brizard. Strange. The Englishman was just saved by the bell, the referee was conferring with the officials, and the crowd was loudly demanding murder. I crouched low in my seat and let my eyes wander over the faces around me and along the sections on the other side of the ring. On that far side, the faces merged into a speckled backdrop; human countenances were transforming into nothing but black eyes and screaming mouths. Faces closer to me were carved into ritual masks by the razor-sharp klieg lights. The wooden structure gave off a musty smell, the smell of a forest with spit, urine, cigarette butts, and greasy paper. The crowd, responding to the age-old instincts of the arena, produced an almost unbearable din.

Suddenly I remembered the immoral manuscript – God knows why I thought of it just at that time and place – and took a deep breath; the air filling my lungs had the nauseating smell of the masses, in whose name we were about to exorcize the heretical novelette. When these masses had freed themselves of capitalism they got rid of unemployment, but not of their arrogant coarseness. The same old vulgarity. Who knows – perhaps with the demise of capitalism they may have even lost some ancient virtues. Behind me, Comrade Andres was instructing his neighbour on the finer points of Soviet boxing technique, while red roses continued to sprout on the referee's white shirt.

Roses. One rose was physically far, far away from this worldly stage, though she, too, played some allegorical part in the grand design, a part that was still unclear to me. That rose was speeding away on the night train to Liberec; at the moment, she was probably playing chess with her director. And the other flower, a bit wilted, was probably shedding secret tears in another theatre in this city. No doubt she had figured out the reason for my absence just the way I hoped she would – all wrong. Perhaps the rest of my plan was starting to work, too; perhaps she was just beginning to put into effect the customary female desire for revenge, with my best friend as a handy tool. My plan was perfect, except that the girl had three fatal disadvantages: she was pretty, she was a ballet dancer, and she was my mistress. Would my best friend be able to overcome these forbidding obstacles?

In the ring, the victim won a stay of execution. The referee, an old pro, was not cowed by the *vox populi* and declared the bout ended by a TKO. The crowd groaned, finally applauded, rose and streamed for the exits, to wet their parched throats during intermission.

*

I went out to a tavern across the street where young Hartman was parked behind a tall table with Dasha Blumenfeld cosily leaning on his shoulder. Hartman was arguing with Andres, and from Dasha's animated gestures and shrill shouts it was clear that she was fiercely defending Hartman. I winked at her. Her companions hadn't noticed me, but nothing escaped Dasha's eagle eyes. She returned my wink in a conspiratorial way, apparently well disposed towards me in spite of her recent slap in the face. She playfully pushed a piece of her sausage into young Hartman's mouth, while rubbing her legendary bosom against his chest. I finished my beer and went back to the stadium.

Now came another scene in the grand parable of humanity. The loudspeakers blared out the announcement of the upcoming lightweight match – Vasko Kolakovic of the Federated People's Republic of Yugoslavia versus Stanislaus Andrzejewski of the Polish People's Republic. A perplexed wrinkle split the forehead of Comrade Andres sitting behind me.

This was the first time during the evening that the wrinkle appeared. It was not there when he was encouraging, to the limits of his lung power, Czechoslovak or other socialist heroes to beat the hell out of capitalist boxers ('Kill him! Murder him!'); it wasn't there when he was showing somewhat more restrained loyalty towards Czechoslovak boxers taking on representatives of other People's Democracies ('Let's go! That's the way!'); it wasn't there when he comforted Czechoslovak pugilists being decimated by Soviet Russians ('Hang on, Franta!'), when he gave sportsmanlike credit to Russian technique ('Great uppercut!'), or when he praised the level of the contest ('Great match!'). Nor was the wrinkle in evidence when foreign People's Democrats fought with each other; on that occasion he neutrally rooted for both sides ('Go to it, boys! That's the spirit!'), with a mild preference for Soviet athletes.

But now he was facing a cruel dilemma. After all, Poland had recently begun to publish Western-style detective stories, and only a few days ago Comrade Kaiser had made some unexpectedly critical remarks about Yugoslavia.

It occurred to me that Andres might solve the question on the basis of class origin. Kolakovic was presented as a member of the Yugoslav police, Andrzejewski was a machinist. It was difficult to estimate the quality of their class affiliations, and there was no time for further deliberation. The bell rang. Policeman and machinist began pounding each other. The crowd in the arena began to scream. I pricked up my ears.

For two rounds I heard nothing significant; Comrade Andres' problem seemed insoluble. It was not even possible to find a purely sporting answer – the rivals were quite equally matched, the crowd roared impartially at each bang of each skull, and Andres could not find a winner to cheer for.

The solution came in the third round. At the beginning of the second minute the machinist succeeded in landing a hard punch to the policeman's solar plexus. The Yugoslav gasped audibly, a stomach cramp bent him double, the din in the hall swelled. From high above us, from the cheapest seats just under the roof, came a voice loud with beer, the divine voice of the people – three clear, unambiguous words filled with healthy hate: 'Kill the cop!'

These words brought Andres to life.

'Kolakovic, hang on!' he yelled, unaccountably supporting the underdog. 'Kill the Polack! Hang on! Go to it! Kolakovic, kill him!'

But it was too late. The Yugoslav plainclothesman crumpled to his knees, lay down on his side, rolled over on his back, and was laid cold. The crowd broke into an orgy of jubilation. Kolakovic was carted away on a stretcher.

It's a strange world, I thought to myself, the world in whose name we are suppressing the manuscript. But I had been wrong in my estimate. Capitalism had left behind not only an egotistic vulgarity. Some virtues remained, too. Some rather important virtues. It was hard to make it all out. I pushed my way through a dusty, beery corridor and I felt quite peculiar, as if some old certainties were deserting me. The Chief's wife hugging Marie Brizard. Lenka Silver. Dasha Blumenfeld. And then there was the little ballerina poised on her slippered toes, her eyes filled with tears. I finally managed to get out of the stadium into the fresh air, to the quay bordered by chestnut trees, their crowns rustling.

The blue ball on top of the trolley station shone in the distance. I felt very strange. High in the sky floated the moon, whose fishy eye had followed me all the days of this passion week. This same moon was accompanying Lenka on her journey to Liberec. I held on to that image, to that dusky rose. Perhaps she could save me, lead me to new certainties, safe certainties. My heart ached. For the first time in years it occurred to me that I was all alone in the world. For the first time in years it mattered.

Lost in thought I almost stumbled against a couple hidden in the broad shadow of a chestnut tree. A pair of gazelle-like, oriental eyes glistened out of the darkness. I heard the sound of heavy breathing. It was Dasha Blumenfeld in the embrace of trembling, panting young Hartman.

I walked on quickly and soon disappeared in the night.

9 *Editorial conference*

The night passed, and with the fresh morning my peculiar mood had passed too. The trolley was filled with girls riding to work in transparent nylon dresses. The Chief had left a message that he would be out all day, freeing me from having to submit an opinion on Cibulka.

Nothing much happened that day. I waited for the telephone to bring me news of dramatic events that had taken place during the night, but the phone remained silent.

The following day, too, brought little of consequence. Except that Blumenfeld – sporting an imported blouse I had never seen before, with a décolletage calculated to devastate Prague – visited me in the afternoon and recapitulated the issues surrounding Cibulka.

This was the situation as she saw it: of the six outside reviewers, four would support publication – Kobliha, Brat, Hezky, and young Hartman. When she mentioned Hartman I gave her a meaningful glance, but she ignored it with sphinx-like disdain and continued: only Dudek and Benes would oppose publication, both of them being realists in the literary as well as political sense, and staunch members of the Chief's iron guard. As far as the six inside reviewers were concerned, after the surprising positive response of Pecakova, only Andres and Zluva – the senile editor of Czech classics – remained outside the fold. And ... 'What about you?' she asked me directly, and shot a gazelle-like, under-the-chestnuts bolt at my eyes.

What about me? 'You know,' I said, 'it's not bad, but it's not exactly a sensation.'

'Come on now, don't make me mad.' Her eyes narrowed to two slits. 'What sensations are we publishing around here?'

I looked down. My editorial motto flashed through my mind: *non edemus, ergo sumus*. He who publisheth not, perisheth not.

But such a Cartesian reply seemed hardly appropriate at the moment.

'Well, if you compare it with something by Alois, for instance . . .'

Alois was a brilliant stylist who at one time had written some provocative social novels about Prague nightlife. More recently, however, he had joined the general trend and taken to writing histories. That's what Dasha jumped on, of course: 'Who needs him? They keep yelling they want raw life – so here it is!'

'But they'll tell you it isn't artistically mature.'

She frowned. 'In other words, you want to scuttle it.'

For the first time since I'd known her, Dasha's pleasant Jewish face showed a trace of possible enmity. In some strange way it seemed more dangerous to me than the enmity of the Chief, even though Dasha had no tangible power over me. The threat posed by Dasha's hostility was remote, but real. It was not like the ephemeral enmity of the Chief, who had long since adopted the custom of our society in which the most devastating attack was accompanied by a friendly pat on the shoulder.

I quickly protested: 'Not at all. But you know what standards they use to measure prose. We'll have to talk to her, get her to cross out half a dozen "assholes" . . .'

'But will you support us?'

'If she crosses out all those . . .'

The gazelle eyes flashed with contempt. Mild contempt. 'You simply want to have an alibi for dear old Emil, right?'

I shrugged my shoulders. 'I am not sure whether this manuscript is the one that's worth going out on a limb for.'

'What book would you consider worth going out on a limb for – Tolstoy?' She yelled this out so loud it must have been heard on the other side of the building. 'Well, if you want to wait until our little Czech sprats grow into Tolstoys, you'll have one long wait, believe me. And I am not sure they wouldn't butcher Tolstoy if he was around and writing today.'

'Don't get excited, Dasha. I'll support the book, with reservations. That should do. Can't we keep a little objectivity?'

'Objectivity? When the other side doesn't have a scrap of it?' she screamed in her notorious aggressive tone. 'Let me tell you something. Even if the Cibulka stuff were written with a broomstick, which it isn't, I'd be all for it. Sure, it's full of all kinds of crazy quirks, but it's still infinitely better than all those slick turds that win all the prizes.'

She was as excited as if she had written the book herself. She got up and strode out of the room, slamming the door behind her, and leaving me feeling quite uncomfortable.

Saturday morning, the Chief showed up for the editorial conference at the last moment.

'You have your report?' he asked me quickly in a low voice.

'Yes. You weren't here yesterday so I couldn't give it to you.'

'Good, good. I'll read it later.'

He seemed nervous, and his mood at once infected me, too. His worried expression contrasted strongly with the flushed, energetic face of Dasha Blumenfeld. That's how Cleopatra – not the fictional one, but the historic, not overly glamorous one – must have looked when she was about to snare Gaius Julius. The Chief sat down at the head of the conference table and uneasily surveyed the assembled company. The laureate Zluva sat on his left, Dudek and Benes on his right; young Hartman was facing him from the other end of the table, and the rest of us were scattered in between. Brat was absent, of course, and for some reason Andres was missing, too. He hadn't shown up at the office the day before, either. But I had no doubt that he had turned in his report, nor did I doubt its verdict.

Happy summer street sounds resounded through the open window; the Chief turned around morosely and asked Dudek to close it. He took off his jacket and uttered the usual comments: that with the window open you can't hear yourself think, and that we should make ourselves comfortable because it was liable to get warm shortly. He wasn't speaking figuratively. As soon as the fresh gasoline-scented air stopped streaming in, the room became hot. We all took off our jackets, and Blumenfeld opened one button on her blouse.

'Well, then, Comrades,' said the Chief in an affable tone of voice, wiping his forehead with a handkerchief although his forehead was still perfectly dry. 'I welcome you to this council concerned with the interesting, promising, but of course rather problematical manuscript of Comrade Jarmila Cibulka. At the very outset I want to make it clear that I do not share the unqualified enthusiasm of some of you, in particular Comrades Blumenfeld and Kobliha. They refer to this manuscript as an artistic discovery, but it is, after all, only the work of a talented beginner.'

'Which represents an artistic discovery,' Kobliha interrupted. The debate promptly turned into a fracas. 'I don't say that this is a masterly work,' continued Kobliha. 'But it shows unquestionable talent, and I can't see any possible objection against publication.'

The first beads of perspiration appeared on the Chief's forehead, allowing him to use his handkerchief quite functionally. It won't be long now, I thought to myself.

'Comrade Kobliha,' he said in a voice that started to tremble, 'you are not employed in publishing. You see everything, so to speak, from a purely ideal viewpoint. But we in publishing must take many things into account. I realize that until recently our literature consisted primarily of formula novels so that young writers are now swinging to the other extreme ...'

'What young writers? I haven't come across anything by any young writer, except maybe a story or two in *The Torch*,' said Kobliha.

'But those are highly significant!' shouted the Chief, not without a touch of desperation. Then, true to his reputation, the Chief pressed the attack: 'I wouldn't want our literature to deal only with model party members. On the other hand, to present our society only from the blackest side, as Cibulka is doing ...'

'She is writing about hoodlums; and they make up the seedy side of any society. How can you write about them in any other way?' Blumenfeld said, adopting a venomously arrogant tone at the very start.

The Chief quickly shifted tactics. 'Yes, that's true. But you must remember one thing: more and more young people are reading novels these days. If we were to publish this, we would be swamped by protests from parents and teachers. Let's face it, this book is a textbook of gangsterism.'

The Chief's cohorts snapped into action. Benes said: 'From a pedagogic viewpoint, it's really awful. There is no question that the pedagogic function of literature was regarded too simplistically in the past, but to feed impressionable young people on this kind of naturalism ...'

'Read yesterday's Soviet *Literary Gazette*, Comrades,' the Chief said, to prevent his side from losing the initiative. 'It contains reviews of two books by young authors that Comrade Blumenfeld is promoting around here. The critic Nikolajev found strong elements of naturalism in these books and rejects them categorically. '

'But those are war novels. It's impossible to write about the horrors of war without naturalism,' objected Blumenfeld.

Dudek piped up: 'It can be done! Why not?'

The corpulent Zluva could no longer stand the heat. He opened the window a crack. The clanging of streetcars made it hard to hear the Chief, who was trying to steer the discussion away from highly controversial practice: 'Say what you will, from the publishing viewpoint we cannot afford to make our first venture into youth readership with this kind of material. Naturalism, modernism – that's a pretty rough way to start. And this novel is a compendium of every questionable "ism". Comrades ...' He pronounced the word as if it were an incantation. 'Let's look at this from a pragmatic, yes, I am not afraid to say it, from a strategic point of view. All of us sitting at this table are deeply interested in the development of new literary trends, and as human beings we have a soft spot for young authors. We cannot be indifferent to their professional or personal fates. We're among friends here, so I can confidently tell you the reaction of Comrade Kaiser to recent developments. And you know that Comrade Kaiser always has the inside track.' He paused to let this sink in, and took a sip of coffee.

'Comrade Kaiser,' he continued in a solemn tone, as befitted that awe-inspiring name, 'keeps well informed of literary discussions that take place in our office and elsewhere. I saw him recently and we talked precisely about the critical reviews of Nikolajev. Nikolajev is a highly respected Soviet critic – a very *influential* critic, Comrades.'

He glanced around the room to assess the impression made by his remarks. Blumenfeld looked scornful, Kobliha raised his eyebrows, Dudek and Benes nodded their heads, young Hartman looked distressed, and a sticky mugginess hung over all. It was a critical moment. I glanced at Blumenfeld. She, in turn, glanced over at the only young author present (Hartman was young by calendar age, at least). When she saw the war going on inside him – duty struggling with love – she stuck her devastating breasts under his face and whispered something in his ear. His face suddenly relaxed into a lecherous smile.

'Busy as he is, Comrades, nothing that's going on in the field of culture escapes the notice of Comrade Kaiser,' the Chief continued huskily. 'For example, he recently took the trouble of counting all the photographs of women in the last volume of *Young Life Magazine*. He found that there were three hundred and seventy-nine of them, as compared to only two hundred and twenty-three pictures of men. That wouldn't be so bad in itself, but two hundred and ninety-five pictures of women – in other words, two thirds – showed women in bathing suits or in scanty clothes!' Everybody automatically glanced at Dasha's monumental curves. There was a painful pause. The Chief went on. 'And of those women in bathing suits, exactly one hundred wore bikinis! As I was leaving, Comrade Kaiser said to me confidentially: "Comrade Prochazka, I can only tell you this much. We have always supported socialist realism, we are supporting it now, and we will in the future. Anybody who tries to defend naturalism, modernism, or any of those other foreign *isms*, is going to find himself in serious trouble."'

Dudek and Benes nodded their heads like marionettes. But in general, Comrade Kaiser's threatening dictum failed to produce its usual chilling effect. Young Hartman apparently had not heard it at all, for he was still captivated by Dasha's décolletage. Kobliha scowled. Hezky's mouth took on a strange curve, expressing God knows what. Then I noticed that he was resentfully following Dasha's flirtions with Hartman. Perhaps that explained it.

'In serious trouble,' repeated the Chief, shaking his head. 'I am transmitting to you the authentic sentiments of Comrade Kaiser, and, as you know, he always knows what he is talking about. I therefore ask you to keep this in mind when you're evaluating Cibulka's work. Modernism, naturalism . . .'

'In my opinion, this book has little to do with naturalism,' Hezky said heatedly and with a sharp look not at the Chief but at Blumenfeld. So that was it! Blumenfeld caught his glare and responded with a coquettish smile. The curve of Hezky's mouth straightened out. 'Really, this has little to do with naturalism,' he repeated, returning Dasha's smile. 'We must not be fooled by certain superficial naturalistic stylistic traits; these do not mean that the basic concept of the work is naturalistic,' he said professorially. 'Not at all. I would say that the harsh – and admittedly somewhat marginal – subject matter is treated from the moral standpoint of socialism, and ...'

He continued in this vein for about fifteen minutes, a theoretical, academic dissertation. Now and then the Chief tried to interject the opinions of well informed Comrade Kaiser, his personal adviser on top-level policy, but Hezky seemed much more interested in Dasha Blumenfeld's reactions.

Everything Dasha did that day was to her advantage. Young Hartman, in spite of his notoriously slow reaction time, noticed the encouraging glances she was lavishing on Hezky, but instead of getting angry he decided to compete for her favour. He took the floor and emphasized – not with the elegance of Hezky, but with even greater forcefulness – that Cibulka's novel could be an excellent study guide for youth council workers who had until now neglected young people on the margins of society. He went on to suggest that we might negotiate with the youth council publishing house to cooperate on a joint edition for mass circulation. The Chief could only roll his eyes in stunned amazement.

Even Dudek and Benes were confused by Hartman's behaviour; without taking time to think the matter through, they launched into a violent argument with the aggressive Kobliha about the essence of realism, using obsolete concepts such as 'rebound theory' and 'typicalness'. Because neither of them was very bright, they didn't realize that the opinions they were defending were defensible only in times when Kobliha's opinions were indefensible. It didn't take long for Kobliha to demolish them.

Thereupon Pecakova dealt the Chief another painful blow. She said: 'Comrades, I was deeply moved by this novel. If I were editing that manuscript,' Pecakova went on, revealing traces of her old orientation which the persuasive Blumenfeld had obviously been unable to dislodge, 'I would ask the author to tone down some of the language. I believe it's unnecessarily vulgar. But the central problem – the inner struggle of that unhappy girl, when her boy leads her to the abortionist – I believe that part is rendered beautifully.'

Her eyes filled with tears. The Chief used his soaking handkerchief to wipe his forehead, then rose and shut the window. This may have been the reason why I gradually began to feel hotter and hotter. Or perhaps it was the way Pecakova continued to spread her sticky sentimentality. Then, too, the moment was getting ever closer when the Chief would call on me for my opinion. The window was intermittently opened and closed. Trolleys clanged and fell silent. My stomach was full of butterflies, and I felt slightly feverish and dizzy. The debate was getting more acrimonious, the Chief was losing one trump card after another, and my moment of truth was near at hand.

I was unexpectedly saved by a *deus ex machina*, or more precisely, by senile Zluva's incurable tendency to lean on authorities. He had said at the outset that he was not an expert on contemporary prose, but on the Czech classics, and while others debated he rustled a pile of reviews which he proceeded to peruse. Zluva was an old reliable whore – stupid, but in contrast to Pecakova, stupidly devious. Now, he said, he regarded Cibulka's novel as misleading. This was best expressed by the report of Comrade Andres, declared Zluva, with which he was in complete agreement and which he would now take the liberty of reading aloud. All the pros and cons were extremely well formulated, he explained – and at this point the Chief interrupted him.

I didn't understand what was going on. Why was the Chief opposed to a reading of Andres' report – a report which, in spite of some favourable comments, was surely on the right side of the issue? Surely Andres wouldn't . . . no, that was impossible. I couldn't understand why the Chief wanted to postpone it 'to a more fitting time', as if a more fitting moment could possibly arise. I was still more puzzled by Blumenfeld's insistence that the report be read. Zluva, who was aware of nothing at all, simply began to read. I noticed that the Chief's forehead was suddenly producing more sweat than ever before.

Zluva read.

The 'pros' that Andres saw in the manuscript were principally limited to generalized statements about the author's 'definite talent'. His 'cons' filled four pages. 'The novel shows signs of an uncritical acceptance of fashionable Western literary phenomena, such as a decadent interest in degenerate aspects of life, the mixing of chronological planes, emphasis on sex, alcoholism, violence, and a variety of esoteric allusions. Recently,' Zluva said, raising his voice before going on with what struck me as being the swan song of a literary epoch, 'our literary taste has been subjected to the terrorism of snobs. Authors who wish to write realistically about matters of interest to the average reader, and who ignore modish waves and wavelets, feel this terror most keenly. They are ridiculed as old-fashioned, provincial, social-realistic. I have no doubt that Cibulka's novel would be greeted by the snobbish circles with the greatest enthusiasm. It is therefore the duty of a socialist publisher to reject such a work and to exert an educational influence upon the author, urging her to think more deeply about the significance of her work so that her future creativity would be free of modish piquancy and so that she would try to portray the whole truth about our lives – lives which certainly have their difficult moments but in which hope and good cheer predominate.'

Zluva stopped. The last ritual sentence was supposed to have been followed by a reverent hush, after which the Chief would take over. And, in fact, for a few seconds there was a hush – silence broken only by the palace guard – Dudek and Benes – clicking their spoons against their coffee cups in a dignified show of approval. A blast of warm air blew in through the window, and a trolley creaked around a curve.

I looked at the Chief. Now, Chief, now! – but he was strangely silent, perspiring heavily. For God's sake, this was the ideal time to trot out Comrade Kaiser again! The report by Andres had a clear message which was certainly not lost on the present company. But the Chief just sat there. Blumenfeld raised her strident voice, not at all wavering and evasive, not at all cowed by the sententious pronouncement of Comrade Andres.

She said: 'Comrade Prochazka, could you tell us why Comrade Andres is not present at this meeting?'

There was a deathly silence, and it lasted for a painfully long time.

Then the Chief cleared his throat: 'He had some important matter to attend to.' He cleared his throat again.

Something was up. I glanced sharply at Blumenfeld. Her eyes were glued on the Chief, who was trying to evade her challenge.

The air was charged with tension. The hot noonday sun lit up Blumenfeld's face. She looked almost beautiful again. Young Hartman licked his lower lip. A passing trolley clanked by. Someone closed the window. So Blumenfeld's next sentence came through loud and clear: 'It has to do with his work on the guerrillas, doesn't it?'

The Chief turned pale and feigned surprise: 'Oh?'

'Yes,' Blumenfeld answered firmly. 'It turned out that almost all of the entries in the county chronicles about a guerrilla movement were written by Andres himself. After the war. After he started writing his book.'

The bomb fell and exploded. The Chief blinked. Benes dropped a spoon on the floor, bent down to retrieve it, and remained in a stooping position. Blumenfeld continued coolly: 'First he would offer the national council to put certain county chronicles in order; then he wrote up a whole batch of imaginary accounts. And now he's filling his book with the stories he made up . . .'

I looked at the faces around me, especially those of the Chief's élite guard. Benes was still pretending to look for something under the table. Dudek sat as straight as a ramrod, his face impassive as stone. The Chief was still trying to act surprised. Kobliha laughed out loud. Hezky grinned at Blumenfeld. Young Hartman was turning his head in alarm. Zluva turned beet-red and quickly stuck Andres' review in his briefcase.

'I don't believe it,' mumbled the Chief.

'It's a fact,' replied Blumenfeld.

'How do you know?'

'I have it from a reliable source,' she said. 'I wouldn't come out with such a story if I weren't absolutely sure.'

The room was becoming stifling; drops of cold sweat were trickling down my spine. I came to the firm decision that, under the circumstances, my review would be positive – with minor reservations.

But Blumenfeld's bomb had turned the meeting into chaos. The Chief's party looked as if they had suffered an irreparable defeat. In their panic, they mumbled about how they couldn't believe it, about rumours, about having been misled. Somebody opened the windows again, and the cacophony of voices merged with the noise of traffic. Hezky and Kobliha relentlessly pressed their advantage, Dasha's voice spurring them on like a tin trumpet of doom. The rattled Benes tried to compare Andres' fakery to the famous controversy surrounding ancient Czech manuscripts allegedly forged by Vaclav Hanka, the nineteenth-century Czech linguist and literary scholar, in order to prove that Czech culture was older than German. Kobliha countered with sarcasm that was so biting that Benes took it personally and it seemed the debate might end in a fistfight. Everybody was standing up by now, and Dasha could be heard above the din, screaming about swindlers – in the plural, no less. Convinced that nothing could prevent the triumph of a cause so just – albeit foolish – I was on the verge of inconspicuously aligning myself with the rebels.

I was once more saved by a *deus ex machina*, this time in the person of the Chief himself. Once again he proved himself a master tactician. He cunningly allowed the dispute between Benes and Kobliha, egged on by Blumenfeld, to reach its crisis. Then, as soon as Benes had landed a clumsy punch on Kobliha's chest, he jumped up, stepped between the two men, and pushed them aside. I had to admire the man: it was the psychologically perfect moment – the only moment in which his words would carry the weight of authority.

'Comrade Blumenfeld's disclosure,' he roared, outshouting the din on both sides of the window, 'has shaken us all so badly that we are clearly incapable of coolly weighing a matter as important as the manuscript before us. Therefore, in the meantime ...' Blumenfeld was beginning to see what he was up to, but it was too late. Her protesting voice cracked and the Chief went on: '... in the meantime, I will keep the matter open, and I will submit it to the editorial board which will be convened after the summer vacation.'

Postponement always ranked high in the repertoire of classical solutions. Blumenfeld promptly challenged the ruling, but the chaos of passions, reservations, confusions, and ulterior motives had become so noisy that it would have been impossible to ascertain the decision of the council. Thus, the Chief's solution was finally accepted.

Both sides retreated from the battleground, leaving behind a mess of overturned coffee cups and scattered notes.

That afternoon, when I came to see the Chief with the preface to a collection of stories, he was sitting at his desk looking utterly dejected. The ashtray in front of him was heaped high with cigarette butts.

'Yes, I'll take a look at it. Sit down,' he said, throwing the preface listlessly into his box of unfinished business. 'What do you think?'

'I think that the editorial board will be reasonable.'

'No, I mean about that Andres business.'

'He's an idiot. He must have known he couldn't get away with it.'

The Chief shook his head. 'I don't get it either. If he had faked a little bit here and there – let's face it, we all do that once in a while – but to dream up a whole phony guerrilla campaign!'

He rested his head on the palm of his hand. 'I read it, and it did seem a bit fishy. So many guerrillas. But I assumed that Andres was an intelligent fellow.'

'You knew it before Blumenfeld let the cat out of the bag?'

'Of course. That's what that meeting with Comrade Kaiser was about.'

'And?'

'Andres will have to leave, of course.'

'What will they do to him?'

The Chief pulled a bottle of vodka from a desk drawer. 'He was lucky this thing exploded while his book was still in manuscript. He'll be shipped off to a labour brigade, and later we'll see.'

'They should fire him. He made one hell of a mess.'

'He certainly did,' the Chief said. 'And he deserves a good spanking. But then again, you know him. He's a good comrade, reliable . . .'

'Do you think he'll get a job here again – after it's all blown over?'

'Probably not. Jaros over in the Children's Publishing Division is supposed to retire next year. Maybe there'll be a spot for him there.'

He poured out a couple of shots of vodka. The afternoon sun burnished the bust behind the Chief with a bronze glow.

'How did Blumenfeld find out?'

'The Jews, Kaja, the Jews. You can't hide anything from them. They've got their people everywhere.'

I gulped down my vodka, and he immediately refilled my glass.

'Now, that editorial board: look, here's my idea. I have something in mind and I want to know how you feel about it.'

'Sure.'

'Look, up till now the voting at board meetings was done by a show of hands. But with the board we've got now I have a hunch it might be better to switch to a secret ballot.'

I hadn't expected anything like this. 'Why?' I said.

'I don't know,' said the Chief. 'I'm not sure. But what that fool Andres writes about the terror of snobs – there's something to it.'

'But why a secret vote?'

'Well, in the past, people were damn slow to come out for some kind of degenerate junk. But now?' The Chief gazed out of the window at the façade of the house across the street. There was a movie theatre in the building, and a big sign advertising the American film *A Jazz Fantasy* was just going up.

'I have the impression now that some people won't feel like voting against Cibulka. They're scared of losing face before Kobliha and his crowd – frightened of the power of the snobs, you understand? You saw it for yourself. Pecakova. Who'd have ever guessed that Pecakova . . .'

'She's not doing it because she's scared of the snobs,' I answered. 'She's a romantic sentimentalist. She was moved by the stuff about the abortions.'

'Or take young Hartman. Karel, tell me the truth, would you ever have guessed, even in your wildest dreams, that Hartman would support such immorality?'

I shrugged my shoulders. I didn't say what I knew about young Hartman's motives or his feelings about immorality.

'And so it occurred to me that a secret ballot would help get these people off the hook, you know? They'll be able to vote against the book without having to worry about anyone accusing them of being chicken-livered or philistines. You can just imagine what people like Kobliha are saying about me.'

I nodded, and suddenly I appreciated the beauty of the Chief's idea. It fitted in so well with my own needs that the Chief might have dreamed it up exclusively for my benefit. A secret ballot, which fits in perfectly with the democratic trends of the times, a masterly dialectic that succeeds in turning everything upside down and turning everything to its own advantage. The Chief had just convincingly demonstrated that he could rise to any challenge.

I would be well advised to stick in his corner. 'I think it's a good idea,' I said. 'In fact, I think it's an excellent idea, Emil.'

The Chief's excellent idea failed to put me into an excellent mood, however. In the afternoon I went for a swim, took several showers, and then tried to read an English detective story, but the sentences slid by without leaving a trace. I thought of Lenka, who would be coming back in the evening by the Liberec express, but this pleasant thought was marred by the unresolved dilemma of Vera. It had been three days since I'd heard from her and I still had no idea whether this was because my plan had failed or because it had been fantastically successful.

At six I went to the Slavia for dinner, where I managed to evade the attentions of the poetess Sintakova – the most over-barbiturated person in Czech literature. After dinner I set out for a stroll along the quay.

The streetlights went on. Neon signs began to blink in the amber evening. I stood by the bridge watching the floating birds and my soul was heavy. Downstream, boating couples were drifting amid foam and debris, an occasional flurry of oars splashing the ruby surface. Girls in summer dresses and young men in linen trousers set out on their inevitable journey to pleasures that were no less enjoyable for being eternally the same, and I felt sad. Lenka was tormenting me with desire; the world was tormenting me with uncertainty.

Suddenly, out of the crowd of pedestrians milling towards me, a young lady materialized. Vera. Wearing dark glasses and striding youthfully in her pale blue dress, she carried her firm, athletic body as if it were a rare piece of valuable private property. From my point of view, not as private as all that.

She didn't see me.

'Hi, Vera!' I called out from the railing.

The dark glasses turned towards me, then turned away.

I unglued myself from the railing and followed her. I should have let her stride off into the amber evening after Vasek or anyone else, but the way she ignored me was a new phenomenon. I was stung. I quickened my steps and soon caught up to her.

I repeated: 'Hi, Vera!'

She glanced at me out of the corner of her eye, and said coldly: 'Hello.'

The shadow of a wheeling bird crossed the pale face of the ballerina who never had an opportunity to enjoy the luxury of prolonged sunshine. Then her figure took on the red cast of a traffic light. She stood under the light, a pale blue, white, black, and pink composition with the massive stone-façaded theatre as background. It was a different, strange Vera, someone who didn't seem to have any connection with my life, just as she seemed to have little connection with the patriotic stone buildings behind her which the sun was gilding with fool's gold.

I tried to sound jovial: 'How was the gymnastics meet?'

In a voice as unfamiliar as everything else about her, she said: 'Great fun.'

The light turned green. We crossed the street.

'I couldn't make it. A party meeting came up at the last minute. I called, but you weren't home.'

'Oh?' She had put on a hard-to-get act before, of course. Except it didn't seem like an act now. I had the feeling that she had definitely changed. And, oddly enough, I wasn't pleased.

'Did you have a good time?'

She stopped at the stage door. She took off her dark glasses and looked me straight in the face. She gave me an exquisitely poisonous female smile – something she had never been able to bring off before.

'I had a marvellous time! Much better than with you, Kaja dear. Lenka Silver is really a wonderful girl.'

Lenka? I felt as if a boulder had crashed down on my head.

'Silver?'

'Vasek, too. Bye.' She stretched out her hand. I shook it, in a daze.

'Wait, Vera.'

'I have to go now. I have a performance.' She slipped by me, turned smartly on her heel, and ran past the bloated doorman into the theatre.

Damn it, what's going on?

'Vera!' I shouted, louder than I had intended.

'A cute trick!' I heard a voice behind me. Still groggy from the encounter with Vera, I turned around, and stared vacantly at Kopanec, the Master of Fuckups.

'Don't take it so hard,' he said, linking elbows with me. 'Let's go have some fun!'

I was still trying to figure out what it all meant. How had Vera got together with Lenka? That meant that the whole thing had been a trick! That my beautiful vixen hadn't gone on a trip at all! She had arranged everything to make me think she had left for Liberec, and then had gone to the meet without a ticket. But why? For Vasek? Was it possible? She had me completely muddled. Anything was possible.

I made a move to follow Vera into the theatre.

'Just a moment,' said Kopanec. 'They won't let you in the dressing rooms now. Buy her a dozen roses and wait for her after the show.'

'Balls!' I said.

'Well, ballerinas can be pretty tricky,' Kopanec said knowingly.

'Balls!'

'Take it easy! It'll all turn out all right! I want to celebrate today. I have scored a great personal victory.'

He took me under the arm and, while I mentally wished him and his personal victory in hell, he led me down Narodni Avenue.

'Do you remember Randa? That great critic who wrote that I had dragged Czech prose into the worst depths of degradation?' he babbled, full of himself and showing no regard for the delicate state of my nerves.

'Yes, sure,' I said, my mind preoccupied with other things. 'What about him?'

'He's in bad trouble these days,' said Kopanec jubilantly and proceeded to give me a detailed account of Randa's habit of stealing things, picking pockets at the editorial offices and using the proceeds to buy booze. I was listening with one ear. I kept turning Vera's words over in my mind and I still couldn't understand what it was all about. Whenever Lenka Silver appeared on the scene, some mystery was involved. As a matter of fact, I didn't understand anything at all. Kopanec was recounting with great relish how Randa had been caught redhanded in the offices of *The Torch*, pulling editor Pacholik's wallet out of his jacket. 'That's the third of the sons of bitches!' exulted Kopanec. 'The third one of the bastards that tried to ruin me! Puchold got killed in a plane crash in China. Rejnoha's already had three heart attacks and it won't be long before he croaks. And now Randa. That leaves young Hartman, but he'll probably be done in by the general state of affairs in this country and Brat could be bumped off by ideological revisionism, which would be a nice bit of poetic justice. Karel,' he slapped my back, 'I feel like the thunderbolt of Zeus. Anybody who crosses me will be destroyed.'

He grinned and jumped in the air like a Slovak folkdancer. We were just passing the Writers' Club. 'Come on up with me. We'll have supper together. You can keep me company until your ballerina gets through working.'

I thought it over quickly. No use going after Lenka until I could find out just what happened at the meet.

'All right,' I said, and in we went.

The iron guard sat in a huddle in one corner of the clubroom. Kopanec made a deep bow in their direction and headed for a table in the opposite corner. After we sat down, he asked me for a briefing of what had gone on at the meeting. When he heard about Blumenfeld's bombshell disclosure he burst into a long, loud fit of laughter, pounding the table with his fist. Several iron guard heads turned to stare.

'Blumenfeld! That's the best part of it!'

'Why?' I asked.

'Well, she's God's thunderbolt, too, just like me. An Old Testament thunderbolt. We're both instruments of God's revenge.'

He was talking in a loud voice. In his position as Master of Fuckups he could afford not to care whether anybody overheard. He didn't have to feign 'correct' opinions, for since his notorious scandal concerned with the *Battle for Brnirov* it was generally assumed that he didn't have any. Also, because the affair surrounding the book had damaged so many people's reputations, nobody felt like rehashing the details, and so Kopanec was left in peace.

'I really don't understand what you mean,' I said. 'It's true that the Chief isn't particularly fond of Blumenfeld . . .'

'Your Chief is one of the most viciously anti-Semitic swine I've ever run into,' said Kopanec. 'You mean you haven't noticed?'

I remembered the Chief's remarks about the Jews: they have their people everywhere. Yids. But remarks like that weren't all that unusual.

'You think so?'

'I don't think so, I know so,' said Kopanec. 'Don't you know the history of his love affairs?'

'He married the daughter of a publisher . . .'

'You simple shit, since when is marriage a love affair? So you really don't know?'

I shook my head.

'Well, actually very few people know this,' Kopanec said, leaning towards me and lowering his voice for the first time since we had arrived in the club. 'I heard this from Kocour, who used to be Prochazka's buddy before the war. This is precisely why Kocour parted company with your boss.'

'Go on.'

'Your little Emil was engaged to a Jewish girl,' Kopanec said. 'But after March 15 1939, he dropped her fast. It was only after he broke off the engagement that he married the publisher's daughter.'

'I didn't know . . .'

'Well, now you do,' said Kopanec. 'She ended up in a gas chamber.

The fiancée. So that, fundamentally, his anti-Semitism is caused by a bad conscience.'

The Master of Fuckups took a deep gulp from his beer glass and added philosophically: 'When you come down to it, a good many radical opinions are fundamentally nothing but bad conscience.'

The supper with Kopanec could have been quite pleasant if my mind hadn't been preoccupied with the mysterious circumstances surrounding the gymnastics meet. Kopanec, in a good mood over Randa's arrest, sparkled with wit. He gave me a thorough rundown of his sexual life and then he turned to literature, a topic I would have gladly avoided. He was no longer interested in anything but women and literature. That might not be very much, but it was something. Some of the iron guard were no longer interested even in women. Kopanec talked about them with some feeling: 'Those bastards have life by the balls,' he philosophized. 'You know why? Because whatever they know they keep to themselves. You have any idea what an enormous number of facts those bastards have at their fingertips? If I knew just one tenth – and if I had some talent – I'd be another Balzac. You know what they really are?' He nodded in the direction of the iron guard.

'Court jesters?' I suggested.

'Are you crazy?' Kopanec waved his arm in disgust. 'A court jester used to tell the king some very unpleasant truths right to his face. These bastards are just the opposite. They're blackmailers. Hands up, Comrade Kaiser! If you don't pay up we'll write what we know. So Comrade Kaiser pays up.'

'Or else shakes his fist,' I said.

'Or he shakes his fist. But recently that hasn't scared anybody the way it used to.'

'I wouldn't underestimate him.'

Kopanec squinted craftily: 'My dear fellow, I no longer underestimate him. That was a luxury I allowed myself before the fuckups. That's precisely why there was a fuckup in the first place. I served as an instructive precedent,' he laughed. His attention was taken up by a young girl who was approaching the table of the iron guard, autograph book in hand and practically bowing with deference. Kopanec turned his head in disgust and cursed: 'Goddammit, you see that? She doesn't even notice me! And I'll tell you why! Because at the last minute they took my picture out of that illustrated series "Our Writers". Now nobody knows what I look like,' he said gloomily, watching enviously as the corpulent laureate Bobr scribbled something into the autograph book with the expression of a bored movie star on his face. 'Lovely girl!' He sighed. 'Shall I go over and introduce myself?'

'As what?' I asked ironically. 'An instructive precedent?'

That snapped him out of his fantasy. 'Why not? I *am* a legitimate precedent.' He took a drink and frowned. 'Sure I am. But they found out that I got away with thumbing my nose at the bigwigs, and now others are trying the same thing.'

The waiter brought cutlets and Kopanec started eating with gusto. As Master of Fuckups he received special consideration at the club. His cutlet was considerably bigger than mine.

'Ah yes,' he sighed meditatively. 'It's true that nothing much happened to me. Except that now they go over all my works with a microscope. And they turn them down for having insufficient artistic merit.' He mused a while, then smiled sourly. 'The worst of it is that they're not all that wrong. I'm not worth a shit. But neither are they. Writers who are worth a damn have yet to arrive.'

Have yet to arrive? And how about Cibulka? They are knocking on the door, my friend. But the well informed Comrade Kaiser has not abdicated yet. Not by a long shot. We'll probably all die first. I frowned. I hoped we would die first.

Kopanec sighed and drank up. 'I think I'll take up translating again. Or I'll write fairytales. There's a renascence in this field now, so I might as well be part of it. Yes, indeed. When the institution of court jesters dies out, the court fairytale tellers proliferate.' He took another swig of beer and glowered at the girl, who tiptoed out of the club like a sleepwalker, her autograph book under her arm. 'What the hell,' he turned back to me. 'We've got our appetite, so what more do we need? I always say that as long as you're out of jail, you're ahead of the game.'

I quickly changed the subject. 'I understand you're after Dasha Blumenfeld.'

'That girl is a whore,' said the Master with absolute certainty. 'She could write an essay about contemporary Czech literature from the viewpoint of "authors I have known". It would never be published, though. I think the only editor she hasn't diddled around with is Brat, and that's only because he can't get it up any more.' Kopanec leaned towards me and took me by the hand. 'In a week Blumenfeld is off on a study tour of the Soviet Union.' He cackled. 'Watch Soviet literature about six months from now. I predict that all the young Soviet writers will turn to lyrical eroticism. Some not-so-young ones, too.'

'That's a capital offence there, isn't it?' I asked in a low voice.

'That's right,' he answered loudly. 'The next purge of young Soviet lyricists will be on Dasha Blumenfeld's conscience.'

Vera appeared in the stage door, but she was surrounded by a mob of her girlfriends and gay friends.

'Hi. We're going to the Olympia. Ivana has a birthday,' she announced to me, as if I were a member of the latter group.

'I want to talk to you,' I muttered like a disgruntled lover. Vera's one-word reply was a beautiful blend of irony, ridicule, and reproach: 'Really?'

Before I could reply, her friends broke in. 'Tonight Vera's going out with us, Mr Leden. We don't put up with any individualism.'

I had no choice but to go along.

A jazz quintet was playing at the Olympia. A singer who looked as if he were recovering from a case of German measles was belting out the latest hit tunes. The lyrics had nothing to do with happiness, building socialism, or even love. It was said that the singer, who was also his own lyricist and song writer, was in trouble with the authorities and that the Olympia was going to be closed any day now.

It wouldn't have surprised me. It was a smoky cellar, full of young men with beards and girls sipping tall drinks. And there were lots of foreigners.

Vera's group had a reservation, and they promptly began celebrating. The waiter brought champagne, everybody drank to Ivana's health. It was her twentieth birthday, and she publicly proclaimed that she was in love with the singer with the German-measle face. After a while, the singer came over to our table, where he was enthusiastically received. I used this interlude to whisper in Vera's ear: 'I couldn't make it.'

'Nonsense,' she snapped.

'Zamberk was there?'

'Yes.'

'I wanted to fix him up with the Silver girl. That's why I bought . . .'

'Stop it!'

'That's the truth. He's crazy about her.'

'And you're not?'

'No.'

Vera bit her lip. She was silent for a while. Her friends were chatting with the singer. The smoke-filled air made everything look hazy.

'Don't give me that stuff,' Vera said at last. 'You admitted it yourself.'

'Admitted what?'

'That you love her.'

She was speaking calmly, but her calm was only on the surface. I remembered the alabaster nude and Vera's tears.

'Love, hell,' I snorted. 'I like her. That's my nature, you know me. But love . . .'

'Yes, I know. So you wanted to get her together with Vasek?'

I shrugged. 'She's not interested in me. I was hoping I could at least help out a friend.'

She bit her lip again. 'You're really mean – you know that? And you're a liar.'

I shrugged again. 'I lie so often that when I tell the truth nobody believes me. But that was the truth, anyway.'

'You thought that Lenka was off on a business trip. That's why you didn't show up. And you called up Vasek as soon as you left my dressing room. You think I didn't see through it? I am not as big a fool as you take me for.'

The singer rose and returned to the microphone. One of Vera's girlfriends leaned towards us.

'Are you two trying to solve the world's problems? This is no time for problems. It's a time for drinking.'

'Let's have everybody on the dance floor,' the singer said into the mike. 'The next number is the foxtrot, "Honey-Coloured Eyes".'

'Let's dance,' I said, taking Vera by the hand. She got up and let me hold her close. We shuffled around on a small platform in the middle of the cellar.

I said: 'It wasn't the way you think.'

'But it came out just the way you planned.'

She seemed completely changed. She spoke coolly, with complete indifference. Had Lenka injected her with some of her cunning?

'What do you mean, the way I planned?'

We were practically standing still now, marking time. The floor was packed, and the semi-darkness gave the cellar an air of unreality.

Vera said at last: 'Three tickets and one doesn't show up.'

'Oh, that!'

'Yes, that. I have a good memory. And I am not so dumb.'

I listened to the loud music. Vera's skin, rubbing against her thin dress, was turning moist under my palm. I said slowly, emphasizing each word: 'Well, if you aren't dumb, as you say, then my plan couldn't have worked – could it?'

I looked her contemptuously in the face.

She looked down, the lids with the mascara-covered lashes fluttered. I could feel a shudder pass through her body. Apparently Lenka hadn't given her a big enough dose of cunning. Any minute now Vera would start to bawl, just like the Vera of old. We danced mechanically. Then all at once, what I had known would happen did happen.

'Let me go!' she shouted suddenly, breaking away from me, and she ran off the dance floor and out of the room. I ran after her. I caught up with her outside the revolving door and grabbed her by the hand.

'Let me go! How can you be such a brute! I hate you!'

'Now, now, calm down, Vera darling.' I felt like the lord and master again, and taking her firmly by the arm, I led her into a side street, where it was darker and there weren't so many people around. The moon hung low over the rooftops. Vera stopped trying to control herself and shivered feverishly.

'You're disgusting, a disgusting brute! To plan a thing like that, so cool and collected. To count on my being unhappy – and then on top of everything you come after me to the theatre and play your disgusting comedy!'

'I meant well, Vera dear!'

'I hate you! I detest you!'

'That's good,' I scoffed. 'At least you'll get over it.'

'I slept with Vasek, for your information!'

That came out of her quite involuntarily. I hadn't really expected it, and I was taken aback. A drunk staggered out of a dark doorway where he had been taking a leak.

'Young lady, behave yourself!' he muttered thickly. 'Young ladies are supposed to be virgins, otherwise they aren't worth a shit.'

Vera instinctively pressed closer to me. I led her quickly away. Behind us, the drunkard began to vomit noisily.

'Well,' I sighed, 'I must say that's a bit of a surprise. I hadn't planned things quite that far.'

Vera made an attempt at sarcasm. 'But I went beyond your plan.'

It was too much for her, though. She started sobbing. 'You can think what you like. You don't understand anything. Have you any idea how I felt?'

'Like a whore,' I suggested.

She slapped my face before I could duck. It was a resounding slap which surprised me with its force. Almost like Blumenfeld's. But in Vera's case it wasn't a matter of practice, but of lithe, ballet-trained muscles.

'Do you have any idea how you humiliated me?' she sobbed. 'And I was so happy when you came to my dressing room with the ticket. You're a bastard! You're such a bastard!'

My face was burning. I stroked it with my hand. I tasted blood inside my mouth.

'You almost knocked out a tooth. You're a fine one to talk. First you sleep with my best friend and then you slug me in the middle of the street. Who else acts this way but a tramp?'

Again I saw stars. Again the same side of my face. Like a whiplash.

A policeman appeared around the corner.

'Calm down, or they'll lock us up.'

She sprang at me like a cat, grabbing at my hair. I gripped her firmly. A taxi came out of a side street. I flagged it down with my free arm and when the driver stopped I shoved Vera inside.

She squeezed into a corner and began to sob. The taxi driver turned on the radio. I gazed out the window, at the houses, my mind a blank. The only idea in my head was how beautifully my plan had worked out. Far better than I ever expected. And yet it didn't seem to give me pleasure. The radio was playing *Eine kleine Nachtmusik*.

Vera calmed down after a while and began to wipe her tears with her hands. I handed her a handkerchief. She struck my arm and the handkerchief fell to the floor. I picked it up without a word. We continued our silent joyride until we reached Nulse.

Before I had time to pay the driver she had already reached the door. But there she waited. She unlocked the door and turned her white face towards me.

'Goodnight,' I said.

She didn't answer. She was waiting.

'I am not coming up,' I said.

She bit her lip. 'I am not asking you up.'

I stood there a while longer, mutely looking at her. 'Goodbye, then.'

'Goodbye...'

I did an aboutface and walked away. I felt a strong pang of regret. I stopped, turned around. Vera was still standing in the door, looking at me. Everything had worked out so well, and – and I mustn't spoil it, I reminded myself sternly. A sob reached me through the silent street. I didn't turn around. When I did a moment later, Vera had already vanished. I heard the door slam shut. I recalled the bathtub, the recriminations, the panic that had possessed me the other day. Today I was calm but sad. Vera had set out on the way of all flesh. Those slaps confirmed it. The chimpanzee-bitten tuba player was a painful maidenly error. I was the so-called great love, and Vasek was a step towards normalcy. Yes, that's the way things went.

That's the way things went in this world. I shook my head, then set out briskly for the Nusle stairway. I was approaching the green vestibule of another familiar building, but the other figure from the Nusle farce was not on stage. As if prodded by a pang of conscience, I walked faster.

No, no let's face it – I thought to myself – it's nothing but a farce, and a laugh is the first step towards normalcy. Vera can look after herself. She's safe now. And she'll continue on the safe path until she gets married. An advantageous marriage, no doubt. A pretty, successful, young ballerina who's already learned a lot about life, a soloist with a good future. That's no tragedy.

And where would life take me? I sat down on a bench in a patch of shadow. A chunk of moon was already missing. A skein of misty clouds ringed the moon. So that's the end of that. But something was still aching inside of me. What? The way of the world: I had just demolished Vera, and Lenka was probably about to demolish me. Well, but if that was the way things went, why was I so sad?

I heard footsteps behind me. A figure sprinted past. It was Vasek Zamberk, and he was racing down the Nusle stairs as if he were late for a train. I frowned. What was he doing here? He had probably been moaning for Vera in a hallway across from her house, and when he saw us together he had lost heart. But then he also must have seen the way we parted. He would recover his courage tomorrow. The sound of his footsteps gradually died away. Case of Vera Kajetan: closed.

What about me? Where am I going?

Where? You know perfectly well, Karel Leden. You've been ditched. Dumped. Demolished. With the mysterious Lenka Silver leading you on, what else did you expect?

10 *A dog's life*

And so on Sunday morning I lay in bed embraced by sorrow, pondering the situation. Or rather the ruins of the situation, for I had originally imagined everything quite differently. Next door, the landlady was listening to an inspirational programme on the kitchen radio, and through the wall I heard some comrade discoursing on love. The affair between me and my tawny rose – could that be categorized as love? I couldn't find the answer, so I immersed myself in old memories. As a student I had once been in love with a girl with chestnut-coloured pigtails, but that was all I could remember about our romance. It was terribly long ago. I couldn't remember what it felt like. I racked my brain, but the comrade on the radio kept breaking in. He was talking exaltedly, using words larger than any conceivable emotion. Desperately I attempted to concentrate my fuzzy brain and to embark on a dispassionate analysis. I had always been fond of detective stories and I read them avidly, even in periods when they occupied a prominent place on the list of Harmful Literature – somewhere between George Orwell and *The Imitation of Christ*. And so I was now forcing myself to play the role of a detective of love.

Take the facts, the pure facts. First of all, the fact of my sadness. I had recently been feeling awfully lonely – a feeling I had never had before. At worst, I used to be bored when I was alone, but now I longed to be near Lenka, to be with her all the time, and I longed to hear her pleasant chatter. Further, when I was in love with the pigtailed girl, it never occurred to me to sleep with her. I simply wanted to be near her. To stroll through the woods with her. To ski down the slopes of the Black Mountain in an icy wind, on that overcast wintry day long ago when everything was poetry. And now Nusle – the prosaic borough where Vera lived – had turned into a moonlit fairyland inhabited by a lovely mermaid. I was no longer preoccupied with sex. A week ago, yes. Even a few days ago, when her shoulder dipped out of her dress. Even last night, when I mused about sex in order to banish pangs of conscience. But not any longer. Not that I was opposed to sex – I simply didn't think about it. So apparently I was in bad shape. It must be love.

I started to daydream. Cool analysis was replaced by a mental movie similar to the one I used to project on to the screen of my closed eyelids when I was very young and had trouble falling asleep. The film whirred noiselessly; my Lenka moved in slow motion close-ups through the wonder-filled events of the past week. After the fiftieth rerun cold logic reasserted itself and the film faded. I became aware of the lofty voice coming out of the radio on the other side of the wall, exhorting all listeners to mutual respect and to honourable human relationships. If I couldn't analyse love, he could, and did – with the cool objectivity of those who aren't in any danger of getting burned by it. For him, love was a clinical problem, one that involved reason, intelligence, and mutual caring.

Was there anything 'mutual' about my relationship with Lenka?

I ran the film for the fifty-first time. I watched it not like a participant but like an observer searching for clues and explanations.

Sunday. On the spotted ceiling of my room flashed an image of the riverside. Sunday started out promising. Not the slightest hint of antipathy from Lenka. Normal reaction and behaviour. Ditto on Monday at the Manes. Ditto Tuesday at Blumenfeld's.

Then a still of the Chief flashed on the ceiling, a baldheaded character actor, no Gérard Philippe. But from that moment something had changed. Something barely noticeable, but damned significant. She warmed up to him, bantered with him, that haughty queen. Why? That stuff about the pleasant feel of a smooth bald head was all nonsense. Why would a beautiful young girl go for my Chief? After all, he was *my* boss, not hers.

Why? The detective in my brain, mindful of the Holmesian rule that the most unlikely possibility is often the truth, considered one such possibility: that she wanted to tease me, to provoke me. The ceiling showed a party at a Barrandov villa, then a closeup of a tawny hand caressing a shiny bald pate. In spite of the insubstantial nature of the image, my blood was boiling. If that was meant as a provocation, it was a damned successful one. But she made no use of my jealousy. She gave me the cold shoulder in the Avenue of November Nineteenth, and a day later ...

Was it deception or accident that she didn't go to Liberec? It was hardly deception. That would have meant extensive preparation and painstaking planning of alibis; after all, the people at her office confirmed her story. In any case, what possible motive could she have for playing such a trick? To meet the reticent Vasek alone, without me? But then she had no way of knowing that I was not planning to be present, unless she was aware of my scheme regarding Vera. But at the time she told me about her trip that scheme had not even existed. All this would necessarily presuppose clairvoyance and telepathy. Nonsense.

No. Liberec was definitely on the programme, but for some reason the trip was cancelled and she appeared at the gymnastics meet. Why? So many whys. Was she hoping to meet me there? But she could have easily called me on the phone; she had the opportunity to do it. Or perhaps I was wrong and all her talk about feeling sorry for Vasek was not just bunk, as I had thought. Maybe she really cared for him. She went to the show, that was a fact. But Vasek threw her overboard and slept with Vera instead. That was a fact, too.

And a very significant fact. A fresh scene was unfolding on the ceiling, this one shot in the studio of my imagination. Vasek is standing in front of the stadium, two beautiful girls come rushing towards him, one from each side. The two girls cordially hate each other. Cut to Vasek, nervous and chagrined, sitting in the front row between the two lovelies. During the performances on the parallel bars he is regaling them with carefully rehearsed comments about the new book of poems by Vrchcolab.

And what about Lenka? How has she managed to become so chummy with Vera? Probably she's one of those beautiful females who has a knack for fascinating persons of the same sex, even when they are as healthily heterosexual as Vera. Then I recalled Blumenfeld's admiring glances at the party and I cut to a new scene. Vasek, painfully struggling with his inferiority complex, is taking the girls home. First he says goodnight to Lenka, who lives at the beginning of that fateful avenue. Then he gallantly accompanies Vera to her door.

A huge corny moon lights up the ceiling screen; it hangs over the silent avenue. Vera's lobby beckons. A big closeup of Vera, hurt and insulted, a big closeup of the trite moon; a big closeup of Vasek who could be Errol Flynn if he weren't so shy. Medium shot: Vera, in that familiar female mood of not giving a damn about anything any more, is inviting Vasek up for coffee. Stiff with stagefright, Vasek crosses the fateful threshold – big closeup of threshold. At that moment, however, the projector went dark and the pictures vanished. What Vera did after that escaped my fantasy. But she did it, that was clear. Ironic that it took a girl like Vera to deprive that thirty-year-old virgin of his innocence. But she managed. And I managed. I succeeded in turning another quite decent girl into a slut.

Vasek, of course, immediately fell in love with Vera. He would have fallen in love with Comrade Pecakova if he had succeeded in sleeping with her. So that was the situation. Not really favourable at all.

I got out of bed and stepped to the window; the show was over. Outside it looked like a pleasant Sunday morning. What, then, is the result of your analysis, my dear chap? Tell me, Watson, what's behind the mysterious behaviour of that enigmatic young lady?

I don't know. I still don't know. I'm stumped. Time to call in Scotland Yard.

A few things were clear enough, though, as clear as that miserable, boring Sunday morning. I was no longer Vera's lover. Vasek had taken over that role. Ergo, Lenka's solicitude towards Vera, as well as her pity for Vasek because of his lack of female companionship, had lost their *raison d'être*. In other words, it was time for Casanova to get moving again.

The comrade behind the wall had finished his sermon with a sentence fairly reeking of incense, something about love being life's greatest blessing. All right. If I am to be denied this greatest blessing, I'll have to settle for something less. I opened my dresser with a firm decision: this very day I would visit Lenka in her apartment, room mate or not.

*

But I had hardly stepped out of the door of my house when I changed my plan. On a fence across the street from my building was a poster which caught my attention:

DOG SHOW
also featuring award of title to
CHAMPION DOG OF CZECHOSLOVAKIA

The show was being held in the People's Park of Culture and Relaxation that Sunday – opening time: 9 a.m.; arranged under the auspices of the Military Sportclub, canine section, and Bio-Ex.

Anything sponsored by Bio-Ex was likely to include a certain young lady who was devoted to the welfare of animals.

It did. She emerged from a white tent and the morning sun provided an ideal setting for her beauty. She was again wearing her pink-and-white striped dress – what a tiny wardrobe! – and she was accompanied by a little fellow with a camera. Behind her came a lady who weighed at least a ton and who was leading a dog on a chain. The dog's expression was so incredibly stupid that I was amazed to find it on a creature other than a human being.

They climbed a wooden podium. 'The title of champion of Czechoslovakia in the category of terriers,' said a voice that thundered from the loudspeakers like the growl of King Kong, 'was won by the bull terrier Rexy. The breeder was Mrs Hadrbolcová. Mother, Gita von Orstleben. Father, William of Needsbury ...'

The giant lady lifted up Rexy, the dog stuck out a long pink tongue and with a practised motion licked its owner's face. The shutter clicked; a heavy-set gentleman drew near and hung a medal with a red-white-and-blue ribbon around the terrier's neck. Then Lenka put her arm around the animal's neck, placed her lovely head next to the idiotic face framed by the ribbon, and flashed a Hollywood smile.

The photographer became inspired; he kneeled, got up, quickly kneeled a bit closer, and gave hurried orders. Lenka froze in her movie smile; the mechanized dog tried to lick her gorgeous face. He was sharply reprimanded; somebody behind the photographer meowed like a cat. The dog promptly pricked up his ears, and with an expression of idiotic distrust, stared into the lens. The photographer pressed the shutter.

I remained lost in the crowd for more than two hours, until the midday intermission. Lenka worked tirelessly. She posed successively with a St Bernard who was almost bigger than she, a schizoid Pekingese who was so spoiled that he left half a cube of sugar lying in the grass, a Maltese pinscher with black snout and no eyes, a yellow-toothed mastiff who almost knocked her down with affection and who gulped down cubes of sugar whole, and a wildly mustachioed miniature poodle who looked like a black African idol. It finally dawned on me that the friends of God's creation were probably planning to put together an illustrated calendar. I decided that for the first time in my life I would buy myself a calendar. I had never needed one before, because I had never planned ahead.

I stopped the photographer in front of the men's room.

'Excuse me, please. Could you – would you make me a series of prints – privately?'

He looked me over with a commercial eye, took down my name and address in a matter-of-fact way, and promised to send me the pictures within two weeks.

This was another first in my life. I had never felt any need for photographs – I always had plenty of originals in the flesh. Now I was ordering an entire set.

In the cafeteria I got into line right behind Lenka. She didn't notice me, because the cafeteria was full of noise and confusion. As I pushed my tray I eagerly breathed in her lily-of-the-valley aroma.

When she had sat down at a table in the dining room, I came up, tray in hand. 'Is this seat free, Miss?'

Lenka turned her familiar opaque eyes on me.

'Ah, it's you!' she said coldly 'Sit down.' I sat down with a distinctly queasy feeling in the pit of my stomach.

Silently, I watched Lenka. She was toying with her lemonade

glass, staring at the table. At last I said: 'That was quite a trick you pulled on me!'

'What do you mean?'

'I believed you when you said you were going to Liberec, and instead you amused yourself with Vasek at the show.'

'I had no idea you wouldn't be there.'

'You could have guessed it. There was no reason for me to go.'

She thought that over. 'You gave your ticket to Vera, didn't you?' she asked.

'Yes. So that she could solace herself with Vasek. And it worked. I'm free now.'

Lenka's rosy lips formed something like a sneer. 'Congratulations.'

'And Vasek is all set,' I continued. 'He doesn't care for you any more. He's fallen in love with Vera. So you're free, too.'

'You think so?'

'As far as I know, anyway,' I added quickly. 'Not that I know very much about you.'

'Never mind. But you think that Professor Zamberk does not love me any more?'

'Positively not. Vera deprived him of his virginity.'

Lenka gazed out at the flags fluttering over the green lawn. 'What does that have to do with love?'

Eagerly I offered an explanation: 'In cases like Vasek Zamberk, it's got a great deal to do with it. People like him confuse their suppressed sexual needs with love. Any girl who helps them get rid of their physical torment they promptly fall in love with.'

'That's a very simple theory.'

'It's based on simple experience.'

This time she sneered quite openly. 'Perhaps you'll have to dream up a more complicated one.'

'If I have the chance for more complicated experience . . .'

Lenka peered through the glass wall of the restaurant at the clock in the tower of the exhibition building. Then she said: 'Love has a special characteristic. Experience is a drawback. Those who are most successful are generally those with the least experience.'

I was trying to counter with a *bon mot* of my own, but a stray pup mistook a man's trouser leg for a fire hydrant. Suddenly the pup was the centre of attention – everybody started feeding it dumplings, including Lenka – and I was completely ignored.

In the afternoon the programme resumed. Lenka was again pecking away at the typewriter, transporting lists, chatting with owners, and posing for the 'Beauty and Beast' series. By four o'clock it was all over, and the portly gentleman stepped up to the public address microphone and invited everybody to watch the greyhound race, which would start shortly on the adjoining track.

Lenka collected her things and disappeared into the tent. When she came out I joined her.

'Are you free now?'

'No. I am a judge at the finish line.'

'Where?'

'At the greyhound race.'

'Can I enter the race?'

She glanced at me contemptuously. 'Your wit is a little under par, isn't it?'

'You think so?'

'Yes.'

'I'm sorry. Do I really rub you the wrong way?'

She lowered her head. She poked her high heel around the edge of a mousehole, the wind gluing her skirt tight around her body. Then she looked me in the eye. 'You wouldn't . . . if you listened to me.'

'On what subject?'

She sighed. 'You know perfectly well. I've told you more than once. I really mean well, Mr Leden. Abandon all hope.'

'You talk like Dante.'

'I am talking like Lenka Silver. I have no idea what Dante has written on this subject, but I believe that my meaning is quite clear.'

'Dante wrote a book on this subject. It's called *The Inferno*.'

Again she poked the soft soil with her heel. 'I am not an educated person,' she said. 'I do know, though, that you're talking about one of the greatest literary works of all time. But your inferno is just a petty, ordinary, little inferno, if you can call it that at all.'

'It burns all the same,' I said.

She scrutinized me again. 'Deservedly.'

She turned, and like a beautiful pink and white flamingo, she strode towards the racetrack.

She again sat behind a typewriter – this time at a table at the top of a rise which marked the finish of the race. A pudgy gentleman was running the machine that released the mechanical rabbit. The dogs were racing along a narrow corridor after a piece of rabbit fur, pulled by a steel cable. They were wearing red, white, and checkered cloths that bore large numbers, and they sprinted after the fake rabbit as if their lives depended on it. Lenka was now standing at the end of the track, paper and pencil in hand, and in the sudden dusk brought on by the passage of a long black cloud, her pink and white dress shone all the more radiantly. After each race she and the pudgy man in riding breeches pulled the rabbit back to the starting line. The thinning throng which surrounded the track watched them carefully.

Again the greyhounds broke out of their gate, took off after their deceitful prey.

By the time the next-to-last group of dogs reached the finish line, the first drops of rain began to fall.

From the covered veranda of the park restaurant I watched the white tent, where the animal lovers had taken shelter from the downpour. There I met Miroslav Kruta, who had been expecting a girl who hadn't shown up, and who was now regaling me with stories of his harem. His car was parked in front of the restaurant. I wasn't really listening to him; my attention was focused on the tent.

At around 6:30, Lenka appeared, followed by the stout gentleman. He strode briskly through the rain with his jacket collar turned up; Lenka held a small briefcase over her head for protection against the downpour.

'Listen, Mirek, are you a real pal?' I said, interrupting his lengthy account of amorous escapades. And before he could answer I implored: 'I need your car. Tonight. It's a matter of life and death.'

Kruta's experienced eyes quickly spotted Lenka's rain-soaked figure. 'That dripping pink one?'

'Yes. It's only for two or three hours. It's really terribly important to me.'

Kruta could always be depended upon in any conspiracy involving women. He had already lent me his car on several similar occasions, and it was unlikely that his girl would show up this late in the day. He pulled the keys out of his pocket and handed them to me with a sardonic smile. 'If it doesn't work out, I'll be in the Film Club until eleven. Otherwise give them to me in the morning. But for God's sake don't smash up my buggy. You look like you're completely drunk with love.'

I drove up elegantly alongside Lenka and opened the door. 'Jump in! You, too, sir. In the back.'

The look she gave me from underneath her briefcase was not wildly enthusiastic, but the portly gentleman accepted my offer with sincere gratitude. He scrambled over the tilted front seat into the back of the Felicia, his head bumping against the car's canvas top. Lenka slid in beside me and slammed the door. We were off.

My friend in the back considered it his duty to keep up a conversation. 'A nice little car.'

'It isn't mine,' I admitted. 'I borrowed it when I saw you getting soaked. Where to?'

'You can let me off in Karlin,' he said, and launched into a discussion of the capabilities of various animals to undergo automobile trips.

Lenka remained silent. Big drops of rain spattered against the windshield, but the wipers faithfully kept the wet grey world in view. Actually, that world looked quite gay. Sunday throngs filled the streets. Few people had umbrellas or raincoats. Giggling girls held their boyfriends' sweaters over their heads and the young men heroically ignored the weather. Lenka said nothing; neither did I.

I broke my silence only after we had let off our passenger in a dingy Karlin street: 'Are you angry with me?'

'No. I'm grateful for the ride.'

I wanted to say something clever, but I swallowed the first witticism that came to my mind, and the second and third, too. Lenka did not appreciate flippancy. We passed under the Zizkov viaduct and circled the main railroad station. At the crossroad in front of the museum I asked: 'May I invite you to have dinner with me?'

'No, thank you. Please take me home. I am very tired.'

All right then. We'll try another tack. We were silent. The rain beat down harder. As we passed the Botanical Garden it turned into a tropical downpour, pounding furiously against the canvas top of Kruta's Felicia.

'Great, isn't it?' I said.

'It must be hard for you to drive.'

'No. I mean the drumbeat on the roof. Don't you like it?'

'Yes. It's pleasant. Like a tent.'

'You slept often in a tent?'

'Quite often.'

'Is that part of your wild past?'

'What kind of past?'

I took my right hand off the steering wheel. Lenka was sitting with both arms propped against the dashboard. The little rectangle under her elbow shone against her brown skin like a miniature pink Chinese lantern. I touched it with my finger.

'Oh, that!' she said. 'You're right. I did have a rather wild past.'

'How wild?'

'Wild enough.'

'Were you by any chance . . .' I hesitated.

'What?'

'I am now editing a certain manuscript about a girls' reformatory . . .'

'I was in jail,' she said soberly.

'Really?' As if trying to counter a possible bad impression, she added quickly: 'It wasn't my fault.'

'I like ex-convicts. Especially reformed delinquents,' I said, but I didn't dare press the matter any further. I turned sharply from Nusle square up the Pankrac hill. The rain was not letting up. The car skidded around the curve. I expertly brought us out of the skid. Lenka remained cool and praised me: 'You drive well.'

'Thank you,' I said, and took advantage of the favourable moment to pursue my inquiry. 'By the way, that wild past somehow doesn't fit you.'

'No? Why not?'

'You're as virtuous as a young girl fresh out of finishing school.'

She seemed to smile slightly. 'There are certain reasons for that.'

'What reasons?'

'You wouldn't understand.'

'Jail?'

'Maybe. But others, too.'

'The literary fellow who was so cruel to you?'

'To me? . . . Ah yes! Of course.'

'Will you let me read his writing?'

'No.'

We drove at last down the Avenue of November Nineteenth. The dark shop window, which a week ago mirrored the moon, now burst into flame from the reflection of the red Felicia. The tyres plopped against the asphalt, then splashed through a puddle as I pulled up in front of the green portal.

Lenka wriggled in her seat. 'Thanks very much. That was kind of you.' She reached out her hand.

I left my hands holding the steering wheel. 'There is one favour I want to ask of you.'

'Yes? What is it?'

I took a deep breath. 'Look. I know what you must think of me. And I admit that I used to be a bastard, and that I shouldn't have pulled that hoax on Vera. It was a dirty trick,' I said contritely. 'It was just – just habit. I always used to pull stunts like that. But nobody has ever mattered so much to me as you.'

Lenka blinked her wet lashes and wiped the corner of her eye with her little finger. 'What is it that you want from me, anyway?'

'To ask me up for a while.'

'I will not.'

'Is your room mate at home?'

'No.' Pause. 'That's why I won't let you come up.'

'Just for a cup of coffee. I mean it. I swear that's all I want. I feel lonely, you know.'

She threw me a mocking look. 'Lonely? You?'

Her voice was so sarcastic that I almost shuddered.

'I am not such a monster that I don't feel lonely now and then.' And I added: 'Just now I feel like dying.'

Lenka concentrated on an indefinite point in space. 'Aren't you deceiving yourself? And what good will it do you if I ask you up?'

'You make me feel good,' I said. 'Even if you only keep repeating how much you hate me, it's better than being alone.'

It occurred to me that I was talking just like Vera. Perhaps for that very reason Lenka might thaw a bit. Perhaps . . .

She reached for the doorknob. 'I don't want to give you a hard time, you know,' she said softly. 'I don't want to give anybody a hard time, even though at times it may seem otherwise. But there really is no point to it.'

Big drops of rain pelted the top of the car. The windshield wipers were still on and every slow pass of the blades revealed a grey rainbow segment of the Avenue of November Nineteenth, as fresh and clean as a soap advertisement. I shut off the wipers. The inside of the car became silent and the avenue at once dissolved behind a watery curtain.

'I feel terribly lonely,' I pressed on. 'I may be a rat, but I am a lonely rat. I promise you I will only come up for coffee. We'll chat for a half an hour, and I'll be off.'

She didn't answer. A passing car fixed us in the glare of its bright headlights. I was blinded momentarily. The rain slackened, splashing softly against the roof like a lullaby.

'Will you do me the favour?'

The question broke the lyrical mood; the tension of a detective story set in. And her moment of silence. Then she said it – without enthusiasm, but she said it: 'All right. Come on then.'

And she opened the door.

I've got you, my lily-of-the-valley!

I jumped out into the rain.

She had a small flat on the top floor. A kitchenette for half a cook and a room with pictures of animals on the walls. One couch, one closet. A round table with two wicker chairs, a small, black cat with yellow-green eyes lying on the table. No trace of any room mate.

The cat silently sauntered towards me and touched my trouser leg with his nose.

'Meow.'

'Hello, Felix,' said Lenka. Then she turned to me: 'Sit down. I'll make coffee.'

She pulled a red dressing gown out of the closet and disappeared into the kitchen.

I sat down in one of the armchairs. The cat jumped into my lap and gazed at me intently. I returned his stare. He continued to look me straight in the eye and I did not evade the challenge. It's been a long time since I've had a similar experience with a human being.

I examined the room. The couch and dresser looked as if they had been picked up at a bazaar sale. The wicker chairs looked new, but they hardly looked expensive. Neither did the tiny plastic radio.

Lenka obviously spent most of her income on clothes. In that respect she was no different from other young ladies. But only in that respect.

I scanned the room a second time. The atmosphere was strangely gloomy. The only touch of gaiety came from the animal photographs on the walls.

Lenka returned with coffee in two extraordinarily plain cups and sat down in the other chair. She placed a sugar bowl on the table. The cat jumped over into her lap. It stuck its nose close to the rim of her cup, sniffed the steaming liquid, and pulled back.

'May I ask you something quite personal?'

'Why not? After all, I don't have to answer.'

'No, you don't. But I would like you to.'

She spooned up some coffee and poured it out on the glass table-top. The cat lapped it up with relish. I said: 'You and your room mate sleep on one couch?'

The black cat looked up at me, licked himself. Lenka glanced at the cat and smiled. 'Yes. Isn't that so, Felix?'

'Meow.'

I pointed at Felix. She nodded. 'Yes. This is my room mate. I misled you a little. He is male.'

But I was pleased. 'I am rather fond of animals, but I associate cats with old widows rather than someone like you. You're right, though – you certainly did mislead me!'

'It's misleading men that helps me to stay a virgin.'

Lily-of-the-valley! My heart rejoiced. Everything was again like the beginning of beginnings, like the first day on the trampled bank of the Moldau.

'Virginity does you honour,' I said appreciatively. 'But you're not an old maid to be surrounded by cats.'

'I have the cat to remind me of certain things.'

'What things?'

She didn't answer me directly. She lifted up the cat, nuzzled him, then held him straight in front of her. He looked like a little black homunculus.

'A cat is a beautiful animal, isn't he? Elegant, shiny, takes good care of himself. But he is terribly lazy. A terrible egotist. Doesn't really love his mistress, only his own comfort.'

'Interesting.'

'Just like you,' she added. 'And men of your type.'

'I am not lazy. Just give me the word and I will scrub your floor.'

'Yes. Felix is also extremely diligent when it comes to hunting down a pussy cat. That comparison is accurate.'

'But you like him, don't you? Surely you are not keeping him just as a living memento?'

Lenka scratched the back of the cat's head. He closed his eyes blissfully and began to purr. 'Yes, I like him.'

'In spite of his being a lazy egotist?'

'Yes.'

'Then why can't you care for me, since according to you I'm just like him?'

'The cat is an animal,' she said, her eyes flashing with a venomous glint. 'You want to tell me that you're an animal too, my dear editor?'

It grew dark. We were standing by the window, which opened on a fine view of Prague. The rain had stopped. The sun had set. Black clouds, bordered by a thin strip of light blue sky, hung over the city.

The wet roofs of Nusle glistened. The cupolas of churches shone copper green. Yellow lights came on, one by one.

'I love to look out of the window,' she said. 'It is . . .'

'What?' I asked softly.

'One of the few really beautiful things in this world. An old town in the rain.'

'You're one of those really beautiful things, too,' I said.

'I am not a thing.'

'I didn't mean it that way.'

Silence, silence in the rain. An old tune sang in my head, a beautiful song of youthful naïveté. A magic sky hung over Prague. A thin, orange-crowned moon emerged from a cloudbank. You never miss a trick, do you? Lightning flashed in the distance, pink and red pillars of light striped the sky behind the silhouetted church steeples.

'You know, your love for animals – I was almost tempted to take it as a sign . . .'

'Yes?'

'That you don't like people.'

She shook her head. The reflected hues of the city caressed her face. The coal-black diamonds of her eyes mirrored the world: a polished cameo of yellow lights, red and green signals.

'No,' she said. 'I don't like people. And I don't trust them. Animals are all the same. At least from our standpoint.'

'Would you like all people to be the same?'

'In some ways, yes.'

'That would be awfully boring.'

'But there would be a lot less . . .'

She stopped. After a long interval the flash of lightning was followed by a peal of thunder. She was surrounded by symbols; to add still one more, the sound of a saxophone wafted over from the open window of an apartment house across the street.

'There would be less what?'

She shrugged. 'Less disappointment, pain – I am not sure it wouldn't be better that way.'

The saxophone played a slow melody, deep, hoarse. It was a baritone saxophone.

'Your favourite instrument,' I said.

'Yes.'

I put my arm around her waist – and at that instant I lost control of myself.

'Lenka,' I whispered.

'Stop that,' she said, as girls traditionally do. 'Don't do that.'

It was too late. Passion, confusion, the mystery of her secret took hold of me, and I wasn't even aware of what I was doing.

I pulled her close, violently, and kissed her hard on the mouth. She tried to break away, her mouth half open. Her dressing gown parted. I saw white lace and my mouth descended to its border. But Lenka grabbed me by the hair and yanked with all her might. The pain goaded me on. I grasped her by the shoulders and pulled her down on the couch. Both of us stumbled, and I fell on top of her. The thought flashed through my mind that I was acting just like a drunken truckdriver, but I no longer cared. I began to tug at her gown. Suddenly it grew dark before my eyes and I jackknifed in terrible pain. I rolled off the couch like a sack of potatoes; the pain was unbearable. I grabbed my crotch with both hands. The bitch! My God! The whole lower half of my body was in agony. I wailed like a dog. Lenka got up and tied the cord of her gown. Then I saw her standing in front of the dresser mirror, running her hand through her tousled hair.

The cat was sitting on the top of the table, turning his head as I rolled on the floor, following me with unblinking yellow-green eyes. Lenka crossed the room and stood over me. The pain was as agonizing as ever.

'You'll leave this house the moment you feel better,' she said icily.

I hissed at her: 'What's the matter with you? You damn near crippled me!'

'Excuse me,' she said, and changed expression with her characteristic suddenness. 'Don't be angry,' she said in an almost apologetic tone. 'It's all my fault. I should have known better.'

I managed to sit up on the couch. I bent forward and rested my head on my knees. The pain continued, but my fury began to recede. Disgraceful. Like a drunken truckdriver. But damn it, who could figure that girl out?

'Please forgive me, too,' I said hoarsely, my voice breaking. 'I have never done anything like this before. Never. I don't know what got into me.'

She went into the kitchen and I remained alone in the infernal glow of the sunset.

She returned with a glass of water and a bottle of pills. 'Here. Take two. It may help.'

I swallowed two bitter tablets and the pain continued. Slowly, ever so slowly, it was becoming bearable.

'Honestly. I've never done anything like this before.'

'I believe you,' she said. 'You probably never had to.'

She was leaning against the wall, her hands behind her back. She looked at me calmly, without hate, perhaps with a slight touch of distaste. The cat continued to watch me from the top of the table.

I fixed my tormented eyes on Lenka Silver. She was beautiful, light brown, composed of symbols, moonlight, mystery. I didn't understand anything. I shook my head.

'I love you. And I had no intention of doing anything like this. I thought about you all day today, and nothing like this even crossed my mind. Something possessed me when I got up here. By this window.'

'You're not the only man in the world who loves me,' she said coldly. 'But others know how to control themselves. They know how to wait.'

'I'll wait, if you let me. All my life.' And because this didn't sound very convincing even to my own ears, I added quickly: 'Damn it, I mean it! Seriously!'

'You? Seriously?' she said with horrendous question marks. 'Downstairs in the car you gave me your solemn word . . .'

'I was overcome. That's only human . . .'

'Only human? To give your solemn word when you know how easily you are overcome?'

There was no answer to that. I hung my head, raised it again, blinked at my tawny enigma: 'You invited me upstairs. If you invited me up you can't be all that innocent. You must have had an inkling . . . you know that a cup of coffee is a kind of metaphor. And if you're not that innocent, can I believe that you're that ignorant?'

'Maybe you're right,' she said in a funereal voice. 'Of course I should have guessed . . . but I . . . God knows, all of us have . . . but let's not talk about it. Can you walk?'

I tried. I barely managed to drag my legs. I groaned: 'You really hurt me, you know.'

'Maybe you'll behave yourself next time.'

'Next time?'

'I mean with somebody else.'

She unlatched the door. I surmounted my pain and made a pathetic face:

'I have lived thirty-two years, but I have never met anyone like you . . . It's rather unlikely that there ever will be anybody else. I am afraid this is a classical case, my dear Lenka.'

Lenka, the lovely creature of rose petals and dew, was totally unmoved. 'You haven't lived at all yet,' she said softly. 'You've only enjoyed.'

Then she opened the door wide.

The cat dashed out, all the way to the stairway, where he stopped hesitantly. He lifted his tail, and a white feline anus flashed from the dark.

'Felix, come back!' Lenka called, and to me she reached out her hand. 'Goodbye.'

I took her hand and said softly: 'Goodbye.'

'No hard feelings, but . . .' – she paused, during which a last tiny ember of hope glimmered in my heart – '. . . but goodbye!'

Goodbye, then.

The cat guiltily dashed past us back into the room. The pain in my testicles flared up again. I felt that I had to sit down. The door clicked shut behind me. I descended to the next floor and squatted down on the dark stairs.

I stayed there for about half an hour, until the pain had stopped. Then I got up and left the building. When I got to the street I looked up at the fateful window. The moon was reflected in it like an icy monstrance; a table lamp burned weakly in the middle of the pane. The saxophone was still wailing from a window across the street.

I was about to start the car when I felt a strong urge for solace. Vera! I locked the car and set out for Vera's place. After the rain the evening was mild and pleasant. A party of guitar-carrying young men and women was sauntering gaily towards the Nusle park.

I was possessed by an almost physical need to revenge myself on somebody. To reassure myself somehow that this was still a normal world in which Lenka was the sole abnormality. Surely Vera would let me in; yesterday's slaps didn't mean anything. We'd make up, Vera and I. I'd drop her later, of course. After I had convinced myself that all was well with the world.

I convinced myself, all right. As I drew near to the house of the jilted ballerina, the glistening Mercedes of Director Gellen majestically pulled up before the entrance. Out stepped Vera, completely emancipated from knitting needles, sporting a short green evening dress decorated with silver lamé. A beautiful opalescent necklace graced her throat. As she hopped out of the car I noticed her golden slippers, purchased at the price of many bread-and-coffee suppers. She saw me. I opened my mouth, but nothing came out. Director Gellen trotted around the silver radiator grille, not noticing me at all, and took Vera by the arm. She dropped her eyes and opened the door. I was still gaping. Vera went into the vestibule, the director scrambling after her. The lock clicked shut.

I was as numb as Lot's wife. Another guitar-strumming group passed by: 'Rock rock rock! Jailhouse rock!'

Idiot! That's normal life!

I returned to the Felicia and drove to the Film Club, where I was noisily greeted by Kruta, eager for news of my *débâcle*. His company and alcohol consoled me until the early hours of the morning. Then I sat out the dawn on a Slovansky Island bench, and without stopping at home, went straight to the office.

II *A fiery summer*

The next afternoon, when I finally reached home with the intention of taking a long nap, a surprise awaited me: a card from the Army, informing me that I was being given the opportunity of spending the summer in the backwoods town of Medzihorec on a two-month tour of reserve duty. I tore up the card, threw it into the wastebasket, and lay down on the couch.

The wastebasket didn't save me. A week later I was on an express train to Medzihorec, disgusted as hell.

All that week I tried to get in touch with Lenka. The morning after my disaster in the Avenue of November Nineteenth she went on her postponed trip to Liberec, and didn't return until Saturday night. At least she was supposed to return. Saturday night I waited at the station but I didn't see a trace of her black head among the passengers getting off the Liberec express. Nor did she get off the night train. And at four in the morning I was off myself for Medzihorec.

In the office the week passed relatively calmly. We were occupied by routine matters, mainly the liquidation of petty fuckups. On Tuesday we went to the printing plant where we spent the day cutting the picture of a female nude out of a collection of medieval tales, after Comrade Kaiser had concluded that the picture might be morally harmful to our readers. Only a relatively small edition of the book had been printed, so we managed to finish the job in one day.

The illustration had to be cut close to the binding, but without causing the sheet to fall out of the book. The Chief took a personal part in this operation. A certain employee of the printing plant was given the task of consigning the thousands of extirpated nudes to the flames. As it turned out, this 'employee' was not connected with the printing plant at all: when I took a taxi two days later, I found the nude attached to the sun visor, along with a picture of Marilyn Monroe coyly concealed behind the rate schedule.

On Wednesday, the Chief called an extraordinary meeting to deal with a problem concerning Mrs Ehrlich, PhD, our editor of foreign language handbooks. It seemed that Dr Ehrlich had permitted the following sentence to appear in a handbook for travellers called *Dutch on the Train:* 'As a remnant of the former dual mode, modern Dutch has several words which do not undergo normal declension, such as "calf", "cattle", and "people".' The sentence was challenged by the censor on the grounds that such close proximity of people and cattle was insulting to the socialist sense of human dignity. The Chief accused Dr Ehrlich of gross incompetence and ignorance of fundamental editorial principles. In vain did our learned colleague cite a number of Dutch grammars published by various Dutch universities. The Chief personally deleted the word 'people' with red ink, and dismissed Dr Ehrlich from the meeting with the warning that future transgressions would result in her demotion to the rank of proofreader. Dr Ehrlich shuffled off, tears glistening behind her thick glasses. The Chief, virtually in tears himself, gave us a half-hour lecture on the carelessness of intellectuals. Only his own constant vigilance, moaned the Chief, kept his employees from getting themselves in serious trouble. We nodded in agreement, for he was right.

This was proven the very next day, when Dasha Blumenfeld became involved in a minor fuckup. She was being investigated by the police, because a check of the records of a secondhand bookstore disclosed that a certain Blumenfeld had sold a rare dictionary of the English language for 250 crowns, and that the same Blumenfeld immediately bought the book back for 300 crowns, allegedly for our office use. Blumenfeld explained the whole affair as follows: she saw the dictionary in the house of her uncle Feuerstein, a retired former manufacturer, and performed the transaction, knowing that our office badly needed the dictionary but could not purchase it directly, due to a law prohibiting sales by private individuals to government agencies. She therefore paid her invalid uncle 250 crowns out of her own money, sold the dictionary to the secondhand book department for the same amount, purchased it for the price of 300 crowns, and was refunded the money by our office cashier upon the presentation of the sales slip. The secret police scratched their heads in bewilderment, and only after prolonged discussion was Dasha able to melt their distrust and to convince them that neither she nor her uncle had profited unduly from the deal.

It looked as if everything would end smoothly. But Dasha couldn't keep her big mouth shut. As a parting shot she remarked venomously that it was only the State that was the loser. The policemen halted in the doorway, and the merry-go-round of cross-examination began anew. Blumenfeld came under even deeper suspicion than before, and it took her a further two hours before she cleared herself. If the office had been able to buy the dictionary directly from old Feuerstein, it would have cost the State two hundred and fifty crowns. This way, the secondhand bookstore made fifty crowns on Feuerstein, which was paid by our office, so that in effect the secondhand bookstore made a profit of fifty crowns on our office; from an economic viewpoint, therefore, the fifty crowns had only been transferred from one State pocket into another. One of the investigators at last became so confused by the complexity of the case that he concluded old Feuerstein had defrauded the State of fifty crowns, and he demanded that Dasha's uncle be brought to justice. He argued that if Feuerstein had sold the dictionary for two hundred, that store, in turn, could have sold it to us for two hundred and fifty, in other words, the sum which Feuerstein was willing to settle for if he had been permitted by law to sell the book directly. The man simply could not understand the logical fallacy of his argument, and in the end he was defeated by the sheer volume of Dasha's words rather than her logic.

This mishap apparently didn't dampen Dasha's spirits. That same evening I saw her at the movies, where she was taking alternate bites out of four different bars of cream-filled chocolate held to her mouth by young Hartman. After the show, I tried to forget my sorrows in the company of Franta Novosad, a tall, skinny, near-sighted fellow who had written detective stories under a number of English pseudonyms before such novels had been banned, and who was now a bookkeeper for a restaurant. With great enthusiasm, he read to me passages from his new novel, which he wrote when he wasn't busy adding up rows of figures, because he was very hopeful of the current literary developments. The hero of the novel was an ageing Czech detective named Honza Fialka, a figure strongly reminiscent of Inspector Woolstonecraft, the central character of earlier Novosad books. For one thing, both detectives spoke the same laconic hard-boiled Czech not used by anyone else in this country or anywhere else in the world. The plot of the new novel seemed familiar to me, too: it concerned a wholesale grocer, who had hidden an illegal supply of Ivory Soap in his cellar. Under the soap, Fialka discovered the corpse of a man who was later identified as a crippled labourer who had been on the verge of exposing the grocer's black market operations. It soon dawned on me that this was a new version of Novosad's *Secrets of a Blackmoor Cellar*; in that work the grocer was an antique dealer, the buried corpse was Lord Fitzpatrick and the Ivory Soap was smuggled cocaine.

Friday was the least hectic day of all. There was only the merest hint of a *malheur* involving Comrade Salajka. He had overlooked a caption in our house magazine, which read 'This arresting photograph shows the author Joseph Kopanec in a rare moment of relaxation.' The phrasing was most unfortunate, since there was a rumour making the rounds that Kopanec had spent time in jail to expiate his novel *Battle of Brnirov*. Luckily there was still time to stop the presses, so that in the majority of the copies the photograph carried the bland caption: 'Joseph Kopanec relaxing with a group of fellow writers.'

Otherwise, all was peaceful. As I was saying my farewells on Saturday, a new fuckup of potentially major scope loomed on the horizon. We received news that the literary theoretician Manfred Schalowski had defected to the West – only weeks after the Chief had written paeans of praise about Schalowski's incredibly boring essays on German literature. I had no doubt, however, that our experienced Chief would find a way out of this unpleasant predicament. I shook Annie's hand, kissed Blumenfeld, and sallied forth towards the provinces and two months of bone-rattling duty inside a tank turret.

I wrote Lenka several letters from training camp; no reply. I gave up, hoping that I would forget her. I had already forgotten so many young ladies. But Lenka didn't prove to be one of them.

Dasha sent me a postcard from Moscow, with greetings from two well known young Soviet poets – Antolovsky and Glebkin. By coincidence I came across those two names again in a few days; there was a story about them in *Rude Pravo*, which was read to us during a recreation period. The influential critic Nikolajev had expressed himself negatively about Dasha's pair of friends. He attacked them for kowtowing to Western literary fashions and he pointed out that they strayed too far from the authentic life of the people. Blumenfeld, you're keeping company with some fine birds, I said to myself, and shuffled off for a nap in the shade of my armoured chariot.

Dasha's fine birds were soon gone. Two days later I saw a small item in the paper to the effect that the poets Antolovsky and Glebkin were departing on a two-year work tour of Eastern Siberia. They embarked on a long journey to learn the authentic life of the people – and Dasha was clearly up the creek. But I had underestimated the Blumenfeld spirit. Hardly two weeks went by and I received another card, this time from Leningrad, signed by the writer Anatoli Bicenko. His novel *The Dawn* had created quite a furore, but for the time being the liberal atmosphere in his native Leningrad enabled Bicenko to remain safely removed from the authentic life of the people.

Annie mailed me a decorative plaque from Varna. The Chief honoured me with a witty, sarcastic card spotted with red wine. Nothing from Vera. Vasek Zamberk sent only some snapshots of a hiking trip in southern Bohemia, although I had written him a rather long letter. In my letter I had asked him, quite casually, about Lenka.

Whatever was happening to Lenka, she was clearly not thinking of me. At least not in writing. The summer was hot. I dragged out my days across the dusty, deserted meadows of Eastern Slovakia. I gradually wrapped myself up in a cocoon of loneliness, and after a while I no longer had any desire to leave the monotonously soothing army life. Night after night the lights of the tents shone into the warm stillness, and the soldiers griped and mused and longed for wives, girlfriends, children, homes, favourite taverns and even offices – for all those things which give meaning to men's lives.

The meaning of my own life had gone up in smoke. I felt happiest on night manoeuvres, when we rolled through the fragrant countryside like rumbling black phantoms amid the still shadows of shrubs. I stood waisthigh in the turret and watched the soothing eternity overhead; red and green flares blinked among the clear stars, and the camp sparkled in the distant valley like a festival of fireflies. At those times I thought of the young lady from the rainwashed street and I had the urge to write a poem. But when I took out a pencil and paper and sat under the stars on top of the slowly cooling engine, nothing came to mind. Nothing but skilful metaphors which only reflected ten years of professional experience in the manufacture of poetry, and had little to do with the living girl that was in my heart.

I stopped trying to write poetry. I would sprawl out on a pile of hay and listen to the mournful tales of Captain Vavra, who, as a young lieutenant seven years ago in Slana, had given me my tank corps indoctrination. At that time he had just graduated from officers' school and he ate up army life with youthful *élan*. Now he had turned into a dour sceptic. He regaled me with his frustrating love affair; a certain Jana Hloubava, a nutritionist, was rejecting his advances on the ground that she was ashamed to be seen with an army officer. She noted that in this day and age of rockets and atomic bombs, an officer was as outdated as a dinosaur. Vavra, one of the few really intelligent and gifted officers I knew, was thinking of resigning from the army, and he bitterly attacked the atom bomb – not, however, from any pacifist conviction.

I felt sorry for him and to cheer him up I told him that his profession had already been discredited by the author of *The Good Soldier Schweik*, yet officers had managed to survive. He admitted the point, but remained as gloomy as ever. He was thirty-five years old, yet Jana Hloubava had disconcerted him to such a degree that he couldn't pull himself together. He was afraid to shout at the soldiers for fear of appearing ridiculous, so his voice was barely audible and the soldiers made fun of him. Formerly a spit-and-polish ramrod of an instructor, clever but hard as nails, he had turned into a complex-ridden wreck, who put on civilian clothes at every possible opportunity.

I took his fate as a foreboding of my own future. In a surge of sympathy I promised him that on my return to Prague I would have a word with Jana Hloubava, so that the captain could continue in a career in which he excelled and which was his sole profession. Moved by gratitude he showed me a snapshot; it was laminated in plastic and he wore it in the back pocket of his greasy tank-corps overalls. The moonlit photograph of the beautiful blonde stirred my interest. But by morning, as we clumped along in single file through a rocky gorge, I had forgotten all about Jana Hloubava and Lenka again reigned unchallenged in my heart.

The dusty hot summer was over in no time at all. In the middle of August I received the photographs taken at the dog show. I hid them in the bottom of my trunk, but my fellow warriors found them, and while I was out they arranged a photographic exhibit. I told them she was my fiancée, and I put up with their marital jokes with an almost perverse delight. That was about the only really enjoyable part of that summer.

I received one more card from Vasek, showing 'a panoramic view of Doksy Lake'. Evidently he hadn't gone there alone, for it would be hard to imagine Vasek going by himself to that den of iniquity. Usually, though, Vasek's cards were signed by at least five people, all unknown to me. This time, however, the usual tangle of autographs was missing. At first I thought that Vera might have been his companion at Doksy; Vera would not have been likely to sign the card, for obvious reasons. But then I came across an item in the paper, reporting that the noted director Gellen was casting a hitherto unknown ballet dancer as the star of his new film. The director and star were 'shown in this photograph taken at the current Karlovy Vary Film Festival'. On the small, smudgy newspaper, the new face was indistinguishable from any other, new or old, but the ballet pose of Vera's familiar legs was unmistakable. So that matter was settled, too. I no longer had any pangs of conscience, and if I didn't sleep that night it was not because of Vera but because of the mystery of Vasek's unsigned card. It bothered me all night and I was tormented by a strange suspicion. I kept turning the question around in my mind, first one way, then another, ceaselessly. In the morning I wrote a last letter to Lenka.

I carried the letter around with me for two days, telling myself that no sane man could possibly drop such arrant nonsense into a mailbox. It was an idiotic declaration of love, full of pathetic exhibitionism and containing that tritest of excuses: I claimed that I had become a skirtchaser because no woman properly understood me. My reason commanded me with all the insistence of a drillmaster to destroy the letter forthwith. But the letter seemed to exude some paralysing effluvium. On the third day I deposited it at the Medzihorec post office, and the next day I left for home. In the train the discharged soldiers got roaring drunk, returning to their detested wives, troublesome girlfriends, and beloved taverns to the singing of incredibly filthy songs. I didn't join in the singing. I gazed through the train window at the bronze early September sun and wondered about the future. What was I going to do with my life?

Of course, I had never known the answer before. But up till now, I hadn't cared.

12 *Scene with a cap*

I arrived in the early afternoon. At six in the evening, in civilian clothes, I was back in the street that I had dreamed about all summer, the Avenue of November Nineteenth. It had glowed in my dreams like a coloured kaleidoscope, and like a huge theatrical moon, too; I had dreamed about the gentle clipclop of high-heeled shoes, I had heard the soft oboe voice of a tanned girl.

And here I was again before the green portal, at the end of that legendary street of dreams and of perdition, my head tilted back. The shadow of the apartment houses across the street did not reach the top floor of the building, which shone in the setting September sun like a golden fairytale castle. The sound of a saxophone was again flowing out of an open window; even the anonymous jazz aficionado from the street of dreams had remained true to his love.

I entered the building and slowly climbed the stairs. I could have taken the elevator, but I climbed on foot in the manner of pilgrims, filled with contrition. I was filled with foreboding that I was doing something I would soon regret. But Lenka had long ago deprived me of reason, even before I had mailed that schoolboyish letter.

And so I stood before the door with its handlettered sign L. SILVER. I rang the bell. She opened the door.

I never had an eye for feminine fashions, but I always noticed how she was dressed. Somehow her clothes seemed to be organically connected with her beauty. Now she was standing in front of me in a striped grey-and-white pleated skirt, and a blue sweater with honey-coloured buttons. The little black head was surrounded by a sunny corona like a baroque halo, for the window facing the blood-red western sky was at her back. Her eyes were motionless, black discs reflecting my diffident figure – a humble little mendicant of venery.

'Hello,' I said meekly.

'Ah, it's you!'

'It's me.'

'Well ...' she turned back into the room, almost as if she was searching for something.

'Am I disturbing you?'

'N-no,' she answered, remaining standing in the door. The black cat Felix appeared next to her slim ankle and lifted his yellow-green eyes towards me.

'Don't be angry. But I had to see you.'

'Yes.' She swallowed, sending a gentle ripple along the smooth, olive skin of her neck. 'But ... you'd better not come in.'

'I know. I don't even have the courage to ask for a cup of coffee. Not after my disgraceful behaviour last time.'

'Forget about that,' she said, and remained motionless. She showed no inclination to invite me in, nor to slam the door in my face. The cat padded off into the hall and stopped before a narrow door which apparently led to the bathroom. He sniffed the threshold. Then he stood up on his rear legs and made a comical attempt to reach the doorhandle. He didn't succeed, and Lenka didn't help him.

'And ... couldn't I ... really just for a moment?'

'Better not.'

Neither of us moved, and instead of the magnetic radiation that attracted us to each other that day at the river, we were now separated by an invisible wall – a high wall with broken glass at the top, the kind that I had never climbed in all my life. The only sound was the soft scratching of feline paws. It occurred to me that I was in the typical situation of a beggar. In the hall, before a half-open door.

'Did you get my letters?'

'Yes. But don't write to me any more.'

'All right. I won't.'

We lapsed again into silence.

'Goodbye,' said Lenka.

But I wanted to prolong this interlude, no matter how painful it might be.

'Wait a moment. I should go. I know. But ... well, it's just that ...'

I didn't know what to say, but I wanted to postpone this expulsion from paradise. Yes, expulsion. In spite of my *débâcle* I was still an expert in such matters, and I knew perfectly well that it was perfectly useless to stand there, to send letters, to act witty or sincere, simple or complicated, to entice her with poetry or to assault her like a drunken sailor. The game was lost from the very first.

But still I desperately clung to the threshold, where she stood in her black slippers.

'It's just that ... I am going. I see that ... that it's useless.'

'It is,' she confirmed softly.

'But there is one thing ... I want you to believe that what I wrote in those letters – even though it's childish – it's the truth. I mean it. I want you to know that if I can ever be of help ...'

I felt myself blushing. The last time I had said anything like that was when I was sixteen years old, saying goodbye to a pigtailed girl, seriously convinced that a farewell to those pigtails meant farewell to love for the rest of my life. Now I was mumbling the same words; nothing better occurred to me.

'I believe you, and don't be angry with me.'

She moved the door slightly, but I was still unable to listen to reason. I blurted out: 'And then, too, you should know ... that I've really changed ... since the time ... the time I've met you.'

'I doubt it,' she said. 'You've fallen in love. That generally improves people for a time.'

'Isn't that a change?'

'I don't know you well enough to judge. I have no idea what you do in general.'

'What do you mean, in general?'

'In daily life, I mean. At work, among people, and things like that. In general. After all, there's more to life than this.'

'For me, this is my whole life.'

Her eyelids lowered. 'Forgive me, but I have the impression that you haven't changed at all.'

'Why do you say that?'

'Life for you was always ... just you.'

I lowered my head, stared at the delicate, pointed slippers on the threshold. They didn't fit the image of a young lady preacher, but it was precisely the amalgam of stripteaser and evangelist that formed the specificum known as Lenka Silver. A character that totally mystified even me, the renowned Film Club Casanova.

'You're touching on philosophic questions,' I said. 'Can anyone really live for someone else? Can you?'

Her eyes glistened in the honey-coloured oval of her face – the aesthetic culmination of a row of honey-coloured buttons on a blue sweater. And still the same sunlit backdrop. And the same saxophone in a bebop spasm.

'Maybe not,' she admitted hesitantly. 'But a person should at least try. To try and see life through other people's eyes.'

'Are you trying to see life through my eyes?'

Now it was her turn to drop her head, revealing the red semicircle of the sun behind her.

'I believe I am trying. It's just that ...'

'What?'

'You're not the only one.' Pause. Then she added: 'Not the only one by far, you know.'

Yes, I knew. Or at least I sensed. I feared. But who – and suddenly, as if the whole scene had been arranged by a malicious director to climax a tragic farce – a muffled cough sounded somewhere in the apartment. A deep, masculine cough which someone had obviously been trying to suppress for some time but which proved too powerful to overcome. The cat, startled, jumped away from the narrow door which he had been trying to open all this time, and dashed into the living room. The coughing came from the room behind the door. The bathroom.

Everything became clear to me at once. I looked around the foyer. A bright object hung on the coat-rack; it looked as garish in the yellow light as a decoration on a merry-go-round. It was a checkered blue-and-green cap. Incredible! So that explained the lack of signatures on Vasek Zamberk's postcard from Doksy. It was incredible, but it was true all the same. This was the cap that I had last seen on Vasek Zamberk the day he spilled carp roe soup over Lenka's lap.

Life is always tragic, but in its isolated details it has the character of a farce. Schopenhauer. Not that I had read him. Somewhere I had picked up that one quote. I – the Don Juan of Greater Prague –

had stammered like an adolescent at the door of an impregnable young lady, while that clumsy oaf Vasek Zamberk took it all in from his bathroom throne! Was he there just to console himself for having been kicked out of the saddle by Director Gellen? Or had he become a ladykiller in record time?

The cat slowly crept back into the hall. He was again sniffing at the bottom of the bathroom door. I bit my lip. Only now was the full extent of my humiliation becoming clear to me.

'I know,' I said, at last, in reply. 'Goodbye.'

'Goodbye.'

I turned and ran quickly down the stairs. Lenka closed the door behind me.

I headed for the Nusle stairs, thinking, this is the end, my lily-of-the-valley, I swear it! Maybe I'm a bastard or maybe I'm a perfectly ordinary fellow, but I know how to admit defeat. Yes, by God! To hell with your mystery, Lenka Silver. You'll never see me again, even if I die of love.

The way I felt, the sooner I died the better.

13 *Blumenfeld's end*

By morning I was still alive. But I woke up with an aching head and a sense of indifference towards the whole world. I returned to work at the worst possible time. The editorial board was about to meet. Item number one on the agenda: Cibulka. I had already completely forgotten about that troublesome writer. Originally, the subject of Cibulka's book was supposed to take up a whole meeting. Now it was just one item among many, and I had an inkling that some major dialectical turnabout had taken place during my absence.

The happy glow on the Chief's face confirmed my suspicion. He greeted me with a hearty handshake: 'Our brave lieutenant is back! Three cheers for our lieutenant!' He opened the meeting in the good old atmosphere of cordial unanimity.

It was evident that everything was back to normal. It should have been a weight off my mind, but I no longer cared about anything. Rejected by my mermaid, I no longer gave a damn about my reputation, and I probably would have voted on the Chief's side, against the whole office if need be. The dull apathy resulting from unhappy love is a good subsoil for suicidal tendencies.

But as I scanned the editorial board, I saw as clear as daylight that no suicidal heroics on my part would be necessary. The belligerent face of Dasha Blumenfeld was conspicuously absent, for as a junior editor she was excluded from this gathering of the gods. But not even that female Bar Kochba in a bosom-hugging blouse could have affected the outcome of this meeting.

My indifference kept me from identifying with this editorial collective which had witnessed so many apotheoses and so many executions. I watched the proceedings like a disinterested spectator, and *sub specie aeternitatis* my colleagues began to seem ridiculous and their petty actions incomprehensible. What were the motives for their despicable plottings and manoeuvrings? That ephemeral vanity called career, position? Comforts and pleasures? Fear? Jealousy? Surely such trivial lures would be pitifully out of keeping with the veneration accorded to these new, post-religious secular saints by the general public, a public insufficiently informed as always. Or were these men inspired by a naïve, dogmatic faith? Though I was so much younger, less educated, and much more insignificant than they, I found such faith quite unacceptable because of its absurd dialectics of immaculate conception and black sin. Outwardly I professed orthodoxy, of course; the old fuckup with Kocour's manifesto had taught me a lesson. But with me all this was but a ritual, and it was hard for me to imagine that my colleagues might be moved by a real, deep belief springing from the heart and from the brain. It seemed to me preposterous to assume that the ridiculous figures sitting before me had solved the dichotomy of mind and heart that had baffled a host of spiritual giants, including the Doctor Angelicus himself.

Stripped of the aura of popular acclaim, they made a sorry spectacle: the beloved poetess of the people, who had recently sat at this very table and ordered the destruction of the remaining copies of a book by a deceased poet. Why? Probably because she wanted to dissociate herself in a dramatic post-mortem way from a fellow poet with whom she had once been on friendly terms and whose political reputation had now come under a cloud. Moving clockwise around the table, another extremely popular author, who had written scripts for German films during the occupation. An actress I had adored as a boy who had played in these films had been denounced as a collaborator after the war and was barred from public life. Our beloved author, however, had switched from writing scripts for Nazi producers to eulogizing resistance heroes, and he had become extremely popular. Sitting on his left, an eminent literary theoretician whose interests had shifted through the years from 'Novels of blood and soil' to 'The theme of the Virgin Mary in modern Czech lyricism' to 'The Marxist aesthetics of concrete reality'. Next, a popular woman novelist who had spent several summers in the Orel mountains as a child and who continued to celebrate the simple mountain folk. Governments come and go, but every political regime has an abiding love for simple mountain folk, and our novelist had been collecting one laurel wreath after another. Seated next to her, a former surrealist, now an indefatigable sloganeer for the revolution, turning out doggerel for factory posters while unredeemed surrealists worked in the uranium mines. Continuing to move clockwise around the table: an eminent literary critic, ever ready to transubstantiate the bread and wine of Comrade Kaiser's directives into the flesh and blood of literary aesthetic theory.

The Chief made a few introductory comments about a problem connected with the Cibulka manuscript; certain aspects of the manuscript were subject to interpretation, and even Comrade Academician Brat had at first reacted positively. Brat himself was still outside the country, and was represented at the table by an empty chair. His book about a deceased poet was really an anthology of literary distortions, but like the *Summa* of St Thomas it had become a second Bible. Next to the empty chair drowsed an aged linguist, whose work had been rejected – largely as a result of Brat's attack – and who ultimately recanted her own dissertation, having been enlightened and set on the correct ideological path by Marshal Stalin's scholarly pamphlet on linguistics.

A more serious and upstanding observer than I probably would have seen these people as a manifestation of the spiritual debasement of the time, a prostitution of scholarship and literature. Or perhaps he might have shown some understanding for their anachronistic beliefs and conversions. But I was only a cultural parasite, though in my youth I had had a real love for poetry. These literary types were for me just a clique which may have had some lustre in the past but which was now darkened by the shadow of the gallows. And though in many ways I was a bastard, I never rejoiced over a gallows. And though, admittedly, it entailed no risk and was motivated by a bad conscience, I did regularly distribute crumbs from the rich editorial table to needy scribblers like Kocour. And I knew that in the long run art was more important than clean hands, that books would survive while hands perished, that Father Time was not a moralist but an art critic.

But my needy friends were all still alive, and so was I. I was no artist, only a member of the Writers Union. As I pondered on these matters, my Chief began to loom more sympathetic in my eyes than all those literary giants. My Chief, that master of prudence, champion of tactical manoeuvres, that defenceless lightning rod of furies, placed at the focus of conflicting interests from above and below. He resisted Cibulka tooth and nail, that's true, but he had his moments of compassion – he raised the fees for translations from various foreign languages, thus helping quite a few writers and editors to keep their heads above water. I was too much of a coward to take the initiative in such matters myself.

To complete the cast of characters: Zluva and Pecakova, the former too unimportant to have a duty to champion a cause, the latter too stupid to be blamed for any transgression. Ferda Hezky, ageing spokesman for youth, frowning at one end of the table – he managed to sit as far away as possible from young Hartman, although the two used to be the greatest of friends.

They were friends no longer. That became apparent during the brief discussion which the case of the Cibulka manuscript – no longer a major problem – called forth. The Chief was calm, jovial, even-tempered; his nervous system had obviously fully recovered from the havoc caused by the Andres scandal. He announced that the manuscript had been turned over to the author for major rewriting. The revisions which the author had made so far were totally inadequate; they had been sent abroad to Comrade Brat, who had forwarded a report.

The Chief cleared his throat and began to read. Brat had made a dialectical aboutface. 'The manuscript is the work of a beginner, which in itself would not be a major drawback. After all, we have the duty to nurture young talents,' etc. 'However, the subject matter presented by Cibulka in a little more than a hundred pages is a concentrate of the worst influences,' and so on and so forth.

I wasn't paying attention to individual words; the general meaning was the same no matter what the words actually said. I was only listening to the familiar intonations, and my thoughts drifted to the Street of Torments, to the army, the July moon. 'The disgusting language spoken by the book's "heroes" and "heroines",' recited the Chief in the tone of a reincarnated inquisitor. Dasha's efforts had obviously come to nothing; young Hartman rose selfconsciously to his feet, tried to speak as counsel for the defence. 'Comrade Brat is not entirely correct in implying that the author should be disciplined by the Morality Squad rather than by the Writers Union ...' I became seized by a schizophrenic vertigo, a dizzying split of the world into the infernal scene before me and the paradise of my imagination. I longed with all my heart for my lost rose – not as a lover, but as a symbol of something else, something pure and beautiful. The devil take it all. Hezky got up and performed a negation of negation. He was no longer defending anything; he played the role of executioner. I didn't give a damn. It occurred to me that perhaps Dasha had become the victim of her own intrigues; I glanced at Hartman, and it was clear that all his courage was gone ... 'Writers like Cibulka were entrusted with an important role by our society: to educate youth in the spirit of Makarenko,' babbled Hezky. '... Art has an important function ... I fully agree with Comrade Brat ...' I was beginning to feel nauseous. A Breughel-like mummery of masks; I was on the verge of fainting. A Greek mask of Hypocrisy said '... Let us not be too strict with her ... I understand the attitude of Comrade Hezky, he is still young ...' the eighty-year-old mask smiled at the thirty-eight-year-old youngster. '... We must close our eyes to the mistakes of youth ...' With all my might I tried to think of something else. I remembered last night in Nusle, a checkered cap, and I felt even worse. 'It is a bad book ... when I finished it I had to wash my hands ...' The idea that Vasek was sitting on the toilet while I was blurting out my painful confession made my head spin ... The mask droned on ... 'I ask my colleagues to reach out a helping hand to this girl ... I myself would be quite willing to take her along with me to the Orel mountains ...' A new wave of faintness rolled over me: Vasek, the cap, was Vasek really ... or had he just dropped in ... The Chief was summing up the Cibulka discussion. 'The editorial board is recommending to the organs of the Writers Union to take special cognizance ...' Then the farce of voting. The terror of the snobs was duly put to an end and legitimate order was reestablished. I excused myself for not feeling well and left.

I really did feel quite ill. Out in the street the fresh air helped a little, but while my stomach improved, the inside of my head felt awful. I was driven by a compulsion to find out whether that idiot had really penetrated into my paradise. My fragrant paradise, the balmy shade of which could save me from this madhouse. I was seized by a terrible anxiety.

By the time I reached the university dining hall I had managed to calm myself considerably. In fact, I succeeded in putting on my old familiar mask. I got angry at myself. Idiot! Why give up the fight, especially when your rival is someone as oafish as Vasek Zamberk?

Gritting my teeth, I entered the dining room. I was in luck. Vasek was still sitting at his lunch with some lanky boys in sweatpants, and his fateful checkered cap screamed from a hanger above his head. I had a carefully prepared plan of attack.

'Hi, Vasek,' I greeted him coldly behind his back.

He spun around as if I had hit him. His vacation-tanned face at once turned a shade darker. 'Hello,' he said. 'How are you?'

'Have you got a few minutes?'

'Yes, certainly, of course. What ... what is it about?'

He wasn't good at faking. A bad conscience was written all over his face. I pretended not to notice. I was back in my old form. We both acted as if we knew nothing about Lenka's bathroom.

'I'll tell you outside.'

He got up without saying goodbye to the students, left half his lunch on the table, and put on that hideous cap. Adjoining the dining room was a bar equipped with tiny tables at which a handful of couples – young men in elegant clothes, shady women who looked expensive – sat sipping imported drinks.

'Martini,' I ordered, and asked Vasek what he was going to drink.

'I don't know ... Do you have apple cider?'

The waiter raised an eyebrow. 'Yes, sir.'

I kept silent. Vasek couldn't take it. 'How was the Army?'

'Passable.' I had everything well thought out.

'I was on a canoe trip. We did the Moldau ...'

His words were swallowed by the quiet semi-darkness of the bar. The waiter brought the two glasses, I took a sip of my Martini.

'Now look here,' I stared him shamelessly in the eye. Yes, I was definitely back in my element; the temporary weak spell was over. 'What was going on between you and Vera?'

'Who? Me?' he feigned surprise.

'Right. You.'

'Well ... you know about it?'

'I want to hear it straight from you.'

'Karel ... look ... I only ... well, it was a dirty trick on my part ...'

'Did you sleep with her?'

'Well ... that is to say ... I was ...'

'Thanks for being such a true pal. Vera broke up with me, you know.'

As I expected, the real motive behind my little act escaped him.

'Karel ... believe me ... I really didn't mean to ... well, you know how it was with me. I felt so awful on account of Lenka. And you didn't show up that night, the two of them were there ... I took Vera home ...'

'You don't have to say any more.'

I sipped my cocktail, maintaining a tragic silence.

'Really, Karel, try to understand. It's an awful thing to do, that's true, but it only happened once ...'

'You bring that up as an excuse?'

'No.'

'Just once, and then you sent her packing. And started up with Silver, right?'

'You found that out, too?'

So it's true! I stared at the traitor, thunderstruck. He was writhing with embarrassment, completely unaware of the weapons he had at his command. I pulled myself together and said bitterly: 'When I think of how you were stringing me along about being such a shy, inexperienced fellow ...'

'But I really am. I only ...'

'How you always played the shrinking violet. Your schoolboyish talk. And all this time ...'

'But I ...'

'You've been a double-crossing skirtchaser.'

He didn't answer.

'Not that I blame you. That's your affair. But at least you could show some respect for the girlfriends of your pals.'

'Karel, I swear I didn't have any intention of doing it. It happened quite differently than I expected. My conscience bothered me ... about Vera ...'

'And so on account of your tender conscience you dropped her!'

'I didn't! I didn't know what to do. The next day Lenka came to my eurhythmics class, and I told her the whole story.'

'This is getting better all the time!'

'And she ...'

'You slept with her too, right?'

'No!' he said quickly. 'That is to say ...'

'Well, did you or didn't you?'

'Not that time. I went to see Vera to apologize. She understood everything. She told me that she had gone to bed with me because she was unhappy, too.'

'Unhappy? Did she tell you why?'

Vasek shook his head. 'No, she didn't. But I thought you two must have had a quarrel, or something,' he said, throwing me a tentative, almost questioning glance. I was beginning to feel feverish.

'You screwed up a perfectly decent girl, in case you're interested,' I told him. 'There was nobody else in her life before me. Now she's on her merry way – she's currently whoring around with Comrade Director Gellen.'

If he swallows even this ...

He swallowed it whole. 'Karel ... I feel awful ... I don't know what to do ...'

'There is nothing to be done now,' I interrupted him. My brain was working at full tilt, and the conclusions it was reaching terrified me.

'Karel, don't hold a grudge against me,' muttered Vasek. 'All right, I've behaved like a real swine. Belt me if you like, but let's remain friends . . .'

'Forget it,' I said, waving my arm. Something occurred to me. I added quickly: 'I hope at least that Miss Silver is as good in bed as she looks.'

He blushed, looked at me, then timidly reached out his hand.

'Shake?' he asked, his eyes full of naïve sentimentality.

'Shake.' I squeezed his hand. 'Now tell me. What is she like in bed?'

I almost stopped breathing.

The peasant face of Vasek Zamberk took on a blissful expression. 'Karel . . . I never dared hope . . . that such a girl . . .'

Once again I felt as if his well trained fist had struck me between the eyes. The bar and the barflies began spinning around like a merry-go-round, with Vasek's checkered cap in the middle.

I needed solace. I went to Blumenfeld's office. But she wasn't there.

'Don't you know what happened?' wondered Salajka. 'She's a proofreader now. She's not an editor any more. She had a fuckup in Russia.'

'What kind of fuckup?'

'I don't know. She was called on the carpet by the Chief, and she came back bawling. I didn't ask her what it was about.'

I climbed up to the proofreading room in utter dejection. So they've got you too, my young Amazon. You gave your all for the good cause, even your vagina, and it served you ill, as good causes always do in this world. I found her sitting in the oppressively silent room next to old Vavrousek, who had been chief proofreader since the times of capitalism. She was resting her chin in the palm of her hand, staring moodily at some galley proofs. As soon as she spotted me she dropped everything and dashed out into the hall, where she immediately lit a cigarette.

'Damn it,' she said, 'none of those old bastards in there smokes.'

She sucked in the smoke greedily, letting it flow slowly out of her nose and mouth. It curled lovingly over her cheeks. Her beautiful eyes seemed to read my mind: 'We came to quite an end, didn't we?'

'We sure did. Flat on our asses.'

She sucked in the smoke like a sailor, leaned against the radiator and stuck out her provocative breasts.

'What were you up to in the fraternal Soviet Union?'

'Nothing much. The trouble was that I didn't look up those jerks that Emil recommended. I had bad luck. That jackass Nikolajev had to open his trap just when I was there.'

'Why did Emil fire you?'

'He read my report about my trip. Next time I'll be smarter. Like a fool I wrote down all the names and addresses of the people I met and it read like a directory of troublemakers. Every single one of those names appeared on Nikolajev's shitlist.'

'That explains it. But couldn't our employees' council intervene on your behalf?'

'Stop joking!' she said, adding: 'And what about you? The army? And Comrade Silver?'

'Nothing worth talking about,' I said, trying to change the subject. 'When will you break it to Cibulka that the jig is up?'

She took me warmly by the hand, her bosom rubbing against my sleeve.

'You'll help me, won't you? I have a date with her tomorrow afternoon.'

'I'll help, sure, if you want me to.' I paused. 'But . . . to tell you the truth, today at the meeting I voted with the other side. It was a rough situation.'

'Sure, I can imagine. That's all right. We have to start from scratch.'

'Only young Hartman spoke up for her,' I said, so that she wouldn't feel totally abandoned. I wanted to make her feel good. But she frowned.

'What about Ferda Hezky?'

'Well, he . . .'

'Sure. I understand that, too. You don't have to tell me. Listen, Kaja,' she bent forward confidentially, and once again I felt the supple breasts of my ally – an ally who, unfortunately, could do little to help me in my own struggle. 'That Cibulka affair led to quite a fracas. The two of them slugged it out in the Reduta Bar.'

'What?'

'That's right. Young Hartman punched Hezky right in the nose.'

'And he got you as a first prize?'

She was insulted: 'What kind of remark is that? Did the army dry out your brains?'

'Sorry. In other words, the fight was purely on account of ...'

'What else?' she interrupted heatedly. 'Surely you don't think I can't find better men than that pair. Do you know who I could really go for?'

Her pale Semitic face took on a dreamy expression which I had never seen before. Usually she looked as bellicose as Bar Kochba.

'No, I don't. Me?'

'James Dean,' she sighed, and then sighed once more, bitterly. 'But types like that don't exist in our country. More likely in the Soviet Union.'

'Glebkin, for example?' I asked maliciously.

'He happens to be a very fine fellow,' she said with feeling. 'Now the poor boy is milking cows on a collective farm. But he won't be milking them much longer!'

She had turned once again into a Hebrew warrior.

'Aren't you a bit too optimistic?'

'Not me!' she said merrily. 'All our troubles are just little growing pains. I'll sit them out in the proofreading room. Be seeing you!'

She gave me a wet kiss on the cheek and disappeared.

Go on, I thought to myself. Life will never teach you anything.

And what will it take to teach you, my friend? said my inner voice. What if even Lenka turns out to be as false as a counterfeit coin?

14 *Scene with Cibulka*

Another tormented night. Upset stomach. From all those revelations.

The next day, as part of our cultural lecture series, we were enlightened by a visiting lecturer, on the subject of certain ancient Greek philosophers by the names of Socratus, Platus, and Ariston. We learned that Socratus did not know anything, that Platus had spent part of his life in some kind of cave, and that Ariston died of stomach ulcers. My colleague Salajka was sitting next to me, surreptitiously proofreading galleys of *The Aeneid* under the table; the translation had been turned over to him by the aged widow of a Latinist, so that Salajka could make a little money on the side. The lecturer then passed to Ariston's forerunner Hercules, who had taught that everything was in a state of flux – a concept later formulated more precisely by Comrade Stalin in his work entitled 'On Dialectical and Historical Materialism'.

From time to time our lecturer glanced into his notes, written in a frayed old schoolbook. During his talk he leaned on a grand piano, which our Chief had purchased out of the cultural fund of the office; the balance in the fund had seemed unduly high, and the Chief wanted to make sure that our allotment would not be reduced in the future. Nobody ever played the piano; the keyboard had probably never even seen the light of day. It stood in the corner of the club room like an absurd incarnation of good intentions. A pile of manuscripts which somebody had misplaced was lying on top. Somehow or other, the lecturer had shifted from the golden age of Classical Greece to nineteenth-century Europe. Feuerbaum, he declared, had taught that man made God in his own image. Colleague Salajka was up to the eightieth column of his galley; Dudek began loudly snoring in the back. Our mentor took a sip of water, and then assured us that Feuerbaum's thesis had been turned upside down by a certain German named Hegel.

This unwitting entertainer allowed me to forget my troubles and disappointments, and gave me a charitable moment of peace. My mind wandered back to the past – always better than the present – to the luxurious mountain villa which had belonged to some pre-war millionaire, and which had been converted into an indoctrination centre for cultural workers. Five times a day I used to sit down to consume dishes that had magic French names, prepared by students of the Graduate School of Nutrition who were thus fulfilling their practical requirements. Drowsy from overeating, I attended compulsory lectures on Marxism-Leninism. In the evenings I would hang around the bar, where we played old foxtrots and charlestons, drank wine supplied from the private stock of the superintendent, and danced with the students of the nutrition school till the early hours. Dawn would generally find us vomiting into any of the numerous toilets which the millionaire had installed in the unlikeliest places.

But everything changes. The mountain villa vanished and I was once more facing our curiously trained lecturer. He was informing us that according to Engels, man had arisen through the humanization of apes. This change had taken place after the apes had found out that the thumb can be effectively opposed to the other four fingers.

Long ago, in that mountain villa, one of the students was a tall, slender blonde, very progressive. I provoked her by singing English hit songs, and mollified her by poems which I wrote for her. 'Fate touched the sacred urn and made your beauty burn, Irena ...' I wrote these and much better poems, put them together in my first collection, and that launched me on my career. I even earned a reputation as a mild rebel which has stayed with me ever since.

Could I still? ... but such questions should no longer be asked. My pleasant musing evaporated and I found myself again in the cruel embrace of Lenka Silver, that beautiful, faithless deceiver. My mind's eye saw once more the sun-drenched hall, the checkered cap

– and I refused to believe the facts. The detective story had reached its moment of *dénouement*; the culprit must be someone important to the plot, someone I had known from the very beginning. It cannot be a *deus ex machina* ending. But, then again, why not? Life does not follow the rules of Ellery Queen. How many mysteries were concealed in the body and soul of that mysterious mermaid? Her image obsessed me, the image of her eyes, her legs, her breasts tanned further than my eyes would ever reach, the image of that moonlit street, roofs shining in the rain, the trite midnight sky. Mechanically I pulled out my pen. The lecturer was droning on about a chemist who had synthesized urea, thus proving that man was master of nature. Colleague Salajka turned to column eighty-one, and I – heedless of the total failure of inspiration that night atop the tank turret – began writing a poem to that lunar mermaid, that snake, the Virgin incarnate of Catholic iconology.

I wrote one verse and created one inferiority complex. 'I knew you not, yet hallowed is your street ...' It occurred to me that this was just a miserable echo of a well known elegy, even more miserable than the Orten imitation written by the Jewish lad who loved Lenka's sister. I had simply dried up. Continual versifying on every possible subject had dried me up and it didn't really matter, because that unattainable young lady, that beautiful harlot, that enthralling, infuriating puzzle was so much more beautiful than any sonnet by Petrarch. Where does that leave Comrade Leden, editor and poetaster? 'My anguish blazes now ...' I had written to that girl in the mountain school. But I had never really felt the sting until now. Too late.

The bitter end of a poet. I got up as if to go to the bathroom and went to the office library. Row upon row of books that we had helped bring into this world stood upon the shelves. Mine, too. I pulled it out; it was already yellowing around the edges. The pages were still uncut, except for one section which had got me into a great deal of trouble – a group of seven poems dedicated to Irena, a girl supremely gifted in bed. I could no longer recall her last name, nor her occupation. Most likely she was an editor at the Agricultural Publishing House or some similar outfit. I opened the book, which had stood unopened on the shelf for so many years that it had slowly died of jaundice, and my eyes fell on the title 'Acrostic of Resolution'. The widely spaced poem was printed underneath:

My compass and my pole
Show me virtue is adventure
A journey its own goal
O my guide
Lead me to rocks of truth
Shear my pride
Ease my pain
With your tranquil gaze
Teach me disdain
For the din of praise
Let me learn
To hide concern under a mask.
Light my heart with love.
Let me dare
Seek forgiveness without prayer.

Ikon.
Refuge of the blest
Ellipse of magic signs
Nausicaa of my quest
Amen.

I had forgotten it all long ago, the blonde, the poem, everything. I only remembered that I was taken to task for the 'Amen' at the end. Actually, the expression had no special meaning for me; I only needed an appropriate word starting with an 'A' to complete the acronym. All the same, the incident taught me a lesson for my future career as poet.

I read the poem over once again. Did I really write this? And did I mean it seriously, or were my sentiments as spurious as the 'Amen' at the end? I had even forgotten that. Somehow, it all seemed so distant, so unreal.

I stuck the volume back into its mausoleum and returned for more indoctrination.

*

At five in the afternoon Blumenfeld and I waited in the Mokka coffeehouse for Cibulka. Blumenfeld was on pins and needles, and I, too, was overcome by nervous anticipation. What would she be like, this young author who had plunged the Czech language into hitherto unexplored regions of mire?

She arrived twenty minutes late. She turned out to be a rather bland-looking, angular girl with soggy light brown hair. She reached out a nervous hand to me, greeted Dasha with a 'Hi!' took off a soiled blue raincoat, and sat down at the table in a slightly less soiled pink sweater and grey skirt. She ordered vermouth at once, and lit a cigarette.

'Well?' she turned eagerly to Blumenfeld.

'It looks lousy,' said Dasha.

I saw a twinge on the girl's face. 'It's been rejected?'

'It will be published, Jara dear, don't worry. But for the moment we've got to wait. Those senile shitasses on the editorial board have messed it up.'

Nervous, grimy fingers ground the cigarette out in the ashtray. The girl glanced around the tiny dark brown coffeehouse, the intimate darkness of which was reflected in the prices on the menu. A few couples sat around the small round tables, engaged in happier discourse than we. Her lashes trembled, her eyes began to glisten.

'Don't worry, Jarinka,' Blumenfeld said soothingly. 'To hell with them! You can survive a year or two, and then it's sure to come out in a mass edition.'

'It will never come out!' Cibulka murmured darkly, with such desperation that Blumenfeld put her arm around her shoulders. The girl instinctively drew closer. 'Now, now, Jarinka,' Dasha drawled consolingly, and shook the sobbing girl. A hysterical type, I thought to myself. 'Now, now,' repeated Blumenfeld. 'Fuck them all, those morons. Let them choke on *Tales from a Collective Farm*. Your time will come, Jarinka, believe me!'

The decadent authoress continued to sob. I came to Dasha's aid. 'Please don't cry, Miss Cibulka. Things got a little sticky in the last few weeks. If it weren't for that, the book would have gone through like a knife through butter. It was already half approved!'

'That's a fact!' shouted Dasha. 'It was fucked up by that idiot Brat. I hope he croaks of cholera, the syphilitic moron.'

The girl rolled her head all over the most fantastic bosom in Europe, and at last she sat up.

'It's just that I was counting on it,' she said with despair. 'I was looking forward to it so much! And now on top of everything, they kicked me out of the Home, all on account of me trusting Ondrasova, and she ran out on me.'

'They kicked you out?'

'Sure. I wanted to trust people, you know, the honour system. But Ondrasova flew the coop. They caught her in some house in Pilkovice just as she was carting off a record player, so they threw the book at me.' She went into a coughing spell. 'They said I am experimenting with decadent Western methods instead of ...'

'The bastards!' yelled Blumenfeld, with her usual uncomplicated total conviction. At the next table, a young man who had been disturbed in the midst of a kissing spree by the loud shout, angrily raised his head, revealing a freshly sucked pink blotch on the neck of his beloved. But Blumenfeld continued unabashed in her stridently squeaking voice: 'Where did they pack you off to, the bastards?'

'A secondary school in Bechovice.'

'Sonsofbitches.'

By then the lovers were looking at each other in annoyance, and the girl shook her head in answer to her companion's silent question. Dasha still was not paying any attention to them. Cibulka wiped her tears.

'So, in other words,' she sobbed, 'they didn't like it?'

'Just the contrary,' I said. 'They liked it so much that they became afraid.'

'How do you mean, afraid?'

'Just plain scared. Obviously that's a feeling which you do not have.'

She apparently didn't understand, because she first looked at the empty glass of vermouth and then back at me. The lovers next to us were kissing again.

'And you – you don't think it's stupid? I mean in a literary way?'

Blumenfeld became so furious that a shudder went through the kissing couple.

'If you think that's what we think, you're a jerk!'

I interjected quickly: 'It's the best book I've read since I've been in publishing. Seriously.' Her mistrustful, unhappy, pale blue eyes full of complexes quickly turned on me.

'It's a fact?'

'Fact.'

'There you have it,' said Blumenfeld. 'And it means a lot when Karel praises something. He never seems to have a good word about anything.'

'I read your book – *Here and Now* – when I was fifteen,' she hesitated. She couldn't seem to bring herself to say it – but she did at last: 'At the time I thought the poems were great. Really. It's a fact.'

I smiled. A bitter smile inwardly, condescending outwardly. I well understood the subconscious significance of the phrase "at the time". I knew my Freud.

I waved my arm in a self-deprecating gesture. 'Those were the sins of youth. If I could write as easily as you I'd be a happy man.'

I really meant that. I recalled the afternoon at the beginning of summer when I had first come upon the manuscript of this slender, sad girl. I had felt bitterly jealous, because something pulsated in her words which had long vanished from mine – and from everything else coming from our publishing house. Something that we tried to exorcize with our abracadabras, something we spat on from our exalted ivory towers – something called life.

Cibulka blushed. 'Go on! I can't write poems at all!'

'Yes, you can,' I said. 'Only you write them in prose.'

Before she could answer, the narrow wooden stairway that led up to the main floor of the Mokka coffeehouse creaked, and the back of a familiar head emerged above the floorboards. It belonged to the Chief. It rose higher and higher, until it turned around and recognized me.

'Greetings,' he said without special enthusiasm, and glanced around the room. I couldn't imagine what he was doing here; he certainly hadn't come to see us. He quickly finished his inspection, obviously coming to the conclusion that the object of his search was sitting in the other part of the room, behind a confectioner's plaster conception of the Venus de Milo. The Chief was on the verge of waving goodbye to us, when some devil or other prompted me to do something stupid.

'I don't believe you know each other,' I said with aplomb. Before they knew what hit them, I introduced Cibulka to the Chief: 'Comrade Cibulka – Comrade Prochazka.'

'So it is you,' the Chief said in a severe tone of voice, his cold eyes stripping the angular authoress of her grubby sweater. 'We have rejected your manuscript.'

Cibulka's face twitched again. Cry, Cibulka dear, please cry, I begged her silently. Weep your eyes out! Just for the hell of it! But she didn't.

'It is weak, very weak, Comrade,' the Chief said gruffly. 'You should study some of our better Czech authors, Stary, Zluva, Matous ...'

'Yes,' Cibulka said hoarsely.

'A little theory would not hurt you, either. For instance, do you know Brat's *Rebound Theory in Czech Socialist Prose*? Read it! Right now you don't really know your craft.'

The first tears came to Cibulka's eyes. The Chief noticed them and softened.

'But then again, as far as talent goes, you certainly have talent. There is no doubt about that. You know how to observe people, but you shouldn't choose such an eccentric atmosphere, you know. Get in the mainstream of life, Comrade. Into life. Whenever you have something else to show us, please come to see us. I'll always be glad to look it over.'

He squeezed her hand, turned on his popular yellow smile. Then he disappeared into the other part of the room. That ended it, as far as he was concerned. Now he could devote himself again to new editions of classical authors, and sleep with a clear conscience. And Cibulka could go back to pounding out her stories about morally depraved salesgirls and other eccentric characters. To each his own.

She began to tremble so violently that I was worried that she would do something desperate. Her pimply face turned dark; her pale eyes sparkled with fury.

'That shitass!' shouted Blumenfeld. 'Did you hear him? You don't know your craft! The only craft a clown like him knows is cobbling!'

Cibulka turned to her. 'Tell me the truth, Dasha. Do you really think that my book has some literary value?'

'You jerk! I don't *think* so, I *know* so! And those jackass scribblers know it, too, better than any of us!'

'Then why doesn't he say so?' burst out Cibulka. 'Why doesn't he tell the truth! I'd love to scratch his eyes out! The bald old bastard!'

She jumped to her feet, and it almost looked as if she were about to carry out her threat. We had to grab her, and pull her back. I was almost sorry the Chief hadn't stayed around. A number of authors had said similar things about what they would like to do to the Chief; it would have been refreshing to see somebody actually tear into him.

Perhaps he had had an inkling of what she might do and had disappeared just at the right moment. Anyhow, we proved our loyalty as employees by pressing Cibulka down to her seat as hard as we could. Dasha kept on whispering something in her ear, which seemed to gradually quieten her down. After we had filled her with vermouth, wiped her nose, and calmed her, I got a wonderful idea which topped off our solicitous ministrations: 'To hell with the old bastard! Come dancing with us on Saturday to Zivohost. Our office is giving a party and all our authors are invited.'

Her attack had subsided.

'If you promise to stick by me,' mumbled Cibulka mournfully.

'Look here, our editorial board ordered us to take good care of Comrade Cibulka. What do you think, Dasha?'

Blumenfeld threw me a grateful look.

'I am formally inviting you.'

'Fact?'

The pale eyes, taught by life to look on everything with suspicion, scanned my face. I returned her gaze. I would never have expected the girl sitting across from me to be the author of the novel *Between Us Girls*. She hardly seemed like the kind of person who stirred up a storm of feverish activity – cablegrams racing to distant parts of

Europe, well-paid men and women meeting at urgent conferences, reams of reports full of abstract terms, and foreign phrases pouring out of typewriters. Academician Brat interrupting his vacation. The storm even passed close to Comrade Kaiser himself.

I smiled and answered: 'It's a fact.'

'That's really a great idea,' said Dasha. 'We'll all get roaring drunk, including Comrade Chief, and then we'll work him over until he looks like a ripe melon.'

As we were leaving the Mokka I saw a young lady jump off a bus in front of the coffeehouse. It was hard to tell at that distance, but she looked very much like Lenka. But I was squiring two girls, one on each arm, and I couldn't go back.

The Chief was the only person I knew who was in the coffeehouse. If it really was Lenka, what was she doing there? Vasek was certainly not at the Mokka.

But then again, I didn't actually know who might have been sitting in the back, in the dark section behind the Venus de Milo.

It was possible, too, that I was beginning to suffer from hallucinations.

15 *Office outing*

Blumenfeld came to realize that inviting Cibulka to our office outing was not such a good idea after all, but by that time it was too late to withdraw the invitation. Now she sat in a wrinkled taffeta dress, ensconced behind an oleander tree, safely out of the Chief's sight. From past experience, everybody expected the Chief to get plastered, and he was already well on the way.

Everybody at the table was having a good time and, as usual, Kopanec was in the midst of a lively discussion. He was arguing with Pecakova, who maintained that the new novel by the Master of Fuckups contained certain satirical passages which could be interpreted as reactionary calumnies against socialism. Cibulka was casting admiring glances at the renowned author; the Master of Fuckups gave her a rakish wink now and then. The hall was filling with cigarette smoke; the artificial lake glistened through the broad windows; and the noise level was keeping pace with the consumption of alcohol.

I was drinking more than was my custom. Quite a few of my customs were changing under the impact of the recent developments in my life. The loud argument between Kopanec and Pecakova raged on, interrupted now and then by Dr Ehrlich, atomic physicist and husband of our linguistics editor. But I perceived the debate as well as the noisy pleasantries of the Chief only as a background cacophony which did not quite manage to drown out the moaning in my heart.

'That's like the drumbeat of cannibals,' I heard the Master say, and the strong expression shook me out of my melancholy. 'It brings on a cataleptic fit, and then they're bound to eat their own parents.' I gathered that the dispute hinged on the question of enthusiasm, which Pecakova regarded as 'an inseparable part of the building of socialism' whereas Kopanec saw it as 'a mortal danger'. Dr Ehrlich was sneering sarcastically, while his wife hunched anxiously over her glass of wine. I contemplated the collage formed by the silver rays glued over the surface of the lake, and I thought of a similar collage of moonbeams over the Moldau which I had watched not long ago.

'Nothing is so disgusting to me,' Pecakova was saying, 'as an ironic intellectual who can't get excited about anything and whose cynicism plays right into the hands of decadents, reactionaries, and hoodlums.' The collage was cut by a silver arrow, formed by the wake of a dark boat; two figures were silhouetted in the boat, two heads that somehow seemed extremely familiar to me, even though they were far away, diffused by the shimmering of the silvery surface. I turned back to the conversation. Dr Ehrlich maintained that, according to dialectic theory, every good action requires a corresponding reaction, and for this reason, minorities which oppose the trend set by the majority performed an organic, useful societal function. Pecakova retorted that the only true dialectical opposition in our socialist society was between the good and the still better.

The Chief was dancing with Annie, chanting some unrecognizable song. The black boat vanished from my sight. Kopanec was pointing to the etymology of the word 'enthusiasm', which implied possession by God, and he noted that a person possessed by supernatural powers was hardly a model socialist. The black boat floated back into my field of view, again followed by a silver arrow in its wake, and again I had the uncanny feeling that the two silhouetted heads huddling close together had some special significance in my life. Then I sank below the surface of another, private realm, where a golden-brown mermaid flickered her enticing rear end through an inky darkness. My musing was broken up by Dr Ehrlich's sarcastic voice: 'Capitalism is simply demonstrating a higher economic vitality, and that's why I am beginning to have serious doubts about socialism.'

Then the surprisingly angry voice of the Master of Fuckups: 'Beginning? I have always had serious doubts. The question is how to clear away the doubts and make socialism a fact.' He hiccuped. My mermaid vanished. I took another gulp of vodka.

'To hell with economics!' yelled Kopanec. 'I don't give a goddamn whether they produce more junk than we do, but if they produce more humaneness than we do – then we'd better watch out! I don't give a damn about economics. I care about ethics. That's why you won't hear any of that self-congratulatory stuff from me.' The Chief, stewed to the gills, was loudly singing a ballad about some heroic guerrilla exploit. The mermaid was eluding me. Alcohol was turning to bile in my veins. Bilious waves were staining white sands with hideous black stains. Wave after wave was spilling, receding, leaving behind clusters of slimy bones. I came to my senses with a terrified start; I felt a slight twinge of pain – Blumenfeld was holding my hand and digging her red painted nails into my arm.

The Chief was standing over us, an allegorical image of inebriation.

'Do you mind? ... I'll sit down here,' he blurted, and plopped himself down next to Cibulka. I was still fighting my hallucinations, trying hard to focus on the here and now. 'Shall I sit down ... next to our dear author? Our terrible author?' There was a rustle of taffeta. The pimply face of Jarmila Cibulka materialized before me, blushing fiercely. Her hand on the table was trembling. 'Karel! You have to give this young lady a lesson ... teach her how to write, for God's sake!' With the awkwardness of a drunk, the Chief put his arm around Cibulka's waist; she stiffened and tried to get up. 'Writing must be a beautiful thing. Beautiful. But the way you write, my dear, is not beautiful at all. You think you know how to write, but you don't. Not at all at all at all.'

I was frightened. So was Dasha. I could feel her nails digging deeper into my skin. 'She knows how to write,' Dasha snapped angrily. 'She writes as well as Burdych any day!'

I got an idea, a vague idea, and I decided to act. I decided to drown the impending clash in a torrent of pathos – a technique I had used successfully in the past. But I was too drunk to control either my words or my movements. I picked up the bottle of vodka, poured some into two empty glasses, spilling vodka all over the table in the process, and lifted one towards the Chief.

'Emil, permit me ...' I said with feigned sentiment, 'permit me, my friend ...'

'You mustn't say that, Blumenfeld!' The Chief was ignoring me completely; I lowered the vodka glass and sank heavily into my chair.

I was trying hard to concentrate on the words. 'Comrade Burdych, why, she's a great artist!' declared the Chief vehemently. 'And she writes beautifully and about beautiful subjects. But you, Comrade,' he turned to Cibulka, 'you won't get any prizes for that junk of yours – take my word for it.'

My eyes dropped to Cibulka's waist; her grubby small hand with its bitten nails was trying to push away the Chief's arm.

'I . . . I am trying to write as well as I can,' she said. 'And don't call it junk.' Her voice trembled. I noticed the big urn of coffee ordered by Dr Ehrlich and reached for it.

'It is junk,' repeated the Chief. 'Comrade Academician Brat would call it just that.' The Chief released Cibulka's waist and raised his hand with one finger pointing up in a pulpit-like gesture. 'And he knows something about literature. He has seen something of life. And what have you seen of life to give you the right to write such . . .'

'Don't say it!' The taffeta rustled.

'. . . such junk,' said the Chief. I took a deep gulp of coffee. 'Don't say that,' piped the hysterical little voice. I seemed to recall something. Yes, the encounter in the Mokka coffeehouse. I took another sip. The Chief kept repeating stubbornly, drunkenly: 'I'll say what I please. Yes I will!' His bleary eyes swept over the girl's flushed face, the wrinkled taffeta, the small heaving breasts. 'You're not exactly beautiful yourself but that doesn't mean you've got to write such ugly stuff. But that junk . . .' The scene suddenly exploded into violent motion, like a Disney cartoon; there was a scream, a leap of taffeta. Then I saw the Chief topple backwards, I glimpsed the soles of his shoes, a flash of gartered nylon, a clump of bodies, Cibulka scratching the Chief's face, Dasha pulling her back from one side, Mrs Ehrlich from the other. The Chief got up and hurried towards the bar, almost knocking down a couple who parted awkwardly to let him go by. I rubbed my eyes. Cibulka sat down opposite me at the table, her teeth chattering; the trembling Mrs Ehrlich was holding her by the shoulder. 'Well done, Mademoiselle,' I heard the croaking voice of Kopanec say. 'Too bad you didn't scratch his eyes out. He needed that like a goat needs shearing.'

The trembling subsided, the contours of reality began to reassert themselves.

'Please forgive me,' mumbled Cibulka. 'He just made me furious – the lousy bastard!'

'You did the right thing,' said Dasha. People were dancing the foxtrot. Glancing towards the bar I saw the barman putting iodine on the Chief, who was peering uneasily towards our table. What would be the result of all this? What would it mean for me? I didn't really give a damn.

Cibulka said softly: 'It was embarrassing.'

'What was embarrassing about it was that we let you down,' said Dasha.

'Yes,' I said. 'It was almost ... almost ...'

'Almost symbolic,' said Kopanec.

'Come on,' said Blumenfeld. 'Let's see if we can fix you up a bit.' She helped her get up. I took another gulp of coffee. Blumenfeld prophesied: 'It won't be long and he'll be done in by his own flunkies. To make sure they survive his crash.' She winked at me.

I didn't understand. Why did she say that? And whom did she have in mind? She couldn't have meant me. After all, she and I had found ourselves on the same side of most matters recently. Nonsense. Alcohol makes people look for all kinds of connections that don't exist. And it didn't really make a damn bit of difference anyway. I watched the two girls crossing the dance floor. I saw the Chief hunch down at the bar. I saw them disappear behind the doors. The swinging door slowly stopped swinging.

And then they swung again as two figures in slacks and thick sweaters strode into the hall. A man and a woman.

I reached for the coffee urn, but there was no need for it. I was cold sober. The man was Vasek Zamberk, holding the notorious checkered cap in his hand. The woman – and I gaped as if staring at a magic mirror – was Lenka Silver.

She strode straight to the bar. The Chief sat up and gave her a lascivious grin.

I remained alone at the table, watching the pantomime with a head as clear as mountain air. The Ehrlichs shuffled off to the dance floor, to give Mrs Ehrlich a chance to pull herself together, and Kopanec was bending somebody's ear in the corner of the hall. Lenka reached out her hand to the Chief, and the three of them settled down next to each other at the bar.

At the sight of that cosy triangle all my wounds began to ache. What are you up to, my beautiful lily?

There was a vacant stool next to Vasek. A little further down the bar were perched two blond youths in dark blue jackets – Danish tourists, somebody had said. One of them looked like James Dean. The empty stool exerted a magnetic pull on me. It drew me closer, closer, closer.

I sat down and shouted behind Vasek's back: 'Welcome, friends!'

He turned and greeted me with surprising warmth. Lenka smiled at me, quite pleasantly: 'Good evening, Comrade Editor.'

But she immediately returned to her chat with the Chief. A glass of wine was standing on the bar in front of her, next to a pair of grey deerskin gloves. Her tanned hand toyed with the gloves while she subjected the Chief to good-natured ribbing.

Vasek was explaining something to me, some nonsense about the last days of summer and a tent and how cold the two of them felt in the tent at night. It went in one ear and out the other. I was no longer shocked at anything. Vasek babbled on as if everything he was saying was a sober, self-evident fact. The Chief was drunkenly entertaining Lenka while she gently went on making fun of him. The collage behind the window glistened in the light of the full moon. A big glass of wine stood in front of Vasek. Everything had become crystal-clear to me. I wondered whether it was equally clear to Vasek. I pointed at the wine. 'I thought you were a teetotaller?'

'I still am,' said Vasek, and glanced at Lenka. 'But tonight – you know – we're kind of celebrating.'

'Celebrating what?'

He took me by the hand. 'Come. I'll tell you.'

Then he turned to his young lady – his, not mine – and cooed: 'We'll be right back, Lenka.'

Lenka. We sat down at an empty table. 'Let's have the big secret.'

He looked at me with that sincere, artless look of a hammer thrower.

'Karel, I am walking on clouds.'

'Is this the first time you've shacked up with her?'

'No, it isn't that. We've been together before. But ...'

'You knocked her up?'

'No, no. She ... she's going to marry me!'

Yes. I see. Automatically I glanced at that pretty rear end perched on the bar stool. I didn't hear Vasek's enthusiastic outpouring. The alcohol had loosened his tongue. Normally, he didn't even drink beer. So that's your end, my lily-of-the-valley, I felt like bawling. And what about the rest? What about the rest of the story, which was hidden not only from me but from this big bumbling baboon as well?

I felt like bawling. I got up. Vasek remained seated; then he got up too and followed me. I returned to the bar and sat down next to the lily.

'Go on, go on!' she was saying to the Chief. 'You don't know anything about me. But I know something about you.'

'As it happens I know a thing or two. Hey, look who's here. Kaja! I know a thing or two about him, too! Actually, it's all the same ... all the same ...'

He must have had a litre of alcohol in his veins. Vasek pulled up a stool on the other side of me; the lily cast a rather nervous eye at him, and then said to the Chief: 'Don't let your tongue run away with you.'

'My tongue is all twisted together ... I can't seem to speak ...'

He slapped his cheeks and got to his feet. The barman put another glass of wine in front of Vasek.

'Please ... please excuse me ...' said the Chief. 'Be back in a minute.' He swayed dangerously and just managed to grab the edge of the bar in time.

Vasek gulped down his wine, coughed, and jumped to the Chief's side. 'Let me help you.'

'Thank you, ahhh, thank you, Professor.'

He put his arm around Vasek's neck and the two of them staggered towards the swinging doors marked WC.

*

I remained alone at the bar with Lenka. She smiled at me pleasantly, the second time that evening.

'How do you feel, Comrade Editor?'

As cool as you please. That snake disguised as a lily-of-the-valley.

'Horrible. How else can I feel?'

'That will pass.' I gazed at her, a philosopher gazing at the sphinx.

'Why do you look like that?'

I kept staring at her in a melodramatic way, spurred by alcohol and furious jealousy.

'Brrrr!' she said, pretending to shudder. 'You're staring at me like a murderer. But I haven't done anything to you, have I? At least not intentionally.'

Through clenched teeth, like a movie gangster, I growled: 'What kind of woman are you?'

Her treacherous eyebrows arched. 'What kind? Just a normal girl. Nothing out of the ordinary.'

'Nothing out of the ordinary!' I looked her over from the crown of her tousled head to her trim little canvas shoes. 'You mean there's nothing unusual about being engaged to one man and at the same time...'

She winked at me. 'Oh, I see,' she said. 'But you won't tell Vasek on me, will you?'

I kept staring at her – like a murderer. And I still didn't understand.

She laughed. 'Actually, it doesn't mean anything. At least, not what you are thinking.'

'Vasek is a pal of mine. I think I ought to tell him what he's getting himself into.'

She laughed. 'My dear editor, I didn't know that friendship mattered so much to you.'

'Sometimes it does.'

'After all, you did your best to do him in.'

'But who won out in the end? Not me!'

I held my breath. The lily arched her brows again and sighed. 'Dear me, still thinking only about yourself, nobody but yourself.'

Once again I found myself completely in the dark. She scooped the bottom of her glass with a long spoon, while all kinds of ideas swam confusedly in my head. Then she threw me a coquettish glance. 'Are you really going to tell him?'

I didn't answer. Yes, I will, I thought to myself. I can't stand your marrying that baboon. But what can I tell him?

'You wouldn't do a thing like that,' she purred. 'Try to be a gentleman.'

I looked her in the eye. 'I am no gentleman. I am an egotist, and I want you.'

The smiling face turned cool, serious. 'You'd better save those appetites for somebody else,' she said, and sipped the remnant of her mulled wine. 'The matter you want to tell him about is really something completely different from what you think. But you wouldn't understand.'

'No. As far as you are concerned, I don't understand anything. I am sure I wouldn't understand this, either.'

She brushed me with her opaque glance, and said pensively: 'Actually, who knows?'

One of those two Nordic giants approached us, the one who resembled James Dean. The look of arrogant self-confidence with which he examined Lenka made it evident that the highball he was holding in his hand was far from his first. He said something to her which my ears registered as clearly as if they were attached to a tape recorder, even though I didn't understand a single word: *'Ih, sikke nogle klathager de har, det har jeg aldrig set magen til!'*

Then the incomprehensible reality surrounding Lenka Silver dissolved into a Mack Sennett sequence. Startled, she lifted her head from her glass and looked at the Dane; then with perfect calm she slapped his face so hard that it made him spin around. My ears then recorded another sentence, this time from Lenka's lips, and I was certain that I was hearing the impossible: *'Du glemmer vist, at det er en dame, du snakker til.'*

I stared at her in amazement; so did the Dane. He turned red as a beet; then he began to stammer some apology.

'Ka'du skrubbe af, jeg har sgu nok at tage nig af!' said Lenka. Only the spirit of Mack Sennett could have arranged the Dane's exit from the scene: he stepped back, tripped on the rug, fell, knocking down a waiter carrying a trayful of glasses – fortunately empty – got up, turned, was hit in the face by the swinging doors through which Kopanec had just entered, covered his nose with his hands, tried to squeeze through, was momentarily stuck in the wings of the doors, and at last stumbled out of the picture.

I turned to the mermaid. She was perched on the stool, her face aglow with a mysterious blush. Everything seemed incomprehensible. It occurred to me that I must be drunk after all, that everything I had seen was a mirage, a delusion, which had turned ordinary Czech into a foreign tongue, for the world often seems foreign to drunkards who want to escape into an exotic realm but are held fast by ordinary reality, and so they scream and protest and create disturbances. I closed my eyes. I reached for the tip of my nose, and touched it without any difficulty. No. I was not drunk. Yet I did find myself on the other side of a mirror, in a world where Lenka Silver spoke Danish. That simple, uncultured girl, who didn't know what *coup de grâce* meant and who didn't recognize a standard line from Dante.

I said: 'Who are you?'

'Mata Hari,' she answered.

Yes, the beautiful spy. But what secrets could she possibly be looking for? An absurd premonition of foul play crossed my mind. Kopanec staggered to the bar and made a deep bow. 'Beautiful lady, will you say yes?'

She laughed, ending her role of beautiful spy. She had reverted to a pretty young girl in long slacks. 'It all depends on the question.'

'Will you dance with me?' begged Kopanec.

'Just a minute,' I blurted out gruffly. 'This young lady is going to dance with me!'

'The young lady isn't going to dance at all. She's not dressed for it,' said Lenka.

Kopanec looked uneasily from one of us to the other, then resolved the embarrassing moment by making another deep bow, and left.

'I intend to tell him,' I declared firmly.

Lenka shrugged her shoulders. 'As you wish. It won't do you any good, and you won't hurt me by it. He'll understand once I explain the whole story to him.'

'Will you explain it to me, too?'

The grey, alcohol-soaked world was getting darker and darker.

'I won't tell you anything at all, Comrade Editor.'

Vasek and the Chief came back. They had obviously been drinking in the taproom next door; Vasek's shirt was open at the neck, and he was very flushed. Kopanec had sneakily installed himself on one of the stools vacated by the Danes, and in a grand gesture he ordered drinks for the whole company. Lenka, twittering like a swallow, ignored me completely.

I spun around on the stool and stared vacantly into the hall. All the emotions in my long-neglected inner self had turned into a single feeling of dull indifference. Or perhaps it was the feeling of emptiness so often depicted in novels during moments of catharsis. That's all it was, no doubt. A few couples were still reeling around the dance floor. At a table along the wall, Colleague Salajka strummed a guitar to accompany his beery-voiced friends. I looked around the hall – God knows why – at that moment I could just as easily have stood on my head, drunk poison, sung the national anthem, or beaten the stuffing out of my Chief, Vasek, and the Master of Fuckups. None of it would have made a damn bit of difference. Nothing would have helped. Except, perhaps, for a little time, that one timetested opiate ...

Cibulka and Blumenfeld came striding in through the door. Blumenfeld aimed straight for the bar. Cibulka remained standing in front of the swinging door, awkward in her stiff taffeta dress. She didn't know anyone. In the overhead lighting her face didn't look as pimply. Her figure under the taffeta looked quite attractive. I'll kill you, lily-of-the-valley! But in keeping with my character I took the line of least resistance; I walked over to the rejected author and said with a Judas-like smile: 'Would you care to dance?'

She smiled gratefully and floated into my arms.

With someone like you at least I know where I am, I thought. I cut a fancy step which I copied from the showoffs I had seen at the Café Boulevard. The hell with it all. I twirled her around; she knew what she was doing. Obviously the gay life she had written about had some personal experience behind it. She pirouetted smartly under my uplifted arm; the taffeta skirt swirled high over her knees. With a girl like you I know where I stand, I repeated to myself, and that was a feeling so rare in recent days that it took on a special value. I turned on my heel, then stamped my foot, clapped my hands. I saw Blumenfeld, her face shining with animation, conversing with the two Nordics. The stand-in for James Dean had a swollen face. I recalled that as a Jewish orphan child, Blumenfeld had spent some time in Norway and spoke fluent Norwegian. And I knew from Dr Ehrlich that Norwegians and Danes understood one another quite well.

As expected, Cibulka turned out to be the complete opposite of Lenka Silver. She danced as passionately as if she were going to get paid for her efforts; she consumed tobacco like a Dutch sailor, sucking in the smoke with avid nose and mouth. Her shyness obviously evaporated in an environment which was more familiar. Soon we understood each other perfectly. And soon we both felt quite warm and decided to step outside.

The night was cool. The full moon was no longer fragmented by the lake; the surface of the water was totally calm. The twin lunar disks shone serenely off to the right of us. Close to the shore stood Vasek's tent. I took Cibulka around the waist. A small wooden pier jutted out from the sandy shore, with several rowboats bobbing up and down alongside. They were bumping softly against each other, making a hollow wooden sound.

'Let's go for a ride! Come on!' whispered Cibulka. A ride? Why not. It's all just one long, trite amusement-park ride, so why not try all the amusements? I pulled one of the boats close to the pier. CHARON was written in crooked letters across the bow; the practical joke of some vacationing intellectual. I reached out to Cibulka; she scrambled in, holding her wrinkled taffeta dress, almost losing her balance. I sat down behind her. We pushed off: I silently dropped the oars into the water and leaned into them. We were gliding on the dark surface, the water rustling pleasantly under the prow. In the moonlight, her face looked white and touching. Steep rocks jutted out on the other side of the lake, bare except for a few stunted pines.

We were rapidly moving away from the lighted hotel, from the mystery, from the wailing jazz.

'This is something you should write about,' I said, just to break the silence. 'The Chief would love it. A summer night, a boy and a girl, a silvery lake . . .'

'I wouldn't know how,' Cibulka interrupted me. 'That's for poets. I am no good at lyrical moods and things like that.'

'What are you good at?'

'Nothing. Everything comes back rejected.'

The oars splashed in the water. A strange conversation for such a scene. A fish broke the black surface.

'How did you get started, anyway?'

'What?'

'Writing.'

She paused. Then she said: 'I was unhappy. So I started writing poems.'

'Unhappy love affair?'

'Well, yes.'

I rowed silently for a while, my thoughts drifting back towards my own beginnings. They are similar, almost identical. And then my own end, my literary end. What will be the end of Jarmila Cibulka?

'I used to keep a diary,' she said. 'Like all girls, you know. A lot of useless philosophical twaddle. And then I read Hemingway. It was a lousy translation, it was done before the war, but all the same he made me see that it isn't necessary to philosophize. You just write the truth, and yet the philosophy's there all the same. You understand? So I started writing prose. But it isn't worth a damn. Hemingway knew what he was doing. I don't.'

I wanted to cheer her up. 'I think you write extremely well. A little differently than Hemingway, of course.'

'So why don't they want to publish it?'

'Is it that important to you?'

She paused a long time. Then she said: 'Yes, it is.'

'Why?'

She trembled, pulled a handkerchief out of her handbag, and blew her nose. Some white object fell out of the bag. 'You dropped something,' I said.

She examined it. It was a letter. She picked it up and put it back in her handbag with the handkerchief.

'I'm cold,' she said.

'Shall we go back?'

'Please.'

I turned the boat around and the lights of the hotel weakly illuminated Cibulka's face.

'Why is it so important to you?' I asked again. 'Do you want to be famous?'

'No, it isn't that.' She shook her head, which looked quite dark in the moonlight. 'No, I don't care about that. But I have nothing else. Now they've thrown me out of the Home, and writing is all I've got.'

'No young man?'

She stared at the water, then pulled out the handkerchief and again blew her nose. She turned her white, pitiful face towards me; the lights of the hotel windows sparkled in her eyes, just as the world used to be mirrored in the eyes of Lenka Silver. The boat rubbed against the pier. I jumped out, wound the chain around the post and helped Cibulka out of the boat. I embraced her. 'You poor soul,' I said. She pressed against me with all her might. I kissed her. Everything had become as clear as the calendar moon over the postcard lake.

We returned to the hotel, arm in arm. A man stood before the entrance, smoking. As we passed him he took a puff and the glowing tip of the cigar lit up his face. It was old Vavrousek from the proofreading department. He grinned at us, but didn't say anything. We entered.

In the main hall, the bacchanalia was mounting in frenzy. Blumenfeld was shrieking out some Norwegian song, while one of the Danes – the swollen-faced one, of course – was fondling her magnificent breasts. Salajka and Kopanec had their arms around each other and were bellowing at the top of their voices. Lenka Silver – was not there. Neither was the Chief. I scanned the room. Two couples were still stumbling around the dance floor as if they were the finalists in a dance marathon. At a table in the corner, Annie was hugging a young new editor from the graphic arts department. Benes was lying in a deep coma next to the piano. Not a sign of the snake, nor of the Pied Piper.

'Come on!' Cibulka said, pulling me impatiently by the sleeve. My legs resisted, but only slightly. Cibulka was dragging me up the stairs, towards the guest rooms. She was exuding some sort of penetrating but pleasant scent. Ah, to hell with mysteries! I am not a crossword fan. Nor a researcher. Nor a detective. And you, dear lily, are no mystery, but an ordinary girl who sings stupid songs at a campfire and shivers in a tent. To hell with you, to hell with you, I repeated to myself all the way up to my room. But I didn't succeed in sending her to hell. I couldn't get her out of my head, not even when I was undressing Cibulka, not even when the physiologic moment drew near and I thought I had exorcized her for ever. No. I failed. She appeared to me again, with her black pupil-less eyes, her breasts tanned all the way to the invisible nipples. And in the dream which I dreamt later that night, it was her tousled head – and not that of the author of *Between Us Girls* – that rested on my bare shoulder.

I was awakened by furious banging on the door.

'Karel! Get up! Quickly!'

I recognized Salajka's voice. He seemed extremely excited.

'What is it?'

Cibulka turned over and grumbled something in a half-awake way.

Salajka screamed from behind the door, 'The Chief – he's drowned!'

'You're joking!'

'It's true! Hurry up!'

I scrambled out of bed. Cibulka opened her eyes. 'What did he say?'

'I don't know. He's probably still drunk. Go back to sleep.'

But she was already climbing out of bed and reaching for her bra.

I dressed as quickly as I could and was ready to fly out the door.

'Wait!' Cibulka shouted. 'See if anybody's out there.'

I opened the door a little. I saw the backs of several people who were quickly walking towards the stairs. Otherwise the corridor was empty.

'It's all right.'

Cibulka, back to her shy, awkward self, nervously left. I watched her disappear into her own room. Then I went out myself, locked the door, and ran downstairs.

People were milling around in the dining room. Excitement and sensationalism hung in the air. Kopanec left a group of ladies and nodded at me.

'What's up?' I asked.

'He's had it,' he said happily. 'Remember me telling you about the finger of God? It works! Yesterday he told me in confidence that my collection of stories had no substance and that he was returning it to me for rewriting.'

'So you bumped him off?'

He grimaced: 'Unfortunately somebody else got to him first.'

'What actually happened?'

Dr Ehrlich's wife, obviously terrified, stepped over to us, with the distraught Pecakova at her heels. In a helterskelter manner they told me about it. It seemed that the hotel cook, who was a fanatical health faddist, had gone for his usual early morning dip in the lake, and had found a corpse lying on the shore, where it had apparently been washed up by the undertow. There was a bruise on the temple, but according to the cook this did not at all look like a mortal wound. The anonymous man had drowned. He hadn't remained nameless for long. The desk clerk was called, and he immediately recognized our Chief. Then it occurred to the two men to count the boats, and one of them turned out to be missing. A mist was hanging over the lake at the moment, and it was therefore impossible to see the missing boat, but groups of searchers had already gone out to look for it. The police had, of course, been notified.

We all sat down around the tables and sank into respectful silence.

*

I thought about my dear old Chief, and somehow I couldn't care less whether he was alive or dead. But I thought about him all the same. I recalled how he had interviewed me for my job, back in 1949, in the era of berets and denims. I remember the many years during which he had been in firm control, always active, diligent, well-informed. He had aged, lost his hair, and under the strict guidance of Comrade Kaiser, he had built himself an impressive monument in the history of Czech literature. In this mausoleum were buried manuscripts which would never see the light of day, deleted passages, refined phraseology, censored classics, reams of various forewords, afterwords, and introductions, mountains of dusty socialist-realist novels, translations of socialist-realist novels which nobody asked for and nobody read, piles of memoranda for meetings and conferences which traced the gradual zigzag retreat from those wonderful early, pure days when yes meant yes and no meant no.

With the tactical suppleness of a field marshal, the Chief had always managed to consolidate his front lines, pressed on one flank by the well informed Comrade Kaiser, and on the other by modernistic poets, eccentric intellectuals, avant garde troublemakers clustered around the journal *The Spring*. In the end, he had managed to liquidate that publication, but somehow or other he had been forced to accept its aesthetic norms, at least as far as original poetry was concerned, which was to be my theatre of operations.

In his never-ending battle against the terror of the snobs, he had scored a number of decisive victories; for example, he managed to wipe out a thin volume of dirty folksongs which had originally been collected in the early nineteenth century by the aristocratic, lecherous patriot Honzik, and which had been banned during Honzik's lifetime by Hapsburg censorship. He succeeded in liquidating the translation of a novel by a black writer who used certain offensive words in describing conditions in Harlem. He decimated a poetess who dared to submit a collection of calligraphs that Comrade Kaiser found himself unable to decipher. The mausoleum also contained several volumes of the Chief's own poetry, celebrating the time-honoured virtues of native soil, hammers and ploughshares, Prague the golden city, and the people's revolution – in the time-honoured manner of second-rate poets who disappear into literary archives without a trace.

And then the antique-filled villa, with a headless cupid in the garden. And a wife whom I knew so well, and who thought so little of him. And his first wife, whom he divorced and who was now supposedly a conductor on trolleycar number 22. And the Jewish fiancée whom Kopanec had told me about, dead these many years.

What else did he leave behind? An obituary in the newspaper, obligatory for men of his rank. And the mausoleum. Those are the remains of that wily old prostitute, my Chief.

A pile of junk, that's all that will be left of any of us. We have lost our old peasant heads, our old peasant honour. All of us.

They are all gone out of the way, they are together become unprofitable; there is none that doeth good, no, not one.

I got up and walked out of the hotel.

A group of people was just coming back from the landing, among them Dr Ehrlich.

'We found the boat!' he called out to me. I nodded. I wasn't really interested. I set out along the shore of the lake towards a white tent glistening in the bushes.

The canvas sides were fluttering in the breeze. I approached quietly, listened. The sound of regular breathing came from the tent. I scratched against the canvas with my fingernail. Lenka was awake.

'Who is it?' I heard her familiar voice.

'Me. Leden. Could you come out for a moment?'

'Vasek is still sleeping.'

'Then come out yourself.'

'What do you want?' The voice betrayed neither resistance nor mistrust.

'I want to tell you something. It concerns neither you nor me. Somebody drowned during the night.'

Silence.

'Who?'

'The Chief,' I said. Something rustled inside the tent, the canvas top billowed and out popped a small tousled head. Neither the night nor the morning had left any traces on her. She looked perfectly beautiful, straight out of a toothpaste ad.

'What did you say?'

'The Chief drowned. They found him on the shore.'

'Good Lord!' she gasped. 'How did it happen?'

'I don't know.'

She stared at me with those impenetrable black buttons, then glanced towards the hotel.

'Not a single tear?' I said softly.

She didn't answer me and disappeared inside the tent. 'Venca!' I heard the unbelievable nickname with which she addressed my sleeping friend. 'Venca! Wake up! Something's happened!'

Quietly I returned to the hotel. A police car was just pulling up at the entrance.

The captain in charge of the investigation gathered us together in the taproom, and then called us one after another into the adjoining room for interrogation. Through the taproom window I could see the landing, the boat, and two men who were working on it. They were checking for fingerprints on the seat and on the oars.

Our ranks in the taproom were rapidly thinning out. They had interrogated Salajka, Cibulka, Blumenfeld, the Ehrlichs, who were all sent into the restaurant. My turn came at 9.30.

The captain asked me to tell him exactly and in detail everything I remembered from the previous night that might in my opinion have any bearing on the accident. I said that I had not been paying much attention to the Chief, that in my view he had been extremely inebriated, had apparently gone out for a breath of fresh air, had rowed out on the lake and drowned.

'Did Comrade Prochazka have a quarrel with anyone?'

I shook my head. 'That is to say . . . he had plenty of quarrels, but they were of a literary nature.'

'Was there any sharp exchange of opinions last night between him and anyone else? Did anything of that kind occur?'

Of course I knew at once what he was aiming at. They must have informed him. I looked out at the boat, where the two detectives were still busy at work. An inscription glimmered on the bow. I strained my eyes. Yes. It was difficult to read the crooked, amateurishly painted letters, but there was no doubt what they spelled: CHARON. I turned back to the captain.

'But it was an accident, wasn't it?'

'What makes you think so?'

'What else could it be?'

The captain gazed at me intently. He looked like a detective from an amateur play.

'Prochazka's temple shows signs of a blow by a blunt object. There is dried blood on one of the oars. Also on a cap which we found in the boat,' said the captain and lifted a green checkered cap from the table. I quickly went over all the occasions when I had seen the cap, and it formed a consistent, intelligible chain.

'That doesn't belong to him,' I said.

'No?'

'No. That belongs to a certain Zamberk. The two of them got drunk together last night. But if the two of them had been in the boat together, Zamberk would have been the one who'd have drowned. He was much more soused than Prochazka. And much less used to alcohol.'

The captain pensively turned the cap in his hand.

'He must have borrowed it from Zamberk. He was in a joking mood,' I said.

'We'll check that.'

'He must have banged his head against the oar as he fell out of the boat.'

'Or else somebody banged him over the head.'

'It's true the Chief had a fight with Miss Cibulka. They may have told you about that. She was mad at him because he rejected her manuscript. She's a little hysterical. But it was an unfortunate accident all the same, Comrade Captain.'

The captain continued to mull something over. He reached into his briefcase, pulled out an envelope and handed it to me. It contained a name and address: 'Jarmilla Cibulka, teacher, Home for Delinquent Girls, Pilousy, district of Prague.'

'We found that in the boat,' said the captain.

'When was he seen last?' I asked.

'At 1.30, leaving the hotel.'

'I see. And didn't Miss Cibulka tell you where she was at that time?'

The captain shrugged.

'Did she tell you?'

'No,' I said. 'She didn't have to.'

'What do you mean?'

Clearly, Cibulka had not boasted to the captain about her little adventure. And he probably hadn't hit upon it as yet. He was still collecting information, but he had already formed a hypothesis. And since he obviously hadn't confronted Cibulka with the letter, there was no need for her to give an account of her nocturnal excursion. I felt sorry for the captain, but I had to destroy his neat little hypothesis.

'She was with me,' I said. 'From about one o'clock until dawn.'

The captain raised his eyebrows in surprise.

'At one we went out for a boat ride. In a boat named the CHARON. I remember Miss Cibulka opening her handbag to get a handkerchief, and the letter dropped out at that time. I called it to her attention. She shoved it back. But she opened the bag a few more times and the letter must have fallen out again.'

'Did anybody see you take that boat ride?'

I remembered the old proofreader. 'Comrade Vavrousek saw us get back. Must have been about 1.30.'

The captain thought a while longer. Or at least he pretended to be thinking. He said at last: 'Thank you. You may go now. Please don't discuss the content of this interview with anyone.'

I got up, bowed, and went out into the restaurant. The others were sitting there clustered in small groups, rather dispirited, trying not to discuss the content of their interviews. Lenka was not among them. Neither was Vasek. They will undoubtedly give Vasek a good going over, I thought. I ordered black coffee and sat down next to Cibulka, who was as pale as a wax doll. She was wearing her rumpled taffeta dress, which looked more absurd than ever in the morning light. She was whispering to Blumenfeld.

'So what do you say?' that Amazon asked me eagerly.

I shrugged. 'He got soused and fell in.'

She waved her hand in irritation.

'To hell with that. I mean what are we going to do? I think we should stick Cibulka's manuscript right under the new chief's nose, don't you? You have any idea who the new chief will be?'

16 *Scene with Kopanec*

No decision had yet been made about the new chief. For the time being our realm was governed by Benes, and there was no sense in trying to get anything new past him. His first independent decision was to authorize a collection of essays marking the sixtieth birthday of Academician Brat.

The police investigated the Chief's death a few more days, but then they issued an official statement which declared that he had died as the result of an unfortunate mishap caused by excessive consumption of alcohol. On Thursday, the drowned alcoholic had a glorious funeral, attended by one high-ranking and several not-so-high-ranking officials. Among the floral tributes was a giant wreath wired by Academician Brat from Moscow.

The Chief's wife, the only survivor, wore a black dress with a short veil, and was supported on one side by Zulva and on the other by Benes. She didn't actually look like a woman in need of support. Everyone tried to look grave and dignified, but the atmosphere inside the crematorium was surprisingly moisture-free. Only when the coffin with its immense load of flowers had pompously disappeared behind the gilded gate, was there a sound of sobbing, coming from Comrade Pecakova sitting one row ahead of me.

Then we went home. In the crematorium I kept looking for Lenka, but she wasn't there. Whatever there may have been between her and the Chief, he evidently had not been worth a last goodbye.

I paid a visit to the Chief's widow. She was sitting on the Empire chaise-longue, still dressed in mourning, and amusing herself with Marie Brizard. I tried to express my sympathy but she asked me to stop joking.

'His whole life, he was such a cautious old woman,' she said in lieu of a eulogy. 'But at least he ended in style. To fall dead drunk into a lake! That's what I call a proper poet's end.'

'In textbooks they'll compare him to Shelley,' I said.

'That's about the only thing that he ever had in common with any poet.' Then she changed the topic. 'I understand you're having a little affair with that girl writer who had a fight with him that night.'

I shook my head.

'Don't be coy with me! They saw you dragging her into your room.'

'They? Who is "they"?'

'Annie saw you. That's typical of you. You wouldn't help her get the manuscript published. You'd rather give her a consolation prize.'

'I was stewed.'

'You know they tried to pin Emil's death on her? For a time it looked like murder.'

'I know,' I said. 'I had the honour to serve as an alibi.'

'Don't think for a minute you performed a noble deed. There was no need for an alibi, anyway. Murder! Who would go to the trouble of murdering Emil?'

I pursed my lips. 'I could name quite a few.'

'I know. Pejchold, Prouza, Randacek, Sebestakova, and so on and so on.' These were some of the most notorious of the Chief's victims, who had been liquidated mainly as a result of pressure from above. The poet Randacek suffered the worst fate; he had been convicted of Trotskyism in 1952 and was sentenced to twenty years. The only part the Chief had played in this affair was to order the destruction of Randacek's works as soon as the poet was arrested. When the trial opened, the Chief decided to undergo a gall-bladder operation, saved for many years for just such an occasion. The Chief was thus unable to testify. Kocour had seen the Chief's action as a rather courageous one under the circumstances; after all, every surgical operation involved a definite risk.

At present, Randacek was still in jail. Six months after this affair Sebestakova was fired. It was discovered that she had been the wartime mistress of a resistance hero who subsequently turned out to be a counter-revolutionary revisionist. This disclosure coincided with an attack of post-operative complications on the Chief's part, requiring renewed hospitalization, so that the actual firing was performed by Benes. No, the Chief was certainly no ogre who deserved to be cursed beyond the grave. He simply was not endowed with extraordinary courage.

'I know Pejchold and Prouza very well,' said the Chief's widow. 'Nothing much happened to them, and they are dyed-in-the-wool realists. They'd never do anything like that.' She took a gulp of Marie Brizard brandy. 'No. I expected him to be doused with acid by some jealous secretary or something like that. Any hunches?'

I shook my head. I recalled a string of jilted mistresses, but they had all managed either to get married or to find themselves other attachments. No.

'So our Emil's gone,' she said, her voice turning hoarse. The headless cupid in the fountain glistened from the first autumn rain. 'I hope you'll at least quickly publish one of his books as a posthumous gesture. I'll need the money, so see what you can do.'

I winked at her. 'First thing tomorrow morning I'll suggest to Benes that we put out the Collected Works of Emil Prochazka. He'll be wild about it!'

A cuckoo popped out of the carved clock. I noticed for the first time that the bird's head had been replaced by the head of an infant Jesus wearing a gilded crown – the result of some practical joke. The hallowed bird cuckooed six times, a requiem mass for Emil Prochazka, poet laureate who went the way of all flesh towards complete oblivion.

The next day I received a printed announcement to the effect that Miss Lenka Silver would soon cease to be a miss. That pleasurable epoch of her life was destined to come to an end on Saturday at the Old Town Hall, where she was to become the bride of Vasek Zamberk. I attached the card to the headboard of my bed, and covered it with a piece of black cloth. I lay in bed for quite a while, gazing at this product of gallows humour.

There isn't a thing I can do, I thought to myself, I can't even ruin you for Vasek, my treacherous lily-of-the-valley. Of course, I didn't think this seriously; it was just a little cynical game, and cynicism heals everything. I have no power over you, my dear miss. Unless . . .

A thin thread of an idea ran through my mind. Just a foolish, ridiculous idea, without any substance whatever. Without proof I had no power. Without proof, an idea is just a phantasmagoric image of the truth.

Still, I couldn't get the idea out of my head. I gazed at the card with its banal emblem of interlocking wedding rings. I read: *Lenka Silver . . . Vasek Zamberk . . . take great pleasure . . .* I liked the idea better and better, as if it fitted into some Poirot-like *dénouement*, a triumph not of justice but of . . . I stopped my ridiculous daydreaming and slapped my own face. Madness! Unchecked fantasy run wild! Fantasy, the refuge of failures. Those who can, do; those who can't, fantasize. Faulkner. Unquote.

I got up and went out. It was a mild September evening; there were rings around the streetlights. Following some vague instinct I took a streetcar into the centre of the city. On Wenceslas Square I ran into Kopanec.

As usual, he was in a talkative mood and my reticence provided just the right encouragement. He had just been hit by a strange misfortune: he had inherited two apartment houses from an aged uncle, but both buildings were heavily mortgaged. Kopanec's droll wit turned the story into a political anecdote. We were strolling along, ogling sexbombs that kept emerging out of the light mist. Wild riffs of jazz were blaring out of the wide windows of the old Boulevard. It had been years since I had been there, and years since they had played jazz. I did not resist when the Master dragged me in. As we climbed the staircase, I listened with one ear to his story about the readiness of the State to accept both buildings as a gift, providing the private donor had paid all debts and mortgages appertaining thereto.

Attractive girls were swarming over the dance floor. Kopanec was evidently rolling in money, in spite of his inherited debts. We sat down at a table beside the dance floor sexed up with flashing red, purple and green lights. Kopanec ordered a bottle of vodka and began to read to me the draft of a letter addressed to the office of the President of the Republic.

The letter was based on a rather unusual theory of socio-economic law. Kopanec demanded that since the People were the rightful owner of everything within the borders of the State, and since he, Kopanec, was a twelve-millionth part of that same People, he should be paid out a sum equal to one twelve-millionth of the total assets of the State, minus a sum equal to the amount of the mortgage attached to the two buildings donated to the People, the latter sum to be used to redeem the said mortgages.

It occurred to me that if he was really serious about sending that letter, he was about to commit his last fuckup.

I asked him what was happening to his short stories.

'They are being revised by Benes,' he said drily, and turned his head to follow a girl in a bright red skirt who whirled by us like a rocket. An eccentrically dressed young man went leaping after her.

'You're lucky,' I said. 'Benes is easier to get around than our dear old departed. You should be able to manoeuvre it through.'

Literature did not enjoy a very high ranking in the Master's system of values. 'You see that? See that chick?' he tugged at my sleeve, his eyes shining. Then he turned wistful. 'Too bad I've grown so fat. These acrobatics are beyond me now. Still, maybe if I just went up to her . . . and maybe . . .' He roused himself from his daydream and turned to me absentmindedly: 'What was it you were saying?'

'That we might finally publish your stuff, now that the Chief is with the Good Lord.'

The red skirt disappeared in the frenetic swarm and Kopanec freed himself from her spell. He latched on to the mention of the Good Lord. 'I must say, this was one time God really showed us his divine wisdom. And that doesn't happen too often. Have you noticed that it's mainly the good people who die off?'

'It's a cruel world,' I replied. 'But he sure had a classy end. A poet drowning on a drunken spree – this must be the first such case in Czech literature.'

Unfortunately, the red skirt again emerged on the horizon and monopolized Kopanec's attention. My own attention was drawn to a certain gentleman who was watching the rock-and-rolling girl from behind a table half-hidden by a pillar. He had that professional look of bored persistence that's typical of plainclothes policemen. Kopanec took a drink and returned to our topic of conversation. He said in a strange, almost mocking tone: 'Our Chief's case is certainly unique in the history of Czech literature.'

'What do you mean?'

Contrary to his habit, he didn't launch immediately into a stream of chatter, but he gave me a long, searching look. 'Let's not beat around the bush. You didn't exactly love the Chief, you old bastard, did you? You just kissed his ass to get along, right?'

'That's exactly right.'

I grimaced, and Kopanec did the same. 'Well, let me tell you that Comrade Prochazka had the unique opportunity of becoming the Czech Maxwell Bodenheim.'

'Who?'

'You call yourself a poet, you jerk, and you don't know ...'

'You mean that American ...'

'Of course,' Kopanec said. I didn't get it. I knew very little about the American poet, and I didn't see what he could possibly have in common with Emil Prochazka.

'Just think a little harder,' said Kopanec.

I thought and thought, but nothing significant occurred to me. I had a vague recollection of some of Bodenheim's poems from an old Untermeyer anthology, which I had borrowed from the American Information Service library just before the February coup, and which I thought it more prudent not to bother returning. But the poems seemed to have little in common with the literary creations of our departed Chief.

'I really don't know what you are driving at.'

'Just squeeze your noodle a little harder. I hope you follow the minor cultural news reported in the daily press.'

Minor cultural ... something began to stir in my brain. It was once again the zigzag thread of a ridiculous idea. It led me to a photograph of a dingy hole somewhere on the Lower East Side of New York, a crumpled, vomit-soiled man lying on the ground, a dark spot of dried blood between his shoulder blades. My knees began to shake.

'You're joking!'

'I am not joking, you jerk,' said Kopanec, in an oddly gentle voice.

The detective-like gentleman left his observation post and surreptitiously edged closer to the dance floor, where a young man was gyrating with the red-skirted girl.

'And I know just who it was that performed this benevolent act on behalf of Czech literature,' said Kopanec. 'And I'll tell you, because I am the only witness. I didn't say a word to the police. So if by any chance you lose your nerve and go babbling to the fuzz, I'll deny the whole thing. I'm safe. They'll believe that I dreamed the whole thing up, because I am a notoriously unreliable character, anyway.'

He was ogling the pirouetting skirt, which was bouncing back orange shadows from the glare of the green reflector.

'Let's have it!' I said impatiently.

'Don't piss your pants!' said the Master, but he tore his eyes away from the whirling girl. 'That night I got drunk with your beloved friend, a certain Comrade Zamberk.'

A shiver ran up my back.

'Around 1.30 I felt the need to heave,' continued the Master of Fuckups. 'When I am in some recreational area I hate to throw up into the toilet – I prefer to do it in the grass. So I went outside. It was a beautiful moonlit night.' He took a gulp of vodka.

The ants running up and down my back had turned to drops of sweat. Perspiration ran down my spine, and I felt an almost unbearable tension in my brain. The official-looking gentleman strode on to the dance floor and addressed the girl in the red skirt. Fortunately, the Master did not notice.

'All right, go on!'

'It was a beautiful, cool, moonlit night. The moon was bathing in the lake, which had been formed as a result of socialist planning and building.'

He paused, for he at last noticed the increasingly heated argument between the girl and the man.

'Go on, for God's sake! What happened?'

'The moon glistened on the surface of the water, like an undulating silver calligraph. It was as calm and still as in a temple, the monumental temple of Nature. Then . . .'

Events on the dance floor distracted the Master from the Chief's fate. The man was shouting something about suggestive gestures and immorality and public decency. The Master of Fuckups flushed with anger and got to his feet. 'Quiet, citizen! Do not disturb the well earned rest of the working people with your shouting and screaming!' he outshouted the officious gentleman. He scanned the hall. 'Manager! Where is the manager? Take that man away from here!' he called out like a demagogue and headed for the disputants on the dance floor. 'This man is creating a public nuisance! Where are the police? Call the police!'

Perhaps it was an expression of the Master's gallant, knightly sentiments. But he was in the habit of creating a disturbance now and again, just to legitimize his title as Master of Fuckups. And maybe he wanted to show off before the red-skirted girl, whom he could not impress by his dancing ability. In any case, at that moment I was so furious at him I could have killed him myself. I was so impatient to hear the rest that bloody circles swam before my eyes.

Naturally, the confrontation on the dance floor ended in a victory for the forces of law and order. The gentleman identified himself as a police officer and was ready to arrest the Master as well as the dancing couple. Kopanec seemed pleased at the prospect, but he had bad luck. The manager finally arrived on the scene; he knew Kopanec, and exerted unasked-for influence to have him freed. Soon everything was back to normal. At the behest of the official gentleman, the band put away its saxophones, pulled out its violins, and the lilting strains of gypsy folk music soon exorcized the spirit of rock-and-roll. Kopanec returned to his bottle of vodka, cursing the State and its organs. After a while I managed to steer him back to the events of the fateful night.

'Where were we? Oh yes,' he said. 'Well, as I was saying – moonlit night, lake, and similar beauties of nature. And then, suddenly, I heard the splashing of oars. I was just throwing up in the bushes near the little landing bridge, I was almost done, and I pricked up my ears .... Goddamn it! I should have socked that police bastard in the jaw!' he burst into an alcoholic fit of temper, and it took all my cunning to get him to resume his narrative. 'All right then. To put it briefly. There was a light mist over the lake and I saw the shadow of a boat in the mist. But I couldn't make out who was in the boat.'

He took another gulp. I saw the scene clearly outlined before me, for my own experience that night had been almost identical. A boat. A cool mist over the lake. Moonlight.

'And then the boat sailed into a bright silver strip and I saw the silhouettes of two figures. One of the heads seemed to reflect the moonlight; it must have been bald.'

'And the other?' I asked, outwardly still calm.

'The other looked dark and tousled. The head of a woman.'

I felt cold drops of sweat on my spine. 'Are you serious?'

Kopanec raised three fingers in the air. 'I swear to God, if he exists,' he leaned towards me. 'A few hours earlier your Chief had a fight with a certain Cibulka. A hysterical girl with very little self-control, and with a dark tousled head of hair. And with a motive,' he added significantly.

'Go on! She wouldn't kill him for a lousy manuscript!'

Kopanec grinned.

'People have been known to kill for a pack of cigarettes. And this hysterical young lady, my friend, lives for nothing but literature. I know that type. I have met quite a few in my day.' He waved his arm. My zigzagging idea threaded its way through my mind, but it was still eluding me.

'Graphomania plus hysteria equals homicidal mania,' said Kopanec.

I glimpsed a spark.

'Listen,' I interrupted him. 'You got drunk with Zamberk. What was he doing when you were heaving?'

'Him? About half an hour earlier we took him and his girlfriend into the tent. More precisely, we carried him into the tent. He was really stoned.'

'And the girlfriend?'

'I don't know. She crawled in the tent after him. She must have been trying to keep him alive all night with her body heat, because he was out cold.'

I didn't answer. A definite picture was beginning to take shape in my head.

'Why don't you say something?' asked Kopanec. 'I hope I didn't scare you out of your wits. Just a standard, routine murder. Or rather, the hand of God.' He crossed himself derisively. I felt myself trembling. 'Good Lord, I hope you won't shit in your pants! You look all in! I haven't said anything, you understand? I was just joking anyway. I made the whole thing up as a practical joke. Are you all right? You look like you're dying of a heart attack.'

I was shaken by strange chills. As if the negative of some photograph had suddenly turned into a positive before my eyes. Or as if a puzzle was falling into place, piece by piece, until ... what? Yes. The picture of a man with waxed moustaches, Hercule Poirot, who wasn't playing a part in this tragicomedy at all. The story was ending as his stories ended. Only this was not a story; it was reality.

I shook my head. 'I'm all right. It's just ... the story is so hard to believe ... it's so sensational ...'

'No sensation. Mystery,' said Kopanec. 'My own mystification, actually. My exaggerated phantasmagoria.'

No. My phantasmagoria. And to stretch believability a little further, who should appear out of thin air but Blumenfeld, accompanied by a slightly puffy-faced Dane. She was wearing a fantastic body-hugging dress, with a large abstract design and a deep cutout over her fantastic bosom. Latest imported fashion. Phantasmagoria. She spotted us.

'Hello, gentlemen,' she called out in a voice resembling a tin trumpet. The Dane mumbled something in an incomprehensible language. But I understood. I understood everything. The last piece dropped into place in the mosaic of this crime. I stared at the blue numbers tattooed on Dasha's bare arm, just slightly under the elbow.

17 *Black mass*

And so, in spite of all my resolutions, I found myself once again in the Avenue of November Nineteenth. I was standing on the sidewalk in front of the window from which a baritone sax had once blared into the street, and I gazed at the green portal of the building on the other side, and at a certain window just under the roof. The saxophone was mute, but the sun was still bathing the top floors with yellow light, and Lenka Silver was standing in the open window, examining a stocking by holding it up against the sky.

It was Thursday afternoon, rain was in the air, and on Saturday Lenka Silver would cease to exist. I went up and rang her bell. She opened the door and smiled at me. 'Hello.'

'Hello. Don't get the wrong idea. I'm not here to congratulate you.'

'You're not supposed to, anyway, until after the wedding.'

'May I come in?'

The legendary cat ambled out of the apartment, lit up by the sun like a transparent aquarium. The cat stretched lazily, fixed me with his yellow-green eyes. Lenka Silver hesitated.

'I just want to tell you something. Don't be afraid.'

'Come in then.'

I followed her in. In her black-and-white blouse and stylish metal belt she looked like a jewel set in the gold monstrance of the room. I watched her as if she were far away. She sat down in the wicker armchair, crossed her legs; her knee winked at me erotically. The cat jumped up on the round table, turning into a motionless figurine of black porcelain. The old pink and blue mystic sky of that mystic street hung outside the window.

'So you're getting married on Saturday,' I said.

'Yes. I hope that ...'

'What?'

'That you have no hard feelings ... or bitterness ... or ...

'I certainly do. I wanted to marry you myself.'

'As far as I know, all you wanted to do was to sleep with me.'

'At first. But then I wanted to marry you.'

'Unfortunately, we are living in a monogamous society.'

'At least you will sleep with me then. After all, that's done quite often in our society.'

'But not by me.'

'Not even under exceptional circumstances?'

'Never. On principle.'

'As you think best. Is Vasek coming?'

'No. He went to Moravia to pick up his parents.' She glanced at me. 'But in case you have any ideas, let me assure you that I can defend myself. I think you know that by now.'

I took a deep breath, and said: 'I don't think you'll be able to defend yourself.'

Lenka Silver smiled. 'I trust you are not going to molest me.'

'I'm afraid I am.'

A glass ball was standing on the table, containing the tiny figure of a black cat. Lenka Silver picked it up and snow began to fall inside the ball.

'I wouldn't advise you to try anything like that.' She rested her hand with the crystal globe in her lap; the snow gradually stopped falling.

'A dangerous weapon,' I said. 'It might even kill a man. But you'd better put it on the table. I believe we will come to a friendly understanding. Or at least an unfriendly understanding.'

The cat's green pupils rested on me; the animal gave a brief, distrustful sniff. Lenka Silver did not put the ball away. She said: 'I doubt it.'

'You really think so? I wouldn't rely on that little toy, if I were you.' I pointed at the ball; the miniature cat was now placidly sitting in an immobile snowdrift. 'I'll tell you a story. It happened at Zivohost, during our office outing.'

I paused. The sun touched the horizon, a single golden beam was shining into the room, right into Lenka Silver's eyes. Something was happening right in front of me which violated all the laws of physics: Lenka Silver's eyes glowed with a black, bewitched light. I began to utter my black mass.

'At around 1.30 in the morning I went out for a breath of fresh air. The moon was bright. I saw a boat on the lake. I recognized the Chief ...'

I waited. The pink-nailed fingers clutched the ball tighter. A veil of flakes lifted from the snowbank and began to circle the black figurine of the cat.

I finished the sentence: '... and you.'

She smiled. 'You seem to suffer from night blindness.'

'Then Mr Kopanec would have to have the same ailment. He was there with me.'

She didn't say anything. The black light fell on my face. I felt its pressure. Then it bathed the infernal animal on the table. This dark light emanating from her eyes formed a black link between us. For the first time, I was able to penetrate the reflecting surface. What I saw there frightened me.

I continued: 'In the morning they found the Chief's corpse on the shore. There was a wound on his temple which showed that he might have been stunned by some blunt object. One of the oars had traces of blood. They suspected Cibulka because she had quarrelled with the Chief. But she had a perfect alibi.'

The ebony eyes burned in the pale face; a heavy snowstorm was raging inside the ball.

'What motive could I possibly have?' Lenka Silver asked softly.

'I don't know. But it was you in that boat, wasn't it?'

She bowed her head. The light went out. Somebody opened a well known window across the street and I heard the sound of well known music; a nervous saxophone, writhing like a trapped snake, the hissing of the wire brushes, the pounding of the drum.

'It was you, wasn't it?'

She shook her head. 'God knows what you saw!'

'There was a full moon. It was a very bright night. I saw perfectly clearly. So did Kopanec. We're both ready to testify, if need be.'

My eyes were fixed on the pale Lenka Silver. She gulped. The flames of a blazing pyre seemed reflected in her face, around two infernal coals. The saxophone wailed, the sun was disappearing. All the recurring symbols of that night . . .

Except now it was I who had the upper hand.

'Why didn't you tell this to the police?' she said in a dead voice.

'Can't you guess?'

'Then why didn't Mr Kopanec?'

'He's my good friend. He wouldn't do anything to spoil my fun.'

The pink-nailed hand moved, sank back. Lenka Silver put the glass ball back on the table. The hand hesitantly returned to her lap, found its mate, the two hands joined to form a light brown flower with pink petals.

'In other words, you want to blackmail me,' she said, and looked at me. The darkness was getting thicker, thicker, thicker.

I crossed my legs, pulled out a cigarette. I smoke very rarely, but this seemed like an exceptionally opportune time for it.

'Why do you call it by that name?' I said. 'Let's just say that I want to save you.'

'What's your price?'

I shrugged. 'If you were as poor as a church mouse, you'd have enough to pay me.' But I couldn't stand the sound of my own cynicism, and added: 'I love you.'

The blackness thickened into opaqueness. She said bitterly, almost challengingly: 'You have very peculiar ideas about love, Comrade Editor. But I am not ready to go along with them. Yes, I was in that boat. Mr Prochazka asked me to go for a ride with him. I was rowing. Then he wanted to change places. He lost his balance. He fell. He hit his head against an oar and fell into the water. He was drunk.'

'Why didn't you help him?'

'He must have fainted. He sank right away. I was afraid to jump in after him.'

'Then why didn't you call for help?'

She bit her lips. 'I got scared,' she said. The sneer on my lips was goading her. 'I got panicky, Comrade Editor. Go ahead. Tell the police. It will be unpleasant, a small scandal, but they can't convict me. I simply got scared ... I was a little tipsy ... so was he ...'

'Are you sure that they can't convict you?'

She shrugged. 'Maybe they can. Maybe there is some law about failure to provide assistance or something of that sort. Go ahead and denounce me.'

I waited. Then I said: 'If I tell the police, they'll accuse you of something far worse than failure to provide assistance.'

'What?'

I waited. A long time. They were killing the snake, it was sobbing softly, the drum roared under a rain of sticks. The sun had vanished, the stars appeared in the window.

'Murder,' I said.

Lenka Silver sighed, laughed uneasily. She repeated: 'What possible motive could I have?'

'You want me to tell you?'

She thought it over, then said darkly: 'Yes.'

I reached for the glass ball, lifted it up. The little cat had a snowy cap. I shook it and the cap turned into a white halo. I said: 'It's an extremely long story. But first let me give you a bit of advice: you could claim that you struck the Chief in self-defence, that he tried to molest you and you became frightened. The police will believe you. Any number of witnesses will testify that the Chief was a woman chaser. But no jury will believe that you were afraid to pull him out of the water. Especially not if I were to tell them how efficiently you save drowning people – when you want to. I am sure you remember that incident this summer, when your fiancé nearly breathed his last?'

She bit her lip again.

'But this was at night. And I was alone with a drunkard.'

'That's another peculiar thing. Why would an attractive young lady get into a boat with a drunkard at half past one in the morning – when her fiancé is sleeping in a tent nearby?'

I put the ball back on the table. 'A mystery, isn't it?' I continued.

'But after I tell you what I know, the mystery will become a lot clearer. And a first class motive for murder will become a lot clearer too.'

She was staring at me with hate.

'Go on,' she said.

I blew cigarette smoke towards the ceiling; the smoke drifted down, momentarily covering the window and the girl's face with a steel curtain.

'It all started with that day at the river. I noticed your cosmetically removed tattoo.'

Lenka Silver mechanically ran the palm of her hand up her arm. The little rectangle was covered by the sleeve of her dress.

'Then I tried to start an affair with you. To snatch you away from Vasek. Actually, at that time you weren't involved with Vasek. It looked hopeful at first. You showed up for a date at the Manes, you accepted an invitation to the Chief's party. Of course, you played hard to get, supposedly on account of Vera, but that's the usual way. So you came to the Chief's party, he made a pass at you, and you didn't play hard to get at all. He hugged you around the waist, just as I had done earlier. You got angry at me, yet let him get away with it. And from that moment you turned completely cold towards me. You cut me off completely.'

'I started going with Vasek,' she said.

'Yes. That's true. But you weren't very consistent. Why did you make a date with the Chief at the Mokka coffeehouse? At that time you and Vasek were already practically engaged!'

The question died away in the gloom, without answer. It was getting dark and I could barely make out Lenka Silver's figure. Her nylon-stockinged knees were still glistening, and so was the pale oval monstrance of her face. The mysterious Lenka Silver. No longer a mystery to me.

She lowered her lids.

'When I came back from summer camp and went to call on you, you had a visitor. He was in the bathroom. Possibly he had just felt the need to relieve himself. Or possibly he went in there to hide. A checkered cap hung in the hall. It looked very much like Vasek's.'

She raised her head.

'It was Vasek's.'

'No, it wasn't. First of all, why would he hide from me?'

'He may have been feeling guilty about Miss Kajetan ...'

I smiled. 'You're very clever. But it so happened that I talked to him the next day. About Miss Kajetan. I reproached him for having slept with her. While I was standing here in your door, I was making a declaration of love to you. Whoever was in the bathroom must have heard me. But when I talked to Vasek the next day, it was obvious that he knew nothing about my feeling towards you. I was taking him to task for betraying our friendship – do you think that he would have sat still for it if he had known about the way I had betrayed him? He is a fool, but not that much of a fool. Conclusion: the man in the bathroom was somebody else. Elementary, my dear Watson.'

She shrugged. 'It was Vasek, all the same.'

'A checkered cap was hanging there. But this cap has lately become quite popular. You can see it all over Prague. It could have been anybody in that bathroom. At first I thought that somebody new, quite unknown to me had entered into the case. But that's against all the rules of a sound detective story.'

She glanced at me. 'What detective story?'

'In any good murder mystery, there are only a few characters, tied together with firm, fateful ties. At first, the detective doesn't know all those ties; he learns about them as the story unfolds.'

She didn't raise the objection that we were not involved in a murder story; she knew that we were.

'No, it was no outsider,' I said. 'It must have been somebody who played an important part in the plot. Somebody whom the detective had been watching from the very beginning. And you see, thanks to you, the detective had done just that. The detective was in love with you, and everything that concerned you was etched in his mind. That's one of the by-products of love. When you love somebody as much as I did, every moment you spend with that person becomes an unforgettable snapshot. And when you examine that snapshot later, all kinds of significant details are visible. Or rather, these details assume significance as time goes on. And that's what happened to me. I looked at the mental snapshot of my beloved mermaid, and I noticed my Chief riding a water-bicycle in the background. Lo and behold – he was sporting the very same checkered cap that Vasek was wearing that messy day in the restaurant.'

Slowly, I released another puff of smoke. Lights had been turned on across the street. The smoke shimmered as it lazily snaked its way towards the window. Lenka Silver's eyes were closed.

I said: 'The man in the bathroom was the Chief.'

The puff of smoke had vanished out of the window. I watched the glowing cap at the tip of my cigarette. Lenka Silver sat in almost complete darkness, her tousled little head outlined against the window like a silhouette cut out of black paper.

'We're back to mystery again, aren't we?' I said. 'What possible reason could a beautiful young girl have to flirt with a man like the Chief? Why the Chief? He was an intellectual like me, he was at least as big a scoundrel as me – and yet you picked him. Even though you dislike scoundrels and literati. Why? I'll tell you.'

I took a deep breath, lowered my eyes. The erotic knees were still shining into the darkness. My temples were pounding, but my ideas flowed easily, arranging themselves into a neat logical chain.

'A literary type did you harm,' I said. 'You never told me just what kind of harm it was. And later on you forgot that it was you who were the supposed victim. You remember that? We were talking about it on our way back from the dog races. And you were startled: *"To me? Ah yes! Of course."* I knew then that you were lying. For if somebody had injured you so grievously you certainly would not have been so readily confused.' The cat meowed, gingerly stepped over the ball containing its miniature likeness, and nuzzled its black face against Lenka Silver's cheek. She remained silent. I continued: 'But I know perfectly well who the real victim was. You had a sister, and she received love poems from Terezin written by a Jewish boy. But speaking precisely those poems were not received *from* Terezin but *in* Terezin. "I am writing to you, Salina, from my window I see so far ..." An obvious echo of Orten's *Seventh Elegy*. I am a poetry editor, you know. That elegy was not published until the war was over. Anybody who had already been familiar with it in wartime must have known Orten quite intimately. And anyone who was close to Orten at that time . . .'

The shoulders of the silhouette swayed slightly. Lenka Silver seemed about to say something, but she remained silent.

'Now let's go back to the Chief,' I said. 'There was one dark period in his life, a mysterious interlude. I happened to find out something about it. Long ago, before the war, he was engaged to a Jewish girl. When the Germans came, he broke off the engagement. The girl later died in a concentration camp. At that time, my Chief had already become a fairly prominent literary figure. Do you understand?'

Silence. Only the green eyes of the cat. The others were invisible.

I sucked in the smoke, the cigarette flared up, there was only a short butt left. I ground it out against the glass tabletop. Lenka Silver remained motionless.

'Let's assume that the Chief's fiancée had a sister. A younger sister. Roughly your age. Let's say that in 1939 she must have been five or six years old, and the sister about nineteen or twenty. That's roughly the difference between you and Salina, isn't it?'

Her silence was my answer. I continued:

'Both girls were sent to Terezin. They had lost their mother long before, and the father died in the camp, so that the older sister had to play both mother and father to the little girl. They must have loved each other more than the normal, routine world can ever understand. But in 1939 people were not yet sent to concentration camps. There was enough time for the family to discuss the broken engagement, and what it meant to the older sister. Not just the usual disgrace, but much, much more . . . This made a deep impression on the little girl. And later, in the camp, when the older sister died, the broken engagement grew into a crime. And because the older sister did not die a natural death, but died under the terrible circumstances of a death camp, the young girl began to see her sister's former fiancé as a vicious murderer.'

The silence continued.

'But this was murder of a special kind,' I continued softly. 'There are no laws to cover it. You cannot accuse a man of committing this kind of crime. You cannot bring him to justice.'

I tried to make out her eyes in the darkness. I couldn't. I added, almost in a whisper: 'Such a crime cannot be punished. It can only be . . . avenged.'

The window frame outlined a starry rectangle over the mystical street. My black mass was nearing an end. The lights went out in the other building. The jazz subsided to the soft level which Lenka Silver enjoyed. But now she was silent. Totally still.

'When the war was ended, too many things happened too fast. Freedom brought joy mixed with pain. The name of that fiancé, that murderer, was such an ordinary, common one. And the girl was only eleven or twelve years old. She didn't know where to look for him, everything was full of confusion. Besides, certain Jewish orphans were taken abroad, to Switzerland, to Denmark, to Sweden, adopted for a time by wealthy Jewish families to let them recuperate physically and mentally. Dasha Blumenfeld spent some time with such a family. And now listen carefully,' I urged my silent listener, as I was about to leap a few years towards the present. 'Let's say that our girl, the child who was sent to Denmark to convalesce, grows up, comes back to her homeland, gets a job in some provincial city. She has now turned into a young lady, she starts thinking about young men. The episode of 1939 is almost forgotten. She often thinks of her sister, of course. But with the passage of time, hate has lost its edge. She is transferred to Prague. She meets a young man, who introduces her to an editor. The editor, in turn, introduces her to his Chief. His name is the same as that of the long-forgotten fiancé. He is a well known literary figure. After February he got rid of a wife who was a possible handicap to his career. When our young lady hears all this, one day at the river, she almost faints. And yet just a short while before she had shown exceptional courage and coolheadedness in saving a drowning man. How do you reconcile all this? There's only one way: by assuming that the girl who almost fainted is the same person as the younger sister of the Chief's dead fiancée. If she is that person, then the fainting fit is easy to understand for a description of the Chief had suddenly loosed a flood of emotion-charged memories. Am I correct?'

The blood was pounding so hard in my temples that even Lenka Silver must have heard it. The cat growled out of the darkness. Two jetblack sparks flashed from Lenka Silver's face, as she opened her eyes which had been kept closed all this time. And I went on recounting my true story: 'The young lady has to make sure that the Chief is really the right person. After all, a murder is at stake. She therefore accepts an invitation to the Chief's party, even though the editor already has a girlfriend, and there is nothing our heroine dislikes as much as "breaking up other people's relationships". She knows from her own bitter experience what it's like to be jilted. All the same, she accepts the invitation. To make sure the editor really takes her to the party, she is unusually pleasant to him, feeds his hopes.

'During the party she gets better acquainted with the Chief, and he falls for her. He's a lifelong skirtchaser. He's already bedded all the female editors and hopeful women writers, and our young lady is extremely beautiful. She lets him take all sorts of liberties. He's really hooked. But she still has to be dead sure that he's the right man, and naturally he keeps silent precisely about that part of his life that interests her the most. It is taking a long time. I don't know how the young lady managed to wheedle the information out of him. She certainly didn't ask him directly. She probably tried all sorts of roundabout approaches, and it took a long time.'

I lit another cigarette, I had lost count of how many I'd smoked. As I struck the match the flame momentarily lit up that beautiful face. She didn't look at me. The match went out and I was again facing a silhouette against the starry sky.

'The whole affair gets more complicated for our heroine. The editor falls in love with her, starts creating unpleasant scenes. She herself – and this is one item in the whole story which still isn't clear to me – falls in love with the editor's friend. She has to chase him a bit because he's a dolt. Then again, perhaps I do understand this after all. Love is one area where the greatest success is scored by those with the least experience. You remember telling me that? To the editor, our heroine seems like the very incarnation of femininity. But in her own eyes ... You remember that discussion at the bar in the country? You remember my asking you what kind of girl you were? And you answered: "Just a normal girl. Nothing out of the ordinary." But maybe she isn't quite as ordinary as all that, is she?'

She didn't answer. I continued: 'The Chief makes up his mind he's going to sleep with her, and he pursues her more insistently than she likes. He penetrates into her apartment, where he hides from an unexpected visitor. He clamours for one rendezvous after another. And so the affair continues. I don't know the details, but the affair keeps going. Perhaps the young lady can't make up her mind. She is longing for revenge but it all happened so long ago that it hardly seems real any longer. She can't decide to take the fateful step. Nor can she decide to forgive. That's why the story keeps dragging on, all summer, until the fall. Then they all happen to meet near a lake. The heroine comes there with her fiancé; she has no idea the Chief will be there. And the Chief gets drunk, his tongue loosens. The fiancé gets drunk too, but he isn't used to alcohol. He lies down in his tent and is out cold. The editor who loves her at last listens to reason and stops pestering her; he goes off with some girl author. An ideal situation. At 1.30 everybody's either stoned or asleep. The Chief comes out of the hotel for a breath of fresh air. She sees him from the tent and goes out to meet him. She's still not completely decided but the situation seems perfect, and she's drawn to him by forces which she cannot control. She suggests a boat ride on the lake. The Chief, of course, enthusiastically agrees. And so they set out. It's a little past 1.30 in the morning.'

The room was still, the saxophone had stopped. The jazz fan had gone to sleep but lights came on in other windows, turning the building across the street into a black-and-gold checkerboard. The sky behind the tousled head was taking on a golden glow.

'I don't know exactly what happened in the boat, of course,' I continued softly. 'I don't know what they talked about. Maybe he admitted his guilt. Or maybe he said something that convicted him. I don't know. Or maybe he started to molest her, and she no longer needed any evidence. The devil knows. But one way or another, emotions that had long been dormant were roused. Hate, antagonism, disgust – there are no words for it, and it's not a semantic problem, anyway. She simply picked up an oar and hit him over the head, or else she pushed him and he hit his head. I don't know, and it doesn't really matter. She was wearing deerskin gloves. The editor – or rather, the detective – had noticed them when they were lying on top of the bar. This explains why her fingerprints were not on the oars. Then he fell into the lake, or else she pushed him. That's not important, either. She rowed the boat to the other side of the lake, landed somewhere on a barren, rocky shore, and shoved the boat back into the water. Then she walked around the lake and returned to the tent. The fiancé knew nothing, he was dead to the world. She crawled in next to him. Nobody saw anything, nobody knew anything, nobody could prove anything.'

Lenka Silver lifted her head and opened her eyes. I was facing only complete, black darkness.

'There are still a few minor details. After the war, some Jews decided to change their names, to erase the past. Silberstein to Silver, for example. Not all Jews did that, but some. And our heroine wanted to erase the past quite radically. She not only changed her name, she had the tattooed concentration camp number removed from her arm. Our heroine does not like to boast, and she is very sensitive. In fact, I would say that she is pathologically sensitive. Innocent little instances of literary plagiarism make her as angry as if she were personally affected by them. I am not quite sure why she had that tattoo removed, but I know that she did. Only a small pink rectangle is left.' I grimaced. 'That rectangle excited the editor erotically, because at first he interpreted it in an entirely false way.'

Lenka Silver got to her feet. I remained seated. Her body stood out against the window like an idealized silhouette in a shadow play. The cat jumped off her lap, hissed like a snake. I said: 'And her first name was not Lenka. It was Leona. A lioness.'

I looked at the small, dark figure.

'But she was really a cub. A lion cub that had survived to grow up beautiful. A lion cub which that stupid hypocrite, that editor, wanted to hunt down.'

I paused. My black mass was ended. A small, questioning animal voice sounded out of the darkness. Then I heard something click against the glass tabletop. Lenka Silver had taken off her metal belt and laid it on the table. Then I heard her voice, a rough rubato played on a melodious oboe: 'The lion cub is trapped.'

She lifted her hands to her neck. In the thin light of the stars and windows I saw her pink nails, her slim fingers groping for a button.

'You're just like your Chief,' she said calmly, hoarsely, with contempt. 'Come on.'

I rose, too, and stood motionless. She was standing in front of me, in the glimmering darkness, a little smaller than I. All the joys of my life were hidden in that darkness.

I revenged myself on you, my lily-of-the-valley. Forgive me, it was cruel of me, but I love you terribly. I had to revenge myself. Forgive me. She was still holding her hands high, her fingers on the top button; my whole fate hung on that little bit of mother-of-pearl. I looked into her eyes; they were again opaque, impenetrable.

And then I understood. Ah, my dearest lily, forgive me if you can.

I moved. I felt a stab of pain in my heart; perhaps a blood clot was beginning to claim its right to that tormented muscle. The night was dark, moonless, tattered clouds sailed among the stars, rain began to fall over the distant silhouette of Prague. Through my half-closed lids the lights of the city had dissolved into a wavy golden surface. It was Thursday night, the end of my love affair with the beautiful Lenka Silver.

Josef Škvorecký was born in north-eastern Bohemia in 1924, and was made to work in a German aircraft factory during the war where he attempted sabotage on the V-1 which was luckily interpreted as incompetence. In 1951 he received his PhD from Charles University in Prague and then spent two years teaching and two more in the Czech army. After his military service he worked for three years in the Czechoslovakian State Publishing House of Fiction (later Odeon Publishers).

His first published work was the novel *The Cowards* (1958). Greeted as one of the most important postwar novels from Czechoslovakia, shortly after its appearance it was severely attacked by many Czech reviewers in a campaign directed by the leading conservative members of the Communist Party and subsequently banned. In a widespread purge in newspaper offices and publishing houses, Josef Škvorecký lost his job as an editor of the literary bi-monthly *World Literature* and had to return to Odeon Publishers. He subsequently published a number of novels, translated the novels of Hemingway and Faulkner into Czech and wrote scenarios for feature films.

Josef Škvorecký was on holiday abroad when the Russian tanks entered Prague. However, he returned home in November 1968, and finally left Czechoslovakia in January 1969. Since 1971 he has been teaching in the Department of English of the Erindale College in the University of Toronto. Škvorecký's *The Bass Saxophone* is also published in Picador.